Tales of Water and Blood

Xandra Noel

Copyright © 2023 Xandra Noel
Cover design - mageonduty
All rights reserved.
ISBN: 9798386324308

This is a work of fiction. References to real people, locations, events, organizations or establishments are intended for the sole purpose to provide authenticity and are used fictitiously. But, if you do happen to walk into a forest and find a fae prince, you need to message me immediately!

Tales of Water and Blood

- Tales of Earth and Leaves book 4-

Xandra Noel

Chose the tides ♡

Thank you for following the adventure.

There is a surprise waiting in the final chapter.

Winter

Chapter One

"You...can take us?" I had to blink several times and scan my brother's face. It was very like him to say such things, we'd lived with his half-mockery for so long, I could not distinguish truth from joke.

"Like I said," he nodded again and curled a hand over my mate's shoulder to serve himself some more food from her plate. Anwen didn't say a thing and accepted Vikram's closeness, probably as eager as I was for some sense of normalcy.

"We are all looking forward to hearing the details, prince." Of course, Rhylan had to spit more of his venom, after all we had barely finished breakfast. Even though my head wanted to turn in his direction, I fought the urge, keeping my sight focused on Anwen.

My mate. My beautiful and courageous mate. Memories of her body intertwined with mine, her screams of pleasure and all the sensations I drew from her the night before twisted a knot in my stomach. Would we ever go back to those calm sunny days in the Evigt Forest? Where she would wake lazily and turn to find me with lax movements, where the sheets reeked of our joining and the light of the sky was the only one to dare break our loving trance.

"Are you okay?" my mate's soft skin caressed my hand, drawing me back to the present day. She looked at me with a soft smile, probably guessing what my mind had turned to.

"Always," I answered and raised that hand to my lips. "As long as I can do this," I stamped a kiss on each of her fingers for emphasis. Spectators be damned, I had wasted too much time without my mate as it was.

"Right, before these two start fucking over the breakfast table, we need to establish some rules," Vikram stomped his juice glass on the table with enough noise to make Anwen and I jump. I directed my attention to my brother, to his usual grin of satisfaction, the one he showed every time Anwen and I even dared to get close to one another. The same look had followed us through the time we spent back at home, during every dinner and every time we joined the family for breakfast or any kind of celebration. The smirk of a proud older brother.

"Yes, Rhy, tell the man what he needs to know," Cressida's voice twinkled like a spring lily on a rainy day, forcing us all to capture her words. "Though fucking on the table sounds mighty appealing," she giggled and pushed Fear Gorta's shoulder playfully. Causing him to smirk at her, like he too thought the idea sounded extraordinary.

"Now, now, sunshine, you never showed interest in having a crowd devour you alongside me, but if that is my queen's wish…" Rhylan turned to his wife and started kissing her with such passion, we all had to stop for a second and see if they were actually preparing to occupy the breakfast table with other activities.

"Can we please establish some sort of boundaries while we are all together? I know for a fact that I did not agree to an open-ended sex ceremony before I finished my coffee," Amara spoke.

Causing Cressida to seal her lips and place her delicate fingers over Rhylan's mouth, letting him know fun times were over.

I wanted to laugh at the simple gesture, the way this human had such power over the most feared of the fae and how she controlled him without a dash of fear. Had she ever seen what he can do? How he acted with other beings?

"My lady has a point," Marreth added, always there to support Amara. I blinked at them with a sentiment of endearment, rejoicing in the fact that fate had been merciful to them and united them after such a long time. Some complications added to their happy joining, but still.

"Look at you, all grown up," Rhylan turned to Marreth and smiled, the same pride Vikram had displayed for me, now dripping from the lips of the Fear Gorta. Friendship, obvious for all to see.

"OK, boo boo, so…" Anwen's fingers locked tighter between mine and turned to my brother as if she expected to speak for a long time.

"We need Marrynah's tear," Rhylan cut the story short.

"Why?" Vikram snarled, his gaze stabbing into Rhylan.

"To bring the gods back. All the gods."

"Again, why?" Vikram did not conform with such a short explanation.

"The earth is dying." To our surprise, it was Cressida who spoke, her tone eloquent.

Anwen nodded in agreement, in support of her friend. My mind left the present conversation once more, this time to study all the relationships we had, willingly or not, combined at this table. Anwen and I were mates, yet Anwen's loyalties did not lie with me exclusively. By the way her gaze followed Cressida's words, she would do anything for her friend. A friend, a sister, who had become Queen of the Fire kingdom. Married to the king, Fear Gorta, who was also my mate's father.

I myself had loyalties to someone else apart from my mate. My brother and, unwillingly, my wife, Amara, who was in love with Marreth, whom in turn looked like he would die for both Rhylan and the wind princess. I'll be damned…

"…so either it's the gods or a few decades from now, but this planet doesn't look like it would last for too long. Unless something radical happens," Cressida finished and I had to look around to find that everyone agreed. This human had such power in her speech that she would turn a fireling into the most loyal of soldiers. I only had to remember how she drew Jyanna's loyalty in a few short sentences to be mesmerised.

Vikram himself looked ready to eat from the palm of her hand.

"What if it doesn't work? What if you summon the gods and they seek justice? What if they ask for the territories to fight amongst themselves? What if Belgarath fulfils the fireling's desires and burns the world to the ground?" my brother retorted.

"I too was sceptical, Prince Vikram," Amara's turn came to speak. "The first time I heard the plan I found it to be lunacy. But come to think of the alternative, it is the best option we have."

"Not if you are entrusting the Fear Gorta with the fate of your kingdom," my brother shook his head in disbelief.

"She is not," I felt the need to add.

"Rhylan is not to touch any of the tears and should the plan fail, they are to be returned to safety."

Vikram blinked, his eyes widening with the meaning of my words. I nodded to reassure him. The tear was safe. I was safe.

"After all," I forced a half grin, though dark memories struggled to take over, "Rhylan and his mighty team of fire warriors were incapable of drawing critical information for over a year. I wouldn't place too much worry where they are concerned."

Rhylan swallowed dry and Marreth's features turned dark, he too remembering what they had put me through. And his role in all of it.

"So, the plan is to get invited into Ventilo Regnum, stroll about, have some fun and steal their goddess' tear?" my brother wanted to ensure his understanding.

"More or less." It was Anwen who replied. My mate exchanged a quick glance with the firelings, I wasn't sure if her gaze wanted to reach Rhylan or Cressida, because both instantly shifted their attention to my mate, some kind of darkness to be unravelled.

"Can you get us there, brother?" We had reached the point where we all depended on Vikram, whether or not he believed in our plan and if he had enough trust to let it unroll.

"I can, but I must add a word of caution before we proceed. And that is, that I am unable to take sides. I understand the plan and respect your confidence, I want nothing more than to bring back Catalina, if such a thing is possible. However, I will not choose between my kingdom and love."

"Love?" An army of frowns raised across the table, and I did not have to look around to know that the same expression laid portrayed across everyone's face. We all knew, or at least heard of, in Amara's and Cressida's cases, about Vikram's...enjoyment. For him to talk about love was the last thing I expected to drop into my ears.

"What are you talking about, brother?" My words echoed through the room, a few short seconds after Vikram had spoken. Everyone was either too stunned or unwilling to enquire more.

My brother turned to me with a proud smile. "I'm sure you can understand, little one. Like yourself, I have to protect my mate above all."

"Your what now???" Anwen leaned so close to my brother's breath, I thought she needed to physically catch the words he had just exhaled.

I found myself doing the same, because either Vikram was, once again, trying to play some kind of trick on us, or my brother had just admitted to having a mate. It sounded impossible, unreasonable, and unreal. How could Vikram...*Vikram!*....have a mate?

The brother whom I watched growing up under ladies' skirts, the one who bragged about bedding females and showed his charms on each and every occasion. Impossible remained the word I decided to settle on.

The two couples joining us halted in their actions, I didn't even think they were breathing properly from fear of losing the Earth Kingdom commander's next words. Which came out, as expected, sarcastic and filled with chastising remarks. All directed to my mate, who was the first one to release the question we all thought to speak.

"Anwen dearest, seeing how you've been through three kingdoms now, following the love of your life, the one that was destined to join so perfectly with your own body that makes the sex mind blowing and your pretty little throat call his name on each and every occasion, I find myself fairly dumbfounded by your confusion. You should know by now what a mate is, boo boo sweetheart."

"I...what does that have to do with anything?" she retorted.

"You calling my brother's name when he fucks you or...?" Vikram arched a brow, continuing to play with us all.

"Brother, that is enough," I found myself defending my mate and when Vikram's gaze reached me, I softened my tone. "We would all appreciate a few more details, that is all."

His shoulders relaxed instantly, probably realising that we were not pushing questions out of the need to mock him, but because we wanted to better understand the situation.

"It would be easiest to show you, I just need to find a woman," he announced with determination and pushed the chair back, standing and taking all our attention with him.

Anwen
Chapter Two

"What do you mean, you need a woman? A human female?" Marreth questioned.

Amara nodded to her lover, pleased with the question he had posed. How could a mated male need a woman? I looked around to find everyone as shocked as I was. Even Ansgar's features showed surprise. For some reason, Rhylan was the only one to keep silent and distant. Either he knew what was coming or the events did not earn his attention.

"We are human, Anwen and I," Cressida offered. Then she must have thought better of it, because she felt the need to change her statement. "I am human. And female," she clarified.

It was only then that Rhylan turned to his queen, the prohibition in his eyes evident. The bastard already knew something we all still tried to puzzle together but did not plan to share the information. Not that I was surprised in any way.

"Can someone please explain what the hell is happening?" I snapped. We'd been at it for two hours, going back and forth, with everyone revealing pieces of information as and when they felt like it.

"It can't be just any woman, it has to be a woman that is physically attracted to me," Vikram explained.

"Like I said, I'm a woman," Cressi giggled, more as a joke, though I did spot a dash of pink in her cheeks, making it true that she fancied Vikram.

In all fairness, who wouldn't? He had the body of a god and that midnight skin of his did wonders to accentuate every single muscle. I myself had to confess guilty to admiring his sweaty torso when I caught Ansgar and him sparring on the training ring. In my defence, all three brothers were built like Greek gods.

Amara and I started giggling, which meant that she too, had admired the earthling prince a time or two, but at Rhylan's tensing shoulders, Cressi rolled her eyes. Then added, "unfortunately prince, you landed in my life way too late. I am a happily married woman," she giggled again and spread a long caress on Rhylan's tense jaw, following it with a kiss.

"I appreciate it, Your Majesty," Vikram smirked, "but I would like to keep my balls where they are." We all knew his words landed to Rhylan's benefit, who found himself lovingly wrapped in his wife's arms. "I'll go out and get someone, then I'll be back and show you."

Without waiting for confirmation, he walked out the door and before we even had a chance to speak, he was gone.

"Is your brother always so... sure of himself?" Marreth felt the need to question Ansgar, who only nodded.

"Right then, so that's settled. We'll wait for Vikram to pick up a girl and bring her back here." Cressi blinked then turned to Rhylan abruptly. "This isn't some kind of voodoo human sacrifice party, right?" she accentuated the question, as if wanting to be extra sure.

"What kind of parties have you been to?" Ansgar frowned at Cressi, who waved him off.

"Oh prince, if you only knew…"

Three hours later we were all settled on the sofa to watch a movie, as per Cressi's proposal. It felt endearing to see all three couples cuddled together on the circular couch. As I nestled in the familiar warmth of Ansgar's arms, I glanced to my right to see Cressi nonchalantly splayed on Rhylan's chest, my faerie relative resting his legs up on a small seat, adjacent to match the sofa, like he didn't have a care in the world.

Marreth and Amara sat in the far corner, barely able to see the screen, though none of us thought they minded, the two more concerned with chatting under their breaths and caressing their bodies when they thought no one was paying attention.

I had no idea how we landed like this, all three of us perfectly matched, but I did not mind it one bit that Ansgar's supposed wife was not concerned with paying her husband any attention whatsoever. Because that was my job.

Neither of us paid any real attention to the movie, I didn't know why Cressi chose Harry Potter V, because she had to put herself through the better part of a quarter of an hour to explain what had happened to reach that point. And by the look on all the fae's faces, including Rhylan, they were less than interested.

We all took it for what it was, a mindless distraction that we could all join in and take advantage of cuddle time until Vikram made his appearance. I for one could not focus at all, and even if I knew the heart breaking moment when Harry loses his uncle was coming, I did not feel any emotion. Every time a car stopped, or we heard some chatter on the street, my heart jumped, overly excited for Vikram to show up.

"Why does the youngling need to speak the magic, but others don't?" Ansgar broke the silence, giving Cressi and me an opportunity to jump in.

"Did you just call Harry Potter a youngling?" Cressi burst out while I said, "Honestly, I think they filmed it like that to make it more appealing."

My prince stopped and grimaced slightly, not knowing how to react to both of us speaking simultaneously, but Cressi and I looked at one another and started laughing. As soon as the sound reverberated in the living room, Rhylan followed, shaking his head at the situation, and probably thinking how the hell did he get himself in this.

Attracted by my own shaky breaths, Ansgar followed, giggling alongside me and taking Amara and Marreth with him. The next few seconds caught us all laughing hysterically, all looking around at the ridiculousness of the situation.

"Looks like I missed all the fun." That was all we needed to halt abruptly and turn to the door. To find a cheerful Vikram holding hands with a blonde woman in a massive winter jacket and a scarf wrapped so tightly around her neck that only her eyes and part of her hair remained visible.

She took a step back at the sudden attention she received, all of us instantly shifting to look at the two of them.

"Sophia, meet my friends," Vikram broke the ice and invited the girl in, offering to take her jacket and leading her towards the living room, where I realised, we had left a mess after breakfast. None of us even thought about the guest we were expecting, but as soon as she saw the girl, Cressi jumped into action.

"We have tea, coffee, orange juice, coke and mojitos," she offered with a smile.

"A coffee would be great, thanks," the girl spoke with a thick accent, her hand, once more, wrapping around Vikram's arm.

"Welcome," I said and shifted from the sofa, pushing Ansgar to the centre and almost into Rhylan's lap to make room for Sophia.

She half smiled and took a seat on the edge of the cushion, occupying barely any space.

"Are you ready, sugar?" Vikram laid back and hugged the woman, relaxing her into his arms, which she seemed more than happy to do.

"I am, prince," she spoke with the sweetest of voices, causing all of us to, once again, direct our attention to her. With the corner of my eye, I spotted how Rhylan moved to reach his wife and grabbed Cressida into his arms. Probably spotting the closeness of the two, Ansgar decided to do the same with me.

The voice of the woman sounded different, the strong accent suddenly faded away, as if she had played a part until that moment and only now was she released to be her true self.

A few seconds later, Vikram's lips pressed on hers. I don't know if my imagination played tricks on me, but I spotted the woman lit up.

Green, yellow and an amber-rose embraced the outline of her body. My first instinct was to turn to Rhylan and ask if he made the same observation, but I was entranced. Something about the woman had definitely changed, making her become charming and her appearance breath taking all of a sudden.

Her beauty placed a sort of calling on me, demanding my full attention and breath, as if I had waited for that exact moment for a long time. Watching her became my sole purpose.

She was a very pretty girl before this, but it was as if Vikram's kiss allowed her to transform into…I didn't even know how to put it. The most beautiful human being on earth. Ever?

I had to blink several times, that beauty, the perfection and symmetry of her features, the perfect nose, the straight jawline, one that I only spotted at the Louvre, that perfect natural blush of her cheeks and the plumpness of her lips. Not to mention the most beautiful sea-green eyes I'd ever seen. Did that colour even exist before now?

By my side, Ansgar drew in a sharp breath, and I heard Marreth do the same from the far end of the room. Like me, they must have been bewildered. I didn't even consider jealousy; the woman was so beautiful that even I would love to kiss her. It would, in fact, be the biggest achievement of my life. What else was there but the touch of those perfect lips—

"My sweet…" Vikram's voice sounded far away, even though he was less than two metres from me. His tone came out almost admonishing towards Sophia. But for the life of me, I could not understand why.

I wanted to be close to her and I shifted from Ansgar's arms, whose hold on me had become so tight, it barely allowed air into my chest. I started to shift away from my mate, doing my best to escape his embrace, needing to be closer to the woman, to that beauty. Nothing else mattered.

"Habit, my prince," she giggled and blinked.

She blinked. And all my senses returned to normal.

I was in Ansgar's arms, in my mate's arms. My mate, whom I loved more than anything. The sudden desperation to be near the woman diminished. With a blink of an eye.

"You will have to forgive her, Anwen, she enjoys playing these games way too much," Vikram turned back to Sophia and flicked her nose playfully. Only it was not Sophia that sat next to me on the sofa. I still maintained my opinion; she was the most beautiful woman to ever exist. Though that desperation to be near her had suddenly vanished.

"Who is she, brother?" Ansgar's voice came out a tremble from behind me.

"Eidothea," Rhylan answered in his stead, and I looked back to see that Cressida too was fighting to escape his arms, probably trapped under the same charm as I was. Amara and Marreth were simply...stunned, I don't think either of them even breathed.

"Eidothea?" Ansgar spoke again, this time with a little more courage. "The Second Queen of the Water Kingdom is your mate?"

"I know, right?" Vikram winked and rested an arm across the woman's shoulders, like an eighties schoolboy taking ownership of his first girlfriend, a proud grin splayed across his face.

"She is so beautiful…" Cressi's voice came out from behind and I turned to see that she was physically pushing Rhylan away from her, struggling to get closer to Sophia. Eidothea. I wasn't really sure at this point.

"Can you make her stop?" Rhylan asked while continuing to wrestle his wife. I did not know where she got the strength to push her king away so many times, but he was persistent.

"Of course," the woman threw us all the most charming smile and wiggled her fingers in the most elegant movement, as though she were performing a water dance. Cressi became released from the spell I had been under, and I heard Marreth and Amara take a breath.

"Who are you?" Marreth finally found his voice, even though it sounded so distant that he might very well be in another dimension.

"She is the Queen's sister," Vikram responded in her stead. "And my mate," he smiled again, the pride not giving up an inch.

"It is indeed a complicated relationship, as you can imagine, but my prince and I have been working through the difficulties," she smiled, and her radiant joy made even the sun feel jealous.

"As in, you pick up random women and she possesses them?" Cressi seemed to dot the i we were all thinking, pointing and each of them in turn.

"The females have to be willing to be with me, yes, and it works best on humans. The girl will then remember the fun times and Eidothea and I can find some time alone," he replied nonchalantly, as though possessing human beings was the most normal thing in the world.

"Brother…" Ansgar stopped, and I fully expected him to start admonishing the commander. Instead, he stood from behind me and took the few steps separating him from Vikram, urging his brother to rise into a hug.

A hug!

"My brother has a mate!" Ansgar exclaimed cheerfully and patted Vikram's back a few times, both of them hugging with joy. Vikram was obviously happy to deliver the news, one that, from everyone's reaction, had lived as a secret for a long while.

"Many happy returns to the new couple," Marreth and Amara spoke in unison and even Rhylan nodded deeply to offer silent congratulations. It was only Cressida and me that looked at one another, dumbfounded, unable to understand how everyone was taking this so lightly.

They were using women as freaking ice cream cones so they could eat all the chocolate inside. And then discarded of said cone.

"Why can't you just come here? Why can't you use your own legs to visit your mate?" I reprimanded, my voice sounding more scornful than intended. It seemed to break the trance they were all under, causing Ansgar and Vikram to cut their brotherly embrace short and look at me with concern.

Poor little human who doesn't understand faerie laws.

It was Sophia, or Eidothea, who relaxed into her seat and started speaking, her voice as even and seductive as the first time I heard her.

"I am a siren; I am not allowed to walk the earth every day and have to be confined to specific times. And trust me, princess, my mate and I do make the most of it. But would you be able to see your lover for a night only every few months? Would that be enough?"

The way she blinked at me, curiosity and something else in those stupendous eyes, made me immediately shake my head.

No. Of course I couldn't.

"I want to spend every second by his side," I admitted, part of me defeated, understanding to some extent their need to resort to such atrocious things.

"I completely agree," she tilted her head to me and smiled so sweetly that I was once again ready to jump on top of her and steal that damned kiss.

"Stop doing that," I covered my eyes as if I could block the magic seeping through her. She only giggled.

"Well, my sweet," she turned to Vikram, who retook his seat next to his mate. "Why have I been summoned?"

Rhylan choked on the wine he'd been nursing throughout the movie. "Summoned..." he replayed the word slowly, as if he could not believe it and had to piece the word together by saying it out loud. "The barren prince can fucking summon a siren queen," he murmured his annoyance for everyone to hear, but Vikram simply ignored him.

"Yes, let us get to the core of the issue, since Eidothea doesn't have too much time today and there is yet another core we need to get to tonight," he smirked like an idiotic schoolboy.

I couldn't help but release a smirk. It was nice seeing Vikram like this, fussing over his lady, agitated to get to be alone with her and so, so proud of himself. I didn't know how long this relationship had been going on for, but Vikram looked as if he was living his first love every time he looked in her direction. And Eidothea wanted to eat him whole. I hated to say it, but they were cute together.

And hot as fuck.

"What do you want to ask of me, Prince Ansgar?" The siren turned to my mate, her full attention directed at him, and I felt a clench in my stomach. If she was provoking those kinds of thoughts from me, and I never even considered having a lady's adventure in my whole life, what was Ansgar feeling? Was he as bewildered as I was? Would he be ready to give me up and steal the kiss we all seem to desperately want?

"We would like to merit an invitation into your kingdom, my queen," Ansgar dipped his head low by my side, his voice perfectly relaxed and unaffected by the beauty sitting next to us.

"Yourself and…?" Eidothea wanted to confirm.

"Myself and my wife, Amara, Princess of the Wind Kingdom. As well as the Fireling Royals. As incredible as it is, we are working on an alliance, and we would like to bring a proposition to the siren queens.

"I loved how incredibly diplomatic my prince could be. Who in their right mind could say no to this?

"I will discuss it with my sisters tomorrow," she nodded, a salute amongst royals, then turned to Vikram.

"Shall we?

Chapter Three

My brother is mated. To a siren.

Vikram, the one who bragged about his weekly conquests, the one who wanted to push me in the ladies' ways all my life turned out to be faithful to a single female, none other than the Second Queen of the Sirens.

Damaris' theory had been true all along. Apparently, Vikram fell in love with her during his Keeper Assignment, and since he received the keeping of Tuboran Eriberta in the Mindanao Island, the entrance into the Water Kingdom, he kept seeking out the queen.

And somehow managed to start a relationship with a being whose kisses proved lethal. Not when one is mated to a siren, a fact unheard of until now. Sirens did not have mates, they only used males for feeding and conversion, yet somehow, my brother managed to do the impossible. In true Vikram spirit.

We needed a long time to process the events, while my brother took his lady upstairs and did not come out until morning with a completely transformed woman responding to the name of Sophia. She only accepted a coffee to go from Cressida before asking Vikram to accompany her to her Uber. It was a service to call cars to any location, Anwen later explained.

"Brother, I don't think I have to say it, but just in case," Vikram addressed me directly while coming back through the door. "This is not for mother's ears," he pointed with a threatening finger.

"Vikram, I wouldn't even know how to start such a conversation," I huffed and focused on my orange juice.

The day turned bleak after the tumultuous events of the night before. None of us wanted to go upstairs from fear of what we might hear, or the effects that a siren would have on us, so we lingered on the sofa or in the kitchen until the early hours of the morning.

Rhylan was the only one who took his queen upstairs after she dozed off on the couch in the middle of the night, calling us 'useless pricks' on the way up.

Once Vikram departed with the promise of sending news as soon as he heard back from Eidothea, we lingered either in the allocated bedrooms or back on the sofa, trying on some of the clothes Rhylan had arranged and snacking on new specialties while watching the snow fall.

The village we had been placed in was quiet, only a few younglings or some cars passing by, but as soon as night fell, it all became quiet again. We had nothing to do but wait.

Two days to be exact.

Two days until Anwen rose from bed, keeping her phone high towards the ceiling, as if she was holding a torch of victory.

"Spring solstice!" she exclaimed victoriously and ran out the door in nothing but her lace panties.

"Spring solstice," she shouted in the hallway, making the other two doors open, heads popping out to check on the noise. "The sirens agreed, we can go visit on Spring Solstice," she made the announcement clear for us all.

"Wonderful, we start training after lunch," Rhylan ordered before he slammed the door shut.

The training sessions turned out to be so tiring that we barely managed to find the bed before sleep trapped us until the next morning. Which considerably reduced the time we had to spend alone.

The only time we managed to spend together was during meals, and even those felt rushed and untranquil at times. Breakfast was always quiet and full of yawning and complaints about going out in the snowy terrain. Marreth, Amara and I struggled the most, since none of us was used to falling snow. I, for one, had only seen it three times in my life, and twice had been while visiting the Wind Kingdom on the rare occasions it happened.

We kept communication with our families. I wrote letters, delivered by Vikram, to advise my king and queen of the ongoing situation and also, to ensure my mother and father that I was safe. That we were safe.

Amara did the same, keeping constant contact with Jyanna while Anwen and Cressida used their favourite devices to talk to family and friends. I finally had a chance to meet Jason and Elsa via the mirroring screen and I had to apologise for my shortcomings in the past when they mentioned how they waited for my visit.

Their frowns turned into relaxed smiles when they saw Anwen crying with joy and suddenly, the past did not seem to matter.

Dinners had also become a mandatory group activity, according to Rhylan. "If you plan to fuck like bunnies, you do it in your own time. And with proper nourishment in your bellies."

We did not dispute it, enjoying the company in the evenings. Marreth and I spent most of our day sparring and training, while Rhylan and Anwen used a place called *gym* to work on developing her powers.

Amara and Cressida remained home most of the time, either in charge of ordering the food - they did try cooking a few times, but we all preferred to leave the task to professionals - or teaching each other court etiquette.

Dinnertime became the space where we could all be together and share our findings of the day, the events that happened in the world, which Cressida always enjoyed telling us about or chatting through updates and planning.

Amara and Rhylan became the appointed planners, since they were the only ones to have set foot in the Water Kingdom, telling us about the Air Palace and mermaid traditions. We all listened with fascination, except for Anwen, who always found reasons to judge or scorn the siren activities.

I watched her grow under my eyes, every day she became stronger, more confident in herself and her powers, but spending the full day in Rhylan's company covered her in a shred of darkness I tried my best to banish during the night. Something weighed heavy on her and no matter how many times I tried to ask her to open up to me, there was a part of her heart I did not have access to.

"No breakfast today, be ready in three," Rhylan kicked the door open and made me jump awake, taking Anwen with me. My poor mate was cuddled in my arms when Fear Gorta woke us up and I made her jolt with my abrupt movement.

"What is happening?" I barely managed to ask.

"Two minutes, prince. Move," he kicked the door again for emphasis, then proceeded to do the same with Marreth's and Amara's room, which was two doors away from us.

"What is happening?" Anwen barely spoke before she turned and fell prey to sleep again.

"I don't know, fahrenor, I'll be back soon," I whispered, even though I knew she was already gone in the world of dreams. As ordered, I got dressed in the trousers made of tough fabric, which were apparently the norm here. Jeans, humans called them. Pelvis traps, more likely.

The only positive side to human clothing was my mate's excitement to take them off. And to take photographs of me, every single day, in every single garment, doing mundane things. There wasn't a moment, in the first few days of arriving at the house where she did not follow me and photographed each kiss, each embrace, the way I rested in bed, the way I caressed her hair and many, many photographs of parts of my body.

It took me a while to learn to do the same with her, but I knew how much she enjoyed it. I took her photograph device and pressed on the white button, mirroring my face next to her sleepy self, knowing she would see it after waking up. I took another one of me kissing her lips.

"I love you," I murmured and received a groan as a reply. That was the best I would get, so I settled for it and went down the stairs to find a sleepy commander and an overly-excited fireling waiting by the door.

"Let's go," Rhylan ordered and pointed to a black car that waited outside the house. I turned to Marreth and grimaced, neither of us were fans of cars and avoided them at each occasion.

"Where are we going?" the commander finally asked once we shut the doors and the engine started rumbling, inviting the same movement in my stomach.

"It's Valentine's Day, you idiots," Rhylan scorned us.

The car journey was spent with an exasperated Rhylan trying to explain human traditions that we should already be aware of and with Marreth unable to wrap his mind around the activity. I remained content to sit back, focused on controlling the whirlpool in my stomach and enjoying the show.

"But why do we have to buy them gifts on this particular day?"

"Because humans place a big emphasis on specific dates, and this is the one they chose. Females expect flowers, chocolates and teddy bears," Rhylan rubbed his forehead from having to explain it all, yet again.

"What kind of bears?" Marreth continued.

"Stuffed bears. Females enjoy that. The bigger, the better," Rhylan took another sip from his coffee. He had asked the driver to stop and ordered coffee and a sandwich for him and Marreth along the way. I refused, unwilling to torture my stomach further.

"Huh, that would be great, Amara does enjoy hunting," Marreth confirmed with a smile and at Rhylan's expression, I could not help my snort.

"Oh, like you are so knowledgeable with human customs?" Fear Gorta retorted.

"At least I can grow flowers and don't have to depend on a man on metal wheels to carry me around to buy some," I retorted.

"Shut the fuck up," Rhylan threw a dash of his energy straight to my stomach and I was glad I did not take him up on the offering of food.

Twenty minutes later, we had stopped by a massive store and Rhylan started, ordering us around, naming the brands and some gift ideas he thought suitable.

Never in my life had I thought Fear Gorta to offer payment in my stead for the gifts I picked for my mate, but there he was, offering me a rectangle card which looked to be made of gold. Firelings, I internally huffed.

"Pick what you want, then go to the payment desk. They will have a small computer there and a person will always sit in front of it. Pass them the items you want to buy and offer this when they ask 'cash or card'", he instructed. "Very important thing, princeling," he squeezed three fingers together to make a point, "Do not lose this. They have to return it to you every time you buy something. They will scan it and return it to you along with a small piece of paper. Keep the paper in your pocket, it is rude to show how much you paid."

"Understood," I nodded, suddenly unsure. Rhylan planned to leave me on my own in the massive store with multiple shops, each more sparkling than the other accompanied only by this golden card which somehow needed to be returned to me.

We also had golden coins in the regnum, but they had to stay with the vendors after the purchase, they were not returned, so I was confused on how everything worked.

"I'll go with idiot here and make sure he doesn't actually buy a stuffed grizzly. We'll meet in this exact location in three hours."

With that, he turned and started walking away, forcing a very disoriented Marreth to follow in his steps.

"Good luck," the commander mouthed before getting lost in the crowd.

Not knowing how to proceed, I entered the first store I spotted, a jewellery shop to my right. They had decorated the walls with red roses and floating globes of red light, making the appearance heavy on the eye. The air must have been soaked with some kind of artificial rose aroma, because my nostrils screamed in alarm after the first breath.

"Good morning, are you looking for anything in particular?" A woman jumped in front of me with the question as soon as I took a step in.

"I..." I took a deep breath and remembered Rhylan's words. It could have very well been a trick the Fear Gorta wanted to play on me, but I did not have much choice, the alternative being that I showed up on Valentine's Day without a present for Anwen. Apart from the flowers I was already growing in our bedroom every day, which had already become the norm.

"I am looking for a Valentine's Day present for my...fiancée," I settled on the most human title to describe our relationship.

Before the woman had a chance to speak, I wanted to confirm the truth in Rhylan's words.

"I have this," I showed her the gold rectangle. I later discovered it had Rhylan's name on it.

As soon as she saw the golden object, the woman's eyes lit up, suddenly becoming inviting and coddling me in attention. She proceeded to display diamond pieces, rings, bracelets and so many other objects I did not even know existed.

After I chose a white gold bracelet adorned with leaves and petals and speckled with diamonds and sapphires, I did as told and passed the woman the golden rectangle, which she returned to me in seconds, along with a white piece of paper and the biggest smile she ever showed until then.

I thanked her and headed to the next shop. This was going to be a fun day.

Anwen
Chapter Four

"Morning, sexy. Are you planning to wake up anytime soon?" A gentle caress slid down my cheek and I opened my eyes to find Cressi looking at me. Her hair was arranged in a messy bun, and she wore her perfectly drawn eyeliner, as though she had just finished recording one of her blogs.

"What time is it?" I mumbled and shifted in bed, turning my head to find no traces of Ansgar. I vaguely remembered him leaving in a hurry in the morning.

"Half eleven," Cressi shifted to make enough space for me to get out of bed.

"Half-eleven? We don't have training today?" Usually, we woke up at around seven and by eight we were already gathered at the breakfast table.

"Rhy left early with the boys," my sister shrugged. She didn't have more details. "Amara is helping me get ready for tonight, do you wanna join us or sleep some more?"

"I'll join you," I nodded. "What's tonight?" By the time I asked the question, Cressi was almost out the door.

"Valentine's Day," she replied without looking back.

Half an hour later I sipped my coffee, happy to lay on the sofa and watch part of my reflection in the mirror, along with a stunning golden satin dress that hugged Cressi's every curve, making her ass look plump and so, so yummy.

Amara herself made that very statement, while she fussed around my friend, arranging the beading on the dress and some of the straps in the back for the thousandth time.

"Are you and Ansgar doing anything tonight?" she asked. Amara didn't know about Valentine's but now she is excited," Cressi giggled in the direction of Ansgar's wife. My mind could not wrap around the complicated relationship status I had developed in the past few weeks. Luckily, none of her attention was directed at her husband. Thank all the gods.

"I haven't told him anything. Honestly, I completely forgot about it with everything going on…"

"If it is a day dedicated to love, then it must be celebrated," Amara turned to me, as if to reprimand my lack of planning, so I felt the need to defend myself.

"I don't want to burden him. It's not easy, you know? All the training, the wait, depending on Rhylan's whims…" I pouted and Amara nodded quickly, as if to acknowledge my thoughts. We had all grown accustomed to Rhylan's exigence and even if she was the furthest away from the blow, she still got affected by the rigorousness of his planning and all the demands.

I, for one, had to spend at least six hours a day with him, training at the local gym, which he had rented out for the duration of our exercises with the pretence that a famous actress needed to train for an action film. The face of the owner was the portrait of disappointment when he saw me enter the gym, but he did not protest and gave us the security codes so we could come in and leave as we wished.

Now that I had the ability to draw darkness, my training had become much more intense than in Cressi's living room back in NYC. I had to train physically and mentally, I had to create shields around my mind so the sirens could not use me as bait, and I had to be able to summon darkness in my sleep. Easier said than done.

Still, for some reason and very unlike him, Rhylan kept his calm and explained things to me a million times. He taught me how to breathe, how to hold the air in my stomach and even slow-punched me a few times to demonstrate the decrease of pain levels.

My power grew stronger every day, same as my determination. I had to be able to defend myself in the Water Kingdom, as Rhylan pointed out so many times. But what I was training for, was attack.

It was close to sundown when a knock on the door made Cressi jump from in front of the mirror where she had spent the day. As soon as she opened, various men entered the house without saying a word, all carrying massive bouquets of yellow roses. A constant in and out of delivery men followed, bringing so many roses that the entire living room and kitchen became snowed in yellow. Along with crates of champagne, chocolates and plush whales.

Cressi could not stop giggling and taking pictures with everything she received, while Amara and I stole one of the champagne bottles and helped ourselves to a few glasses.

At six o'clock sharp, the doorbell rang and Cressi jumped into action once more, posing seductively in front of the door, leaning on her hip, and supporting her arm against the doorframe before she opened slowly.

Amara and I peeked through as the open door revealed a very sexy Rhylan, dressed up in his usual black attire, holding a jewellery box.

"Happy Valentine's Day, my queen," we heard him say and we both leaned in to spot that he opened the velvet box to reveal a diamond necklace, perfectly tailored to Cressi's taste.

"Happy Valentine's Day indeed," Amara snickered next to me.

It was enough to draw Rhylan's attention, who looked in our direction and spotted us spying.

"You two should head to your rooms, the Queen and I will be back late. If at all," he shifted his attention back to Cressi, looking at her with hunger and enthusiasm.

"Yeah…I'll wait for Ansgar, thank you anyway," I retorted, causing Rhylan to frown.

"Fuckboy is already up. They returned an hour ago," he looked at Amara and me in confusion, but decided that we did not merit his attention and his next gesture was to escort Cressi out.

She turned to us with a wide smile. "I covered for the boys while they were bringing the flowers in. You two have fun," she winked before disappearing out the door.

"Ansgar?" I instantly moved from my seat, causing Amara to do the same.

"Marreth?" she joined me in the calling as we ran up the stairs. Or better said, tried to, the champagne had already started to affect us.

We barely reached the upper floor when Marreth opened the door, holding a massive white teddy bear with a red bow wrapped around its neck.

"Happy Valentine's Day," he jiggled the bear as he spoke, making it look like the stuffed animal was saying it.

Amara joined her hands over her chest with delight, a gesture I had only seen in Cinderella or Snow White and ran to hug the commander. And then attacked his lips ferociously. I took my queue and headed to my room, hoping to find Ansgar in there.

For a moment, I thought I was back in Evigt, because my room, our room, spiked competition with the array of bouquets Rhylan had sent to Cressida. White flowers bloomed everywhere I looked. The bed was covered in gardenias, they bloomed on the covers, over the pillows and cascaded to the floor. The walls became wallpapered with white roses and the ceiling snowed tons of small white petals.

In all this conglomerate of whiteness and bloom, Ansgar waited for me with a wide smile and, just like Marreth had done for Amara, he handed me a small teddy bear that was holding a heart to say, "I love you" and a heart shaped box of chocolates.

"Happy Valentine's Day, fahrenor," my prince closed the distance between us and welcomed me with a kiss, which I was barely able to return due to my surprise.

"How?" I looked at him with the widest gaze I probably gave him in my entire life. "I didn't..." I shook my head. "I didn't prepare anything for you, I thought—"

Ansgar's hand cupped my jaw, and his lips stopped the words from coming out. A long line of kisses travelling down my neck made me forget about my protest.

"Is my mate ready for presents?" he whispered the question in the shell of my ear. That was all I needed to hear before I jumped in bed with excitement, making all the flowers wrestle underneath my abrupt movement.

"You know I love presents," I giggled. "But… I didn't know we were doing this, I didn't get you anything."

I hated myself for not planning ahead. Knowing Ansgar, of course he would go all out when it came to a celebration of love, and here I was, stealing Cressi's champagne and gossiping with Amara instead of showing more consideration to my non-human boyfriend and trying to introduce him to our customs.

"I can think of some presents you can give me," he stared with a hunger that made my insides twist, but before I had a chance to reply, Ansgar started carrying boxes and bags in the bed, to the point where he drowned all the flowers with presents.

"You bought all of this?" I looked around incredulously. There were probably thirty gifts for me to open.

"Rhylan was not too excited, but Cressida helped me carry them in," he smiled with pride and urged me to start opening them. Which took the better part of an hour. All the while, Ansgar sat next to me and absorbed my reaction with joy and enthusiasm.

They were good presents too. Chocolates, of course. Expensive ones. A box of macaroons. A set of personalised champagne flutes with our names.

"A Birkin bag? How on earth did you get one of these?" I could not believe my eyes. Cressi and I had to wait two years to get one, and here Ansgar was, telling me that the sales lady just offered it to him. Offered it to him! As soon as he walked into the store.

"She took me to a room behind the main shop, they had some sort of security and let me choose the one I liked most," he explained as if what had happened to him was just a casual occurrence.

"She let you choose the bag?" My breath stopped in my chest. "You could choose it?"

It took me a good few minutes to calm down enough to open presents again. Luckily, my mate anticipated my needs and opened one of the gift bags which had a vintage bottle of Dom and poured me a glass in our brand-new flutes.

I had to admit, for a person who had no idea how to work a DVD player or choose a movie on Netflix, the man had very good taste. He went for luxury and style. Must be that royal blood of his. *Like calls to like*, I internally snickered and proceeded to open more presents.

The cherry on top was a white gold bracelet with diamonds and sapphires, shaped to look as if leaves twisted around my wrist. The piece of jewellery screamed Ansgar and all the memories we shared. I simply adored it and even shed a tear at the emotion it awoke in me.

"There is one more," Ansgar announced after he helped me clear the bed from all the boxes and gift wrapper, "but it's not just for you. It's for us…" he threw me a playful smirk.

"Now I really have to know," I jumped up and followed him to the wardrobe, from where he picked another small box and handed it to me.

"The female assured me it would bring fun times?" He was so uncomfortable, he had to reach and scratch the back of his head and I could not hold my laughter.

"You bought me a sex toy?" I giggled like a schoolgirl and jumped for the box, opening it eagerly while my prince felt the need to explain.

"I initially entered out of curiosity, because they had so many penises in the window, I just had to know what was happening. And when the lady asked me if I was looking for anything in particular, I said I wanted something for Valentine's Day. Then she asked me if my partner is male or female and gave me this. It is called a ring bunny," he shrugged as if he thought the name sounded ridiculous.

And indeed, I opened the box to find a ring bunny. Which was some sort of combination between a penis ring and a bunny vibrator.

"OK…"

"I don't know what it does," Ansgar alerted me.

"Don't worry, we'll figure it out," I grinned and left myself fall prey to the sudden need to devour my mate.

No matter how many times we did this, I remained amazed by his body, the way his torso arched and the eagerness of his hands, ready to conquer every part of me. He squeezed my breasts while his tongue travelled towards my navel and my stomach twitched with anticipation, knowing full well what his tongue would do when it reached my panties.

Ansgar bit my clit with intent, ripping through the lace underwear I discovered he loved me to wear. Black lace turned out to be his kryptonite, so I made it my mission to wear only that. Every day. One could never be too prepared.

"Fahrenor," he grunted from between my thighs, his fingers squeezing at the newly conquered territory while his mouth remained on me, slowly licking his way down.

"Gods," I twitched under him, for some reason I felt so sensitive today and the way his tongue rolled down my centre made me go crazy with the abundance of sensation.

"You can pray baby, but that won't help you," I felt more than heard his smirk before he plunged mercilessly at his task, his tongue entering my core while his fingers kept my clit occupied and in sweet pain.

"Ansgar…" I murmured, begged, I did not know exactly, I felt him everywhere. In me, on me, around my centre, his fingers did wonders while his tongue kept lunging in and out, just the way he knew I liked it.

"Please, please, get to the point already," I let go of the corners of the pillow I kept squeezing for dear life and tried to grab at his hair, his shoulders, to make some kind of action to draw his attention back to me.

We didn't always start with oral, but for some reason, Ansgar took great satisfaction in tasting my very first release rather than drawing it. So, it became a tradition. Not that I minded one bit, but today I felt too restless to wait. I needed him inside of me, I needed to be connected to my mate and draw the same sensation he was eliciting from me.

"It's my Valentine's Day too, baby." Those were the last words my brain was able to process before I started going mad with pleasure. Ansgar changed the position of his tongue, using it to torture my clit while two fingers pierced deep into me, rubbing at my insides with velocity and determination as a full orchestra of moans marched from my mouth, my stomach tensing, thighs squeezing him in between my legs, hand trapped in his golden locks.

He did not stop until I was a mess. He did not stop until he drank every single drop of my pleasure, and I remained limp, exhausted and totally at his mercy.

He gave me about a minute to rest, offering the superb view of his backside while I assumed, he struggled to fit the ring he had bought around his thickness. I adored seeing his wide back, the way his muscles arched and relaxed with his casual movements, forming that trapeze shape all gym junkies struggled to achieve. Add his gloriously round ass into the mix and, may all the gods spare me.

My eyes travelled to his chest as he turned, that sculpted figure and the way his abs lined so perfectly with the rest of his form and…

"Does it hurt?" I could not help but worry at the sight of that ring squeezing the hell out of his thickness, but Ansgar grinned.

"A bit, but I think I like it," he arched his brows only slightly with the strangeness of his confession.

"Well, well, prince, is someone discovering a kinky side?" I giggled back and instinctively spread my legs to welcome him in. Which he took advantage of with a single deep thrust, causing my lungs to release a sharp breath.

"That feels…" I had to breathe once again to get used to the sensation. I had Ansgar fully inside of me, forcing me to spread wider to receive him, especially with the abruptness of the movement, and the fucking bunny that vibrated straight into my clit.

"Sensational," Ansgar completed the sentence and started moving inside of me with long and deep thrusts.

I had to hold onto his shoulders because every new pumping motion pushed my body back and with the vibrations added, it felt like he was drilling into my core. Deeper and deeper, harder and faster, Ansgar did not stop until he set a savage rhythm which barely allowed me to breathe. All my body knew how to do in that moment was release pleasure and scream his name. Over and over.

Until I forgot the world around me, until I didn't even know who and where I was. The only thing that mattered was him, the way he was pumping into me, the way he made my insides twitch with every movement and how my lips screamed his name. That was the only word that mattered, the only one I remembered. Ansgar.

"Anwen!" I felt soft pats on my cheek, just like when I was young, and my mom struggled to get me to wake up in the mornings. "Anwen, please," I heard the calling of my name again, the movements becoming more rigid and worried.

"Yes…" I responded, half-annoyed. I needed those small slaps to stop, they were irritating as hell.

"Baby, please," I heard again. Baby? What the...then everything returned to me. The memories and the sensation. I was in bed. With my mate. On Valentine's Day.

"Ansgar," I opened my eyes to smile at him, expecting to see his usually cheerful face and those eyes that always devoured me with hunger. Instead, I found worry. Terror even.

"What is it?" I replied with the same caressing tone he had used before.

"Fuck..." he threw his head back, as if allowing himself to finally take a breath and relax. "I thought... you were gone. You were gone," he kept repeating, then rethought his stance on relaxation and hugged me to his chest, continuing to caress my face. "You were gone," he repeated.

It took him a good few minutes to calm down enough to tell me that I fainted during sex and as soon as I fell into sleep, I summoned the night. Enough to fill the room and leave him in complete darkness. It was only when he made me open my eyes that the electricity did its job again and the waves of darkness disappeared.

I'd left him terrified and alone, not knowing if I was alright or how to get me back. Ansgar had to take a while to release all this information because it looked like he was having a full breakdown in front of me.

"I am so sorry, Ansgar, sometimes I can't control these things. I can't control this fucking power that runs inside of me... I don't know what to do," I leaned against the bedframe and hugged my knees to my chest, covering my naked body, suddenly uncomfortable and ashamed.

My body language must have been so evident that my prince read it for what it was.

"Never, you hear me?" He reached for me and wrapped me in his arms. He then reached for a blanket and placed it on my shoulders, sensing my need to be covered. "Never be ashamed of your powers, fahrenor. They are new and will take some time getting used to, but they are a gift," he started to slowly caress my hair and plant a few calming kisses on my forehead.

"A gift?" I huffed. "A gift just ruined the best night we had in a long while."

"It did not ruin it. I just…I got scared. I did not know what was happening," he tried to explain and squeezed me even harder into him.

"Of course you were, 'cause these damned things are only there to harm." That was it. I had spoken out loud what I had always feared and hearing my voice pronounce the worry, releasing them into words turned on a tap of emotions. Along with tears.

Ansgar allowed me a few minutes to embrace my feelings and cry, to lament what I had become. Against my will. All the while holding me tight and offering me that cocoon of love I obviously needed.

Only when I calmed down enough, did he let go, with minimal movements, as if to let me know he was not planning on going too far away. Ansgar left the bed, not before making sure I was fully wrapped in the blanket he'd found for me and stood up straight, displaying his perfect naked body to me.

"Then let's use them for love," he stated.

"What do you mean?" I frowned in confusion and squeezed the blanket to my chest, the sudden loss of his arms making me search for new warmth.

"Use your powers on me." he explained, his eyes the perfect reflection of confidence.

"You don't mean that," I shook my head. "I could hurt you."

"You won't," he relaxed his shoulders as he spoke, another sign of his devotion and confidence.

Terror overpowered my entire being. What if I hurt him? What if I did something to damage him? What if I reminded him of his enemy, of all that he'd endured in the Fire Kingdom. Of all the torture and pain.

"Ansgar, no, I can't do this," I immediately jolted in bed, wanting to put an end to this, but he reached out to stop me.

"Fahrenor, I trust you can do it. Please try," he voiced unrelenting confidence.

The way he looked at me, the way he believed in me gave me new strength, new confidence. My mate trusted me. My mate wanted me to use my powers to show him love.

The jolt in my stomach relaxed.

I loved Ansgar. No, I adored Ansgar. Nothing, no other feeling came to mind that was not a positive one. I trusted this man, I loved being with him, I admired him. I found him funny and intelligent and above all, I was lucky to have him.

Think of where you want the power to go. Direct it and bend it to your will. Rhylan's constant directions sounded in my mind. Direct and bend it to my will.

I looked at my mate, focused on his breathing, the way his chest rose and fell with ease, the way he showed no speck of fear towards what was coming for him. I wanted to caress that torso, the muscles that had become my pillow and my haven. I adored resting there, it was my own little heaven.

I let myself go. I let the feeling surround me.

My eyes grew wide to find a line of darkness travel from my midsection straight to Ansgar's chest to…caress the very section that I had been admiring a second before.

"It tickles," he giggled, looking down at the swirl of darkness with…affection.

God, how I loved this man. And how he loved me! He even loved this part of his worst enemy, just because it was mine.

Gaining more confidence, I sent another line to caress his cheek, causing him to lean into the touch and smile.

"How does it feel?" I had to ask, I had to know. The last thing I wanted was to put him in danger somehow.

"I feel *you*," he smiled again.

"Mom, he can't answer if you keep telling him to eat and ask him questions at the same time," I came to the defence of my poor mate, who struggled to gulp down huge chunks of steak so he could free his mouth to speak to my mom.

We arrived home five hours ago, and since then, mom hadn't stopped talking and grilling my boyfriend with a million different questions. Which he answered heroically every single time, with unrelenting patience.

He must have been exhausted after his first flight, which turned out to be full of unexpected turbulence, shopping for my parents and meeting them in the span of a few hours.

"I believe it was discovered in the sixteenth century, but by then chrysanthemums had already become the new fashionable flower, which is why they appear in so many of the royal portraits," he took the time to respond to another one of mom's questions.

Ever since Ansgar told them about his knowledge of plants — I decided to go with the story I had thought in Evigt and tell everyone Ansgar was a biologist — mom bombarded him with questions about every single plant there ever was. And he seemed to be enjoying telling the stories.

I hadn't even realised how passionate he was about plants. He had always told me of his interest in them and the members of his family confirmed it, but to see him share his passion with such excitement was a completely different story.

I thought mom was a fan of Rhylan, since she kept insisting that I could have done more and not offer him on a silver platter to Cressi, but it took my prince a few hours to make her take a 180 turn. She was now team Ansgar.

I looked at my dad and shrugged. Both of us had been excluded from the conversation a while ago and simply enjoyed gazing at our loved ones and how they behaved with one another, as if they had known each other for decades. I couldn't even remember the last time I saw mom this happy.

Dad took advantage of my attention and threw me a proud smile that screamed "I like him", causing me to beam with joy.

We did it. We were finally here. Mom and dad and Ansgar. The people I loved the most, sharing dinner and casual conversation. How I wished Erik were here to see this.

"How long do we have you for?"

I sprinted to answer, mentally thanking dad for taking the turn in the dinner chat, probably seeing how Ansgar took yet another bite and mom, once again, prepared to ask something else. The poor man needed a break. And some time to chew his food.

"Almost a month," I replied cheerfully. I couldn't even believe we had this long to just enjoy ourselves and spend time together. "We need to travel to see Ansgar's parents as well mid-March and then we're going back to Canada to meet Cressi and Rhylan."

"Oh? Did they not want to come see us?" Mom jumped in.

"They wanted some time alone, you know how it is. Newlyweds and all that," I waved my hand as if to show how busy these two had been with their marital duties. Which, come to think of the noises coming out of their room each night...

"And where will you be travelling to next?" dad asked.

"The Philippines. We'll spend a few weeks there. It'll be in the forest, so not sure about the signal," I announced, already preparing the plan. They had to know I would be, once again, out of reach.

"Ansgar, dearest, you have to tell this girl to settle already. Travelling all the corners of the world, all the time, out of reach for weeks…it's not good for a young lady," mom interjected, and I was about to roll my eyes and start defending myself. But it seemed I had a mate who planned to do just that.

"No man has power over your daughter, Mrs. Elsa, you must already know that." I didn't have to look at him to know he was smiling. "I consider myself fortunate to be spending the time by her side. Though, with the hope of…providence, we shall endeavour to spend more time at home if all goes well in this holiday."

"That's what I like to hear, my boy," Dad relaxed in his seat and took a celebratory sip of whiskey. Then he turned to me. "I have some travelling scheduled in March as well, but if you let me know the dates in advance, I can make sure the jet takes you to the Philippines."

"Oh, no need dad, we need to travel back to Canada first anyway. We're meeting Cressi and Rhylan there."

"Why would you go back North?" Dad frowned, always the calculating businessman.

"There's another couple who remained in the house we shared while doing business there. They don't really like to travel alone so it was common agreement that we all return there on the twentieth," I explained.

The mixture of terror and joy I saw on Marreth and Amara's faces was something I'll never forget. They were so happy to finally get the privacy they obviously needed — that we all did, in fact — and terrified to be left alone, in the human world, to fend for themselves. They did calm down pretty much instantly when Rhylan told them he had hired a driver to take them wherever they needed and take care of payments and all the 'human things' they were so scared of.

For some reason, after returning four days after Valentine's, Rhylan had an epiphany and gave everyone a month off, deciding it was more important for us all to enjoy the company of our partners rather than follow his obsessive training routine.

It was all I needed to hear, I immediately booked flights for the next day and stopped to thank Cressi for the miracle she had performed. Such a blessing could have only come from her, that was for sure.

And here we were, two hours later, when mom finally decided it was time to let us rest after the tiring day...and evening, we both had.

Finally, I thanked all the gods. There was the awkward conversation about Ansgar's sleeping arrangements, which was, of course, brought up by dad, but I was adamant that my boyfriend would spend the night in my room.

I would not, for the love of everything sacred, give up on this and after a few other suggestions and a bit of back and forth, Jason Odstar had to accept defeat.

If we had a month to spend together, I had to make sure we did it properly.

Ansgar

Chapter Five

"They are not going to hate you," I tried to convince my mate. She was obstinate about remaining in Evigt and refused to travel back to the regnum with me, fearing the reaction of my parents. No matter how much I insisted, no matter how many examples I gave her, her stance was the same: no.

"You cannot spend days with Matthyaz and Faelar, they also have work to do and cannot be your hosts until my return," I tried a different route. Anwen had always proven to be a polite guest, so I hoped this new strategy worked.

In a way, I understood her worries, though she had absolutely no reason to hang onto them. I myself had been in the same situation with her parents and even after almost a month of living with them, I still felt uncomfortable at times, especially when her father invited me to have a drink at the bar and discuss my plans with his daughter or when Elsa kept introducing me to her friends as Anwen's boyfriend.

I started to care for them and what I loved the most was to analyse their gimmicks and gestures. It was fascinating to me to see how Anwen had inherited simple gestures or traits from them and how the same reactions and motions came out at oddly specific times.

Like the evening when we had lamb with mint sauce for dinner and both Anwen and her father wrinkled their noses at the exact same time, how Elsa scratched her forehead when she had to write something down, just like I'd seen Anwen do so many times and so many phrases that followed the exact same gestures my mate and her parents performed to perfection.

It had been a blissful month and I absolutely adored the routine we started to get used to. Since her parents and I proved to be early risers, I got used to drinking something Elsa loved to call a *ristretto* early in the morning, while we discussed the weather, daily events and Jason talked about his meetings for the day.

I became invested in the kind of business they did and loved to know how they were sourcing or growing the plants needed for the products. He and Anwen even gave me a tour of one of their production warehouses and some of the growing plantations, then we went to a laboratory where the products were tested on parts of skin they had grown from nothing.

I remained amazed with the power of technology and the struggles they went through in order to produce everything 'ethically and sustainably.' That was Jason's favourite phrase.

After the morning coffee with her parents, Anwen joined us for breakfast, usually half-asleep and grumpy. She needed the better part of an hour to turn back to her sweet self. After which we either went sightseeing, shopping with Elsa, spend some time alone or visited some of the places that were significant to my mate and their business.

Dinner was always a family gathering, which I loved, where Jason told us about his day and we either made plans for the weekend or talked about technology and politics. Jason was a very knowledgeable man, and I took advantage to learn as much as I could from him.

It impressed me to find out how much we did not know, how much of the real human world was filtered through the teachings we received.

The nights were, of course, reserved for love making and soft caresses, Anwen and I too eager to spend the time alone and worshiping one another. My mate started making a habit of torturing me with various outfits that left very little to the imagination and I made a habit of ripping apart every single one until I unveiled her naked body. Most of the time using my teeth.

"Ansgar, you deserve some time alone with your family, and especially some peace and quiet," Anwen giggled softly, surely making a reference to the untameable cascade of dialogue that proved to be her mother.

"I am not going without you," I finally decided to give her the ultimatum. I would not abandon my mate for days, just because she feared the reaction of my family. I would not leave her on her own for even one second. "I can summon Vikram here and we can have a chat and pass all the information we have, then we can be on our way." I must have been the portrait of determination because Anwen paused for a second and bowed her head slightly to accept defeat.

"Alright then, we're going to see your parents," she agreed.

I did not want to bring her back to the regnum without offering her some time to get ready, so we spent the afternoon with my cousin and our friend Faelar, sharing some wine and chatting. The forest fared well, the damage I had left after my departure completely healed. Even though everyone looked well, I felt the need to apologise for the way I had left and the issues I caused them.

The elders offered comforting words of understanding and Faelar even gave me an embrace before we headed out to the Cloutie trees to make our way home. Anwen and I kept silent while we performed the powder ritual, my mate already versed in the actions needed to open the portal.

"Ready?" I stopped and turned to trap her in my arms once the gates opened, wanting to make sure she knew I would always be by her side. That we were perfectly safe.

"Ready," Anwen confirmed and rested her head on my shoulder, squeezing me tighter.

"I'm sure I don't need to tell you to keep your mouth shut about specific things, so…welcome home," Vikram's cheerful voice made us cut our embrace short and realise we were already home.

"Hello, brother," I slowly let go of my mate and went to share a quick hug with my brother, who was more concerned with Anwen and after greeting me, he jumped right to her and caught her in his arms, spinning my mate around and making her giggle.

"At least one of you doesn't hate me," Anwen murmured softly, causing Vikram to frown, then look at me in question.

"She thinks the family is upset because of the way she left," I shrugged, knowing perfectly well the king and queen would be overjoyed to welcome her back.

"Nonsense," Vikram huffed before putting Anwen down. Dropping her sounded more like it, as if he was offended by her thoughts.

"Your carriage awaits silly boo boo," my brother said, pointing to the transportation he had prepared for us.

During the journey, he told us that Eidothea had everything prepared for our visit and that he would be joining us. He had told the king and queen about our upcoming travel, though he'd left the destination unmentioned, thinking it would be best for all of us to plead our cause together, mostly concerned about the queen's reaction.

By the time we reached the palace gates, Anwen's pulse drummed so loud that Vikram and I had to ask her to take a breath, but she was too entranced to even realise we were there. Whatever her thoughts on the events, they needed to be put to a halt.

I opened the door on my side and got out, while urging Anwen to come down and into my arms. She had initially planned to wait in the carriage until I spoke to the king and queen, but that was not something I would allow. By the time my family gathered to welcome us at the entrance doors, we already stood hand in hand, waiting for them.

I did not expect any reproach from the royal family, they had been with us in the Wind Kingdom and saw my mate's situation first hand. The fact that she returned as a fireling princess had to be seen only for what it was, an admirable achievement.

"My son," mother opened her arms to me first and I jumped in, wrapping one of my arms around the queen's waist while squeezing Anwen's hand.

"Mother," I greeted her, leaving the royal title to the side. For a few seconds at least, I wanted to be a son that returned home to hug my mother. And tell her that I missed her.

As soon as Queen Bathysia released me just enough to spot who was behind me, she added a deeper smile to her cheerful face and reached for my mate.

"Anwen, welcome home."

The two obviously needed some space to be able to properly reach that upcoming embrace, so I stepped to the side and directed Anwen into my mother's arms. They shared a long hug, and my mate released a few tears, but as soon as the Queen whispered calming and welcoming words into her ear, all was well again. Father followed suit and hugged us with joy, to the extent of slowly bowing to Anwen in acknowledgement of her new title.

"Silly girl, you worried for nothing," Vikram huffed while passing us by, without bothering to share in the welcoming and embracing moments. He'd visited so many times that he had probably already become fed up with us.

"Worry about what?" mother asked, wiping away one of Anwen's stranded tears.

"She was scared you would turn her away," I explained, knowing I would get a good scolding for saying it, when we were alone. Better this than whatever colourful explanation Vikram had in mind.

"It is a blessing that you are here," Damaris' voice came out of nowhere, causing all of us to look around and find him. He looked tired, wearing a full uniform with smudges of dirt and blood on his face. "Training every day is slowly becoming the death of me," he grinned a welcome and, same as mother and father, offered a quick embrace to both of us.

"Is everything—"

He didn't give me a chance to finish the question, already anticipating what I wanted to know. "Everything is fine, no attacks so far, but I want to make sure the armies are always ready."

"We have a date, but it is part of a longer conversation, which is why we're here," I advised, looking at each member of the royal family in turn and observing how they nodded in agreement.

"Where is Takara?" Anwen found enough courage to ask a question, causing the queen and Damaris to share a proud smile.

"She is not having a particularly good day, but she will tell you more at dinner. Come, you must be exhausted," mother invited us in and started ordering staff around to make preparations for our room and for the upcoming dinner.

Finding my old room the exact way I left it before departing to the Wind Kingdom stirred painful memories. I had asked Takara to remove all of Anwen's belongings, unable to think of her while preparing to depart from my kingdom. The seating room looked perfectly in place, as if the soul had been taken away from the chamber and only an empty skeleton of nothingness remained. Until

I heard Anwen's shriek and hurried to the room I had filled with books and liked to call a library.

"What happened?" I asked, my eyes scanning the surroundings for any kind of danger, should I need to defend myself and my mate.

"My presents!" she clapped with excitement, jumping up and down. "I completely forgot about them; I can't believe you kept them."

I had no idea what she was referring to, until my eyes spotted how the bookshelves were in fact filled with wrapped gifts and boxes rather than the books I had once left there.

I sent a thousand blessings to Takara, who had probably arranged for my mate's belongings to be returned to our chambers when they received word of our arrival. A true queen, she had saved me so many explanations and the awkwardness of telling Anwen how I had removed everything that belonged to her, too eager to banish her from my thoughts.

"I...I forgot about them too," I replied and reached for one of the boxes, offering it to her. I needed to be truthful with her, but this was not a conversation that took priority, especially with the dinner planning that we had scheduled.

Someday, when all would be settled, when my mate and I could laugh and joke at all the strangeness and unwanted situations we had been pushed through, I would confess. But for now, I planned to spend the few hours we had to ourselves helping her open presents and rejoicing in that smile I adored.

I did eat a few chocolate pieces from between her thighs, making sure that my tongue took many, many wrong turns on the way to the sweet.

"Finally, we thought you forgot about dinner," Damaris greeted us with slight admonishment when we arrived in the dining room. We had, in fact, gotten so carried away with our game that we had lost track of time.

"Sorry, it took a while to find my clothes," Anwen smiled, but she must have realised what she said, because she immediately added. "To get changed, for dinner, I mean."

"Uh-huh," Takara smirked, "we are all well aware of what that means," the future queen replied. She looked different, spent and sickly, the usual rosy blush adorning her adamant skin vanished.

"Sister, it is good to see you," I kept my observation to myself while pulling back the chair for Anwen to take a seat. They had brought in another chair next to mine, as if nothing had changed. As if Anwen and I were still a couple in everyone's eyes and that none of the recent events affected our family's view on our relationship. I felt grateful for the wordless confirmation.

Takara smiled in return and greeted me, though she did not move from her seat nor made a gesture to invite me to come closer. I immediately became suspicious of the reason but decided not to press on it. If my senses proved correct, she would tell us when she felt comfortable doing so.

"Are you okay?"

Anwen did not seem to share my diplomacy and ignored the seat I had prepared for her and circled the table to get to Takara.

"Is everything alright?" My mate's hand rested on the healer's shoulder, caressing her gently, as if she did not want her touch to affect the princess in any way.

"Just a bad week," Takara groaned and forced a smile. "You don't understand how bad these things are until they affect you directly."

"What? What happened?" Anwen wanted to clarify, unable to understand but I already started smiling to my brother before his wife and mate had a chance to give the news.

"Nothing too alarming," Takara replied softly. "These things are normal with a second youth."

That was it, I burst into laughter and hurried to their side of the table as well to offer my congratulations.

"You're pregnant?!?" Anwen's voice sounded like a raised alarm, causing Takara to frown and tilt her head to her husband.

"You did not tell them?" she reprimanded.

"I didn't want to take away your moment," Damaris grinned and pointed to Anwen who started shouting with joy and bouncing up and down while holding Takara's hands.

After I congratulated my brother and his wife and wished them a healthy and happy youth, Anwen released enough of her joy to be able to take her seat.

"We are to depart in two days, so if I am needed for the blood blessing, I think this would be the best moment to do so." I did not want to push them into the celebration or raise any alarms, but if my blood was needed, I would rather give it while it still ran smoothly through my veins.

"Why do you have to give your blood?" Anwen asked.

Goddess, please allow me to be truthful to my mate. I had prayed for this so many times, yet every single attempt ended in silence. I could not tell her. Fortunately, mother took over.

"Ansgar is the youngest member of the family, so a drop of his energy given freely is considered a blessing to the new generations."

"We do have another Ansgar, who barely managed to fall asleep before dinner," Takara added, "but he does not hold true energy of his own yet."

"Of course, brother, we did not want to ask for it, but all is prepared. As we are on the cusp of war, a celebration would not be indicated," Damaris responded.

"Very well, we can do it after dinner," I agreed, and watched their faces relax in such a way that both of them looked a decade younger.

"We did not want to assume, especially since your energy is not only your own," father admitted.

Goddess, please allow me to be truthful to my mate.

Poor Anwen looked at each of us in turn, unable to understand the situation. And none of us could do anything to change that.

"We will continue as it is," I advised. "If the youngling is to be blessed by both earth and wind, then he will be the first to receive the merits of two goddesses."

"May the goddess bless you, brother. We are beyond thankful," Damaris replied.

We spent the rest of the evening discussing the possible outcome of our impending travel to the Water Kingdom, advising Damaris on our findings and about Rhylan's plans and trying to establish the best connection to summon the armies, should the need arise.

The morning of our departure arrived sooner than planned. Anwen and I spent two nights in the kingdom, but they turned out to be filled with requirements and tasks that kept us awake and away from one another. After the first dinner, the Queen and Takara prepared the blessing elixir and we all gathered in the garden to invite the goddess to the ceremony. The blood in my veins was thick, and even though I pierced a deep cut in the palm of my hand, it felt as if oil dripped rather than my own essence.

After Takara performed the rite, we allowed ourselves a few hours of celebration under the stars. It had been so long since it was just us, the family members, without any ceremonious routines or wardrobe requirements, without having to bow or watch our stance, measure our words and our gestures. We could simply be and enjoy, celebrate the arrival of another nephew, son and grandchild.

The following day was filled with preparations. Vikram and I accompanied Damaris and father in his daily inspection of the armies, while Anwen stayed with the queen and princess to receive as much training and advice as she could about the Water Kingdom.

We returned for dinner just as Damaris had the day before, bloodied, sweaty and filled with grime, to find the ladies of the kingdom exhausted after spending the full day locked in the library, drowned in manuscripts.

Dinner consisted of more sharing of information and preparation. All of us were determined to help with every strand of energy we possessed in case it proved useful in the upcoming days.

Anwen and I must have had three or four hours of sleep before Vikram announced the time of departure.

Even though we all tried to be cheerful and keep the planning as positive as the evening allowed, we knew that no matter how hard we tried, if one single step turned amiss, it would all end in war.

And we could not afford to lose.

Anwen

Chapter Six

Ansgar took a long while to say goodbye to his family, probably experiencing the same longing I had when I left home. Even though I had abandoned my parents three times in a row, it never got easier.

In fact, the uncertainty and constant danger we seemed to be living under made everything more difficult. While my prince and his mother shared a conversation, I took advantage to spend a bit more time with Takara. I was so happy for her, I knew how they struggled for years to have a child, and now, luck knocked on their door yet again. The birth of a child always caused reason for celebration, but I saw how in a royal family, it meant much more than that. The new baby offered a future. And hope.

Something we all needed.

"Take good care of our boy, Anwen. And trust your skills," Takara gave me another hug, this time with a kind word of advice.

"I will. And you take care of Damaris and the kingdom. And baby Ansgar and that little treasure growing inside of you," I smiled while my fingers instinctively reached towards her belly, and I stopped only inches away from touching her. I don't know why I did it, why my hand pushed towards the place I knew the babe would be growing in her lower belly.

"Please," Takara encouraged and grabbed my fingers gently, to then place them over her belly, just like I initially wanted to do. "Another touch of the gods can never hurt," she smiled softly while letting me feel the warmth of her abdomen.

It took me a good few seconds to realise she was referring to me. I symbolised the touch of another god, since I held Rhylan's power. I instantly removed my hand.

"I don't think it's the kind of energy you want touching your son," I pressed my lips in silent apology.

"On the contrary, that is where the power of creation came from. That's how we all came to be," she nodded, her attention drawn to Ansgar and Vikram, who were preparing the horses, which meant we were ready to depart. "Embrace your powers, Anwen. They might save many lives in the days to come."

I nodded and smiled again, then headed back to Ansgar, who grabbed me in his arms and placed me on the horse. It meant I would be riding in front, which I absolutely hated, but I chose to focus on the royal family instead and joined the princes in saying my goodbyes.

A few minutes of my boobs bouncing up and down and Ansgar's horse trotting on the stone pavement and we were back in the forest. We kept silent on the way there, choosing to watch how the kingdom opened for us to pass through and focusing on details and sceneries rather than our destination. Words became unnecessary. By the way Ansgar squeezed me in his arms, I already knew everything he had to say.

That no matter what, we were in this together.

"Welcome back to the house of madness," Vikram grinned when he made us appear in front of the house we had left around a month ago. The snow had mostly cleared, leaving way for the pavement and the lawn that tried to bring the neighbourhood a community feeling.

The prince made sure we landed on the outer side of the courtyard, hidden from the spying eyes of the neighbourhood, which allowed us to spot the inside of the house through the kitchen window. Amara and Marreth spotted us and hurried to open the back door and welcome us in. We hadn't set a time of meeting, and by the excitement on their faces, we were the first to arrive.

"Welcome, welcome, welcome, how was the journey back home?" Amara beamed and jumped in Ansgar's arms, then did the same with me. The princess only offered a kind nod to Vikram.

It took me a while to realise that the woman I was looking at was truly the princess of Wind. Because the one in front of me looked like a teenage girl, the autumnal version of a young adult instagram influencer.

Her hair was held up in a ponytail, the rest of the strands curled to fall into the neck of an oversized cream jumper. She wore tight black leggings and UGGs, the only thing missing to complete the look was a pumpkin spice latte.

"Look at you!" I did not hold back my surprise. And admiration. She had reached the peak of indoor winter fashion in less than a month, changing from the elegant gowns that always made her cold, which she insisted on wearing every time Rhylan suggested she embraced the human fashion.

"Once I realised how fun it is to go shopping, I decided to accept the changes," Amara smiled and offered a small curtsy, as if she was on stage.

"I cannot get used to the tightness of human trousers," Marreth appeared from behind her and greeted us with a smile.

"Right?" Ansgar and Vikram responded, almost in unison. I had heard Ansgar complain various times about how he needed more space to move in the jeans he had started wearing, but my oh my, his ass looked glorious in them. Marreth too had adopted part of Amara's style, with chinos and the same colour oversized jumper, though his choice of shoes were crocs, which made me laugh.

"Did you have a pleasant journey?" Marreth asked while welcoming us in.

"Anwen's parents are great!" Ansgar responded with excitement, then he started telling Marreth about his adventures and everything he learnt about the human realm while Amara offered to order us some lunch via Uber Eats.

"Sure, that would be great," I half frowned with surprise and watched in amazement how Amara grabbed the latest iPhone and started typing so fast that I doubted even Cressida's typing skills could match.

"Should we order for Cressi and Rhylan as well, just in case they get here before the food arrives?" I suggested but Amara was already ahead of me.

"Cressi texted before they got on the plane, they'll be here at around 4pm and we'll leave straight after," she announced.

OK then…

True to what Amara had announced, at quarter past four Rhylan and Cressi made their appearance. Both of them looked as if they formed part of the royal family and had just completed an overseas tour.

Cressi wore an oversized Louis Vuitton bag and Louboutin knee-high boots, her top half wrapped on some kind of fur coat. Knowing her, it definitely had to be faux-fur.

Rhylan stunned in his usual Boss attire, though for the first time in as long as I could remember, he did not wear a black shirt underneath, but a soft cappuccino coloured one, that matched his wife's jacket.

"I'm sorry, did we miss the Milano fashion show?" I grinned and leaned into the doorframe. It was my turn to welcome them.

"It was the London one," Cressi beamed and placed a quick kiss on my cheek as she passed, finally removing the oversized sunglasses she blinked through.

"Hello, sprout," Rhylan greeted me with a nod before he focused his attention on more important things. "We will take a shower and then we are ready to depart," he announced to no one in particular.

And that was that. I was one of the lucky ones to even be acknowledged by Rhylan, because he passed the rest of the guests by, including Ansgar, without a second gaze, as if they were all unwanted pieces of furniture. Luckily, Cressi came by to offer everyone equal treatment, kissing them on the cheek while flooding the living room with her perfume.

"That is a whole 'nother level," Marreth made the observation, causing us all to chuckle. After which, we decided to listen to

Rhylan's announcement and get ready for departure. We each checked our rooms, ensuring we left nothing valuable behind or nothing that hinted of supernatural beings renting a place like this.

Amara found it hard to give up all the fashion garments she had acquired and took a long time deciding what to wear, while Ansgar and I settled on the couch and cuddled with hot chocolate and a blanket. Even though it was almost the spring solstice, the weather felt grim, inviting Halloween movies.

We were halfway through *A nightmare before Christmas* when Cressi came down in full regalia, wearing a crown similar to what she displayed in the Wind Kingdom and a black lace dress so fitted to her form that I wondered how she managed to take a single step, let alone come down the stairs.

"Why aren't you ready?" My sister frowned when Ansgar and I turned to look at her, mainly because the tap of her high heels interrupted our watch party.

"We are ready, we've been waiting for you," I tried to defend myself, then realised she was talking about the fact that Ansgar and I wore jeans and sweaters. Along with cosy socks. "We don't really have fancy clothes, apart from the ones we came from the kingdom with, and Amara said fancy dress won't be an issue," I defended myself.

"They wanted the excuse to take their clothes off one more time before we left," Vikram added his two cents from the kitchen, where he'd remained since we decided to put the movie on, happy to rummage the fridge one final time.

"Still, first impressions count. Rhylan has a dress prepared in your bedroom. Also, Ansgar and Amara have to dress the same as they are Wind Kingdom now."

I sighed but did as asked and pressed the red button on the remote control. The last normal, mindless gesture I would probably do in a long while. No more lingering in my mate's arms whenever I wanted to, no more chilling on the sofa, no more surprise dinners and snapping photos of one another.

This was it, the final battle, the moment we had all prepared for. We would finally go to the Water Kingdom. I would finally see the mermaids. And discover my brother's murderer.

"Good evening, all," the soft melodious voice was instantly recognised as the Second Queen of the sirens spoke to gather our attention.

After Ansgar and I changed into the garments that Rhylan had selected for us, we gathered into the living room. Rhylan and Cressi displayed their usual regal attire; the king had chosen to adorn his head with a crown that matched Cressi's while Marreth and I wore the dark grey we had grown used to.

Rhylan had instructed us to be the third invited couple, since it would be difficult to explain how Marreth could be unaffected by their charms were he not with his lover. I groaned and protested slightly but agreed to it in the end.

Ansgar and Amara wore dark blue and crimson belts, both of them wearing twin ruby crowns as per the Wind Kingdom regalia. I displayed a huge grin at the sight of my prince, looking just like one would imagine a medieval royal to be like. His crimson belt connected to some sort of waistband that held a sword and his tunic ended with a cape that barely covered that sexy ass of his.

"Anwen, can we focus?" Rhylan drew my attention. We all had to form a small circle and hug one another to help the connection, since the Fire King had taken responsibility to jump all of us to the entrance of the new kingdom.

Where we waited for almost an hour for the horizon to set. That was all Rhylan told us before he focused his gaze on the sea and kept it unmoved until the voice of the siren called him from deep thought.

"My beautiful," Vikram was the first to react and moved toward his mate, allowing us all the time to take her in. The soft chiffon gown she wore seemed to barely cover her body, which was perfection, simply put. Were I a man right now I would fall on my knees in front of her because I would know that never again could I witness such beauty.

Her hair changed colours and floated as if it were still in the sea, every strand reflecting in the sunset to create colourful hues, while her stupendously turquoise eyes smiled with her greeting.

My first instinct was to catch Ansgar's hand, both in awe and from fear that he would feel the same, but I barely looked over to see that Amara was doing just that. Probably sensing my thoughts, Marreth made sure to catch the fingers I had involuntarily raised into the palm of his hand and offer me a gentle encouraging squeeze.

We all remained astounded at the sight of her and did not unhook our eyes from the hungry kiss the siren and Vikram shared. Whiffs of desire started to rise in me, my lower belly and my core clenched with eagerness, with the need to feel what those two were experiencing. I wanted to grab my mate and take him then and there, to impale myself into him and feel that connection that only his touch could sate.

"Sprout…" Rhylan's tone came as a warning, probably reading all the emotions I released with that single thought. I swallowed hard and took a few deep breaths, choosing to focus my attention on Marreth and start playing my part.

This is what I wanted, this is what I had gone to Evigt for and unveiled all the events that took me to a whole new life. That brought me a mate. That brought me a family member, be him a cruel and sometimes unbearable creature, that gifted me a world I never thought existed and unexpected powers. Now I had to play my role and fulfil my destiny.

"If you are all ready, please follow me," Eidothea invited us with a song in her voice, smiling softly to each of us in turn until her full attention returned to Vikram. The couple stepped through a small opening in the cave we had landed next to, which seemed to have opened at the will of the water ruler and invited us to follow through.

"I hope, for your own good, that no one is going to mess this up," Rhylan took the final chance to threaten us before he copied Vikram's movement and reached for Cressida, offering her his arm to step through what I guessed was the portal to the Water Kingdom.

"I will see you on the other side," Marreth announced and shared a smile, then lifted my hand, which had remained trapped in his as an invitation for me to follow. I wanted nothing more than to hug Ansgar one more time, to kiss him before all this tumultuous visit started, but I knew we could be spotted. So, I settled for sharing a final gaze with my mate, one where I hoped I said everything I could not and by the way his shadow-grey eyes blinked back at me, I knew he understood.

"I'll see you soon," I smiled before following Marreth through the small opening into the cave.

I had jumped from one place to another a few times and entered all the other faerie kingdoms, but reaching Water was a whole different story. After we passed through the cave, we walked through a narrow tunnel illuminated by torchlight, which reminded me a lot of the entrance into the Fire Kingdom. It meant that we were going underground.

Amara had mentioned an Air Palace several times in stories of her visit, but somehow my brain did not process that we would be underground. Yet again, we found ourselves trapped.

Marreth and I followed the two couples without saying a word and only exchanging side glances when necessary. The need to turn and check on Ansgar ripped away at my chest and I had to fight it with every step we took. I didn't even want to think what was going through his mind, how scared he must have felt to be, once again, trapped in an underground kingdom. Where we depended on the rulers to release us. But I kept on going and thinking about my brother, focusing on all the memories that seemed to be resurfacing without receiving a summon.

I remembered Erik's smile, those proud smirks he plastered when he walked in with some sort of business achievement, the way we sang in the shower at five in the morning and how I kept shouting at him to shut up or his spot-on impressions of Elvis Presley.

How he returned from a simple city break feeling sick, how we had to rush him to hospital the next day, having absolutely no idea why my brother could not fill his lungs with air and why the sudden pain in his chest did not allow him to stretch.

How we received the news of his heart condition and how we were told that he had to remain hospitalised, how I watched my brother, the strong, gorgeous man he had become turn into a shell, losing colour in his cheeks, shine in his eyes and so much weight overnight. He'd transformed right in front of my eyes, becoming skin and bone, his breaths heavier and more painful, until it came time to draw his very last one. I could not disappoint him.

I would not.

"I advise you to hold your breath for this next part," Eidothea stopped and shifted slightly to make sure all of us followed. I took advantage and mimicked her gesture, risking a glance at my mate. His jaw pressed tight, the prince looked only ahead, already embracing his royal demeanour. I took note and did the same.

"Thank you for your consideration," Rhylan replied on our behalf. The next second shared the same sound, air inflating all of our chests. I made sure to take a deep breath and fill my lungs slowly, forcing them to expand to their maximum capacity, unaware of what would happen.

Once the siren felt satisfied with our action, she flicked her wrist elegantly, opening a whiff of air, which started growing around us, making it feel as if a plane was taking off and someone had left the window open. Droplets of water came out of nowhere and started mixing with the air, creating some sort of vortex, so strong that it flowed under our feet and lifted us in the air.

I instantly grabbed Marreth's arm, trying to hold tight onto him while looking around at the same time to see if Ansgar and Cressida were with us. If they were safe.

My eyes started closing on their own accord, the tornado around me forcing them shut. I felt more than saw Marreth's chest, which he had pressed tight against my own, holding onto me. One of his hands pressed against my nape, pushing me further into him in an attempt to protect me. Until everything stopped. Until we could breathe again.

"Welcome to the Air Palace," Eidothea smiled, extending her arms in an invitation.

I blinked a few times and made sure that I could, truly, breathe. And indeed, air flowed through my lungs as carelessly as always. Only then I unhooked myself from Marreth, whose expression portrayed shock and slight curiosity.

I once again took advantage to look around, searching for my prince. This time he decided to abandon cordiality and stepped closer to us.

"Is everyone alright?" I heard Ansgar ask, though I knew the question was directed at me.

"Yes," I replied, wanting to make sure he knew I was truly safe. That we made it. I also added a quick smile, which he half-returned, before shifting back to offer his arm to Amara. I followed suit and did the same with my supposed boyfriend.

"This is the entrance hall, if you look to your left, you can observe the transformation of the visitors," the siren announced, making us all shift in the direction she had pointed to. As if on cue, a mermaid swam towards the glass gates, approaching the entrance.

"Cressi, a mermaid!" I could not help my excitement and started giggling like an idiot. Like I was a ten-year-old girl and all my dreams had come true. Because she was everything I had imagined her to be. The half woman part, with her breasts uncovered and hair flowing through the ripples of water, with a glorious fish tail that swished with elegance and fluid movements.

It felt so magical to see the entirety of her body, compared to the one I met at the lake on my birthday, whose torso popped out of the water from time to time.

"If you think that to be exciting, princess, you will love the next part," Eidothea replied, and I knew she was smiling by the tone of her voice.

I watched with amazement how the creature swam to the doors, which opened in some sort of a glass bubble, allowing her body and a chunk of water to come in, until the room filled. A spinning system started, and the chamber instantly released the part of the sea it had swallowed, leaving only the mermaid inside, until it completely emptied. Until there was no water left and the tail that had been swishing around remained immobile. It flicked once or twice while its owner remained on the ground, to then…split?

It happened within the span of seconds, the scales started combusting and drying up, making way for fresh skin and legs. She had grown legs in seconds. As soon as the lower members appeared on her body, the woman stood and pressed a few times on the glass, allowing the doors to open.

She entered the hallway we arrived in, walking as well as any human who'd been able to use their legs since the day they were born would. Completely and utterly naked.

"My queen," she bowed her head while passing us by and greeted Eidothea, who allowed a slow nod in recognition.

"She's not wearing any clothes," Cressida made the observation, and I thanked her for it.

"Indeed, it is not tradition for females to wear garments in the Air Palace," Eidothea replied and while she did, she removed the pin that adorned her dress at the shoulder. The veil instantly fell from her body, silk caressing her breasts, then her navel and her thighs, leaving her completely bare.

What in the hell?

"Does the law apply to visitors?" Rhylan enquired, a pout starting to form.

"You've been here before Fear Gorta. You know how this works. Those of you who possess penises may keep them hidden, lest we want to create displeasure among the sisters."

I looked around to check the reaction of the girls, but Amara had already started undressing. She carefully removed her dress and then asked Ansgar to loosen up her corset.

I wanted to die. Blood boiled in my veins and I assumed my cheeks had become as crimson as they could be.

None of the boys said a word, probably too stunned to speak as Amara finished undressing. Completely. Funny how she didn't think to mention this when she talked about her first visit here.

"Cressi," I barely murmured, my eyes wide, begging my friend to get us out of this situation. She was a queen after all, she could make demands.

"Oh, what the hell, I still have a few good years left in me," she replied instead and started to remove her dress.

Ansgar

Chapter Seven

Breathe, breathe, breathe, I urged myself as a thousand different feelings passed through me. Passion, desire, rage, shame, eagerness, just to name a few.

I was looking at a naked siren, in human shape, and goddess damn me, but my eyes did linger on her body. Everything a male would ever want was displayed in the perfect size, with wide inviting hips and ripe breasts. The image of absolute beauty, Eidothea, just like any siren, represented the embodiment of lust. And my body responded to it in ways I did not imagine, in ways I did not allow myself to think.

That was, until Amara decided to remove her clothing and situated herself as if nothing had ensued next to me, retaking her royal stance, chin perfectly parallel to the glass floor. Instantly, I forced my eyes to avert from my wife and looked down, where I noticed part of the city that hid underneath us.

The darkness of the water made it difficult to spot details, but after focusing on a specific point for a while, I spotted domes and taller buildings, ornate with various kinds of greenery, which I assumed would be seaweed.

Amara's hand tightened around mine, probably to bring me back to the present and alert me to what I already knew but found difficult to play my part in, that a new husband would be ecstatic to have his naked wife by his side.

I drew in a deep breath and did what was expected of me, admired Amara's naked body. I let my eyes gaze at her full and plump breasts, spotting how the nipples peaked, either from the cold or from her excitement, I did not know. I took everything else in as well, observing how the small hairs on her lower pelvis matched the same shade of blonde and how they had been cut in a straight line, pointing right at her centre.

Then Cressida displayed a perfectly round ass and stomped to Rhylan without a care in the world, as she had gotten us used to her sparkling personality many times, acting as though she was on a stage displaying an invisible garment.

Fear Gorta, to his credit, focused solely on his queen, his eyes going wide while a mischievous smirk appeared on his lips. And, true to his expression, as soon as Cressida inched closer to the new fire king, his hands did not remain idle, fingers wrapping around her ass to offer a hungry squeeze.

I watched petrified how Rhylan's fingers slid towards the centre and dipped into his queen, causing her to squeal. Then, fully unashamed, and dare I say it, with a dash of pride, Fear Gorta reached the same fingers to his lips and licked them slowly, letting a hungry groan escape.

That was the reaction of a male in love, of a male that would take advantage of his partner's nakedness, without caring who would be looking or the situation they were in. That was the reaction I was supposed to experience.

I did not know how much of our history my brother shared with his mate. While she posed as Sophia, she spotted Anwen and I in a hug and asked questions about Anwen's feelings towards her mate, yet she hadn't made a single gesture to announce that she remembered this information or wanted to uphold it. The message was clear, I had to comport myself as if Eidothea was the second siren queen and not my brother's mate.

My eyes involuntarily averted to Anwen, the last of the females to remain fully clothed and even though I hated myself for thinking it, even though a feeling of possessiveness invaded me and I did not want anyone else to see my naked mate, desire started building.

I wanted to see the curves of her hips, I needed to gaze at her full breasts, the ones I had bitten so many times, I had become perfectly acquainted with her feel and taste and above all, I wanted to see that curve of her back that drove me absolutely manic every time I took her from behind.

Maybe my thoughts reflected on my face or maybe she could read my feelings, like the many times she had played that very game while we were at her parents' home, but Anwen's eyes pointed to mine, our gazes locking. My mate then proceeded to slowly unzip her dress, focusing exclusively on me.

It was only her and I, nothing else mattered, no one else was there but me, as Anwen uncovered her breasts and proceeded to push her dress lower, the fabric caressing her hips on the way down.

She remained in the lace panties that I loved to remove with my teeth and smiled softly to me, one final time, before her right foot twisted, taking her body away from my view.

Anwen turned to look at Marreth, her back fully exposed to me, as she bent down and lowered her panties in one of the sexiest motions I had seen. She wanted to give me the perfect view of her bent ass, knowing the things it would do to me.

I wanted to fuck her senseless right there and I didn't care who watched. The way she turned this into a game drove me mad with desire, and all I needed, all I dreamed, was to be inside her. To take her against these crystal walls, to bend her down and shove myself into her until her legs started shaking and her throat became rasp with screaming my name.

"We've been married for less than two months," I heard Amara's voice while her arms wrapped tighter around me. I had completely forgotten she was there, but the way she pierced her fingers through my skin to bring me back to reality had the desired effect.

"It is understandable," Eidothea waved her words away, even though the siren's eyes lingered a while longer on me, a half-grin contained on her soft lips before she turned to my brother. I only then sensed my full erection, which poked through my pants and stretched them to the point of pain.

"My apologies, the journey was long, and I did not have time to enjoy my wife today," I forced a grin, dropping my arm on Amara's hips and caressing her skin slightly. I had to play my part, had to take my eyes away from Anwen, had to stop thinking that Marreth would be the one touching her.

"Of course, prince, we are not savages," Eidothea replied. "You will be escorted to your private rooms shortly, I wouldn't get rid of *that* just yet," she pointed at the bulge in my pants.

"We are grateful," Amara smiled too and caressed my face and neck, lowering her palm down my chest, her head resting on my shoulder.

"Shall we?" Marreth's voice came out raw and jolted. I didn't need to look at him to know that he was experiencing the same feelings. He was touching my mate, the same way I was touching his lover and we both wanted this to immediately stop.

"I think it would be best," Rhylan replied. I hadn't even noticed that he and Cressida had walked to the side of the glass hallway to continue the long line of caresses Fear Gorta had adorned his wife with at the very beginning. They looked trapped in desire and overly excited to be alone.

I did not know if Rhylan played his part or if it was a true reaction to seeing his wife naked, though, truth be told, any sane male would have the same urges at Cressida's body. One thing was clear, sirens adored lust, and we had offered them exactly what they enjoyed most.

Eidothea escorted us through the glass tube that represented the hallway entrance to the palace. We walked in silence, each couple joining hands and trying to keep their urges contained as much as possible. The path seemed interminable, it felt as if we had walked for miles and surrounded the palace many times over, but none of us protested, probably too tired and nervous to dare question our host.

Amara continued to hang on my shoulder and walk slowly by my side while we tried to look around and spy on the city below as much as we could. Rhylan and Cressida proved to be a distraction, since they walked in front of us, following Vikram and Eidothea and neither of them had stopped kissing or caressing the other every few steps they took.

My brother did not make a gesture, he walked alongside the siren queen as if it was his right to be there, as if he had done it so many times this had become his second home. I had to wonder how many times Vikram visited the Water Kingdom and lived this secret life he had suddenly decided to share with me.

I tried to remember all the solstice celebrations we lived together, and how, ever since he received his keeper assignment, decided to cut the party short and only do what was required from him as a member of the royal family, choosing to escape into the celebration afterwards. We'd see him randomly appear in the morning, always with some kind of excuse.

Had he been here all this time? With her?

"You will have to forgive us, but your first night will have to be spent in the outer side of the palace, until the Queen approves your entry into the kingdom. I believe these will suffice for now?" Eidothea stopped in front of a pink marble wall, the first part of the hallways that was made from something other than transparent materials. Designed to offer guests privacy.

"Thank you for your hospitality," Rhylan took his self-assigned role as a leader and responded in our stead. "When can we meet the queen?"

"My sister will be free after the solstice celebrations, however she wants to greet the newlyweds tonight. Shall I arrange an escort in three hours?"

I realised then that she was addressing Amara and me.

My wife took the lead and nodded softly. "Three hours would be perfect, thank you, my Queen," she replied with a small curtsy. Seeing how she was utterly naked, the gesture may have looked ridiculous in anyone's eyes but Eidothea's, who bowed deep in acknowledgement.

"Very well, I shall see you tomorrow," she addressed the rest of the group and passed each of the ladies a key. The siren queen handed the first one to Cressida, her equal in rank. Cressi grabbed it with a quick thank you and reached the door to her left. It opened immediately, so Amara and Anwen did the same with theirs while Eidothea watched them.

"The doors will only open at the hand of a female," she explained. "A rule of our kingdom."

We all thanked her, and the queen dipped her chin to us once, veiled in elegance, before she turned to Vikram.

"Shall we, my sweet?" she purred to my brother, who in turn waved at us and started walking away.

"Happy solstice everyone," he wished us before they disappeared through a golden gate none of us had access to.

"Very well, in that case—" Rhylan started speaking but neither Marreth nor I were listening. As soon as Eidothea and Vikram disappeared, we instantly shifted to circle back to our partners. There was no one to see us and we were outside of the palace doors. Might as well take advantage of the few hours we were offered.

"In that case, we'll see you in two hours and a half?" I pointed my question to Marreth and Amara who were already preparing to close the door to their room.

"That works," the commander replied before the door snapped shut.

"That works," I nodded to Rhylan and Cressida, then grabbed Anwen in my arms and slammed the door shut right in Fear Gorta's face.

I didn't care about the rest of the world. I needed my mate.

Anwen

Chapter Eight

Purple, dark green and turquoise. Desire, love and need. All three feelings came from my mate, who had decided to abandon everything and let himself be devoured by need. I did not know if it was due to our location or to whatever effect the sirens had on us, but we were desperate to be together, to join right then and there and forget the planning and all that was expected of us.

As soon as the marble door locked us in, leaving a visibly irritated Rhylan behind, Ansgar allowed himself to do what we knew he'd wanted since I unveiled my naked ass to him.

I didn't expect his desire for me to poke through in such a way, or to continue to remain alert until this very moment. God damn it, he was so ready for me, that bulge in his pants so prominent that I instantly turned liquid.

My body did not compare to any of the other three that had followed through the path of nakedness all of us women were invited to attend. Eidothea turned out to be everything a man could desire. She had full and plump breasts, looking as if they had just been completed by the most skilled plastic surgeon in the world. No boob I ever saw could look like that naturally, so perky and full, bouncing up and down as if it was no one's business.

Her ass did not have a single stretch mark or hint of cellulite, formed only of muscle and plumpness, her legs wearing just enough muscle to look perfectly sensual. The way she moved made it look like she was dancing, her feet placing themselves in a constant waltz.

Then Amara came, displaying her Brazilian to everyone and walking around with a superb straight tummy, not a gram of extra fat showing on her beautiful abdomen. The V shape of her pelvis invited the eye right to her pussy, shining pink and looking inviting underneath that soft veil of hair.

And of course, Cressi. Who was a gym maniac. Who always looked perfect and paraded her body with pride every chance she got. One of the most famous influencers in the world, with naturally big boobs that trained with celebrity fitness instructors.

It was no surprise Rhylan reacted the way he did, I would have done the same in his stead. Cressi always took pride in her hairless body, which she underwent so many laser treatments on a yearly basis to maintain. It meant that she was always ready. At any given time.

And there I was, with a belly swollen by the too many cakes I indulged in at uni that turned into a permanent punishment, with stretch marks down my legs and hips, with droplets of cellulite that fell down my inner thighs, making my mother hate that I could never obtain that perfect triangle every celebrity seemed to have.

That was me. The fat one.

Ansgar did not seem to care, he never cared about my imperfections, how my tummy formed rolls every time I sat, which had inched permanent marks into my skin, how the orange-peel looking skin stretched down my legs and covered the better part of my thighs. He only wanted me, accepting and loving me every single time.

I touched that swollen desire of his, squeezing it slightly in the palm of my hand. Or better said, what I could grip from it, because my prince had decided to go full on erect. I felt his cock twitch under my touch, his thick veins responding to the action, eliciting a groan from his throat.

"Fuck…fahrenor, I can't," I looked up at him to find him shaking his head. "Forgive me, but I can't," he said again, blinking at me with eyes filled with rage, a storm clouding them.

I didn't know what he meant, I could not think beyond that point of connection, the pride I felt in what I could do to him, how he wanted *me*, out of all those other much more beautiful women.

Before I had a chance to ask what he meant, Ansgar removed whatever leash he'd kept himself in until then and grabbed me in his arms while biting into my neck and down my shoulder.

Oh, that is what he meant, I snickered in delight.

I found myself thrown on the bed, the little bounce of the mattress alerting me before my prince grabbed my legs to position me. He pulled me back to the side of the bed and lifted my pelvis to make my legs bend and kneel on the mattress. I supported the top half of my body on my elbows, but before I could even complete the movement to stabilise myself and get into the position he made it clear he wanted me in, Ansgar slapped my pussy hard, covering it in the wetness of his saliva and spreading it around my core. Making me ready, I realised.

Not a second later, my core was forced to split abruptly to take him in. I hadn't even realised he had time to take his pants off, until he pumped into me, forcing me to receive him up to the hilt. I looked back to see that he had only unzipped his pants and taken out his hardness before poking it into me with maddening thrusts.

I screamed, not ready for my body to receive such a blow, the mixture of pleasure and pain forcing me to take a few deep breaths. He was massive, he had always been, but today he did not take the time to prepare me, to allow me to adjust to his length and took me savage and raw, with thrusts so deep that poked at my lower belly and forced my stomach to release sudden breaths.

My core struggled to produce enough wetness to allow the forced movements he punished me with while his hands gripped either side of my hips to use as a support for the hardening thrusts he started to work on.

Ansgar wanted to shove himself into me fully, like he had never done before, his balls slapping my clit in his forced movements so abruptly that he created waves of pain.

"Ansgar…" I moaned. I shouted. I begged. All the above? I didn't know.

He'd never taken me like this, with this urgency, with this madness. Every thrust echoed through my bones, making my spine jolt and my body move away from the force of the push, were it not for him gripping my hips and supporting them against his rage.

"Fuck, Ansgar..." I said again, my fingernails ripping at the bedsheet, trying to hold myself, to find something to keep me grounded, because all I could feel, all my body and my mind could focus on were those savage moments, the way his member entered me and split me in half, forcing my body to take more and more of him. Every thrust felt deeper, as if he planned to drill into me until he left me spent, until my body was unable to produce wetness and that jolt of my core that allowed me to produce pleasure was modelled to his own desire.

"You can take it, fahrenor," Ansgar barely replied in between pants. Then he lifted a leg and rested his foot on the bedframe, next to where my knee was, the movement allowing another part of his cock to shove itself deeper, causing me to scream, my throat screeching with the sensation.

"You can take me. All of me," my prince added and started pistoning into me yet again, this time with even more desperation and need.

I released a wave of madness, which allowed his thickness to ease through my core, pumping at that sweet point of pleasure and pain he had gotten me used to. Still, he did not stop, did not slow his thrusts, forcing my body to produce another orgasm only seconds later. The sensation was too much, the heat gathered in my lower belly proved unable to contain. Each of his movements, every slap of his testicles over my clit brought me closer and closer to another wave of pleasure. My hands started shaking, taking my body along with them. They could not sustain my weight, they could not support the blow that my ass received and forced me to drop on the mattress.

I remained limp and useless, shaking with the desire, with the severe punishing thrusts that rained on me, the only support I had being the same one that cost me my balance.

My face barely touched the mattress, arms limp and falling under me when I felt Ansgar's hand reach up my back and to my neck, gripping my nape and spreading his fingers to catch as much of my scalp as they could, before they closed to gather in my hair.

"We're not done yet," Ansgar groaned from behind me. "You cannot show me that ass and not let me take it," he added, shifting the hand that had remained on my hip to lower and catch my belly, holding me up.

I squealed at the new sensation, the palm of his hand placed right where his dick was poking into me, adding yet more pressure to what was already the most sensitive area.

"Fuck, Anwen, is this how I feel inside of you?" He seemed to ease his thrusts just for a few seconds, allowing himself to discover what he was doing to me, how he drilled into my body.

"Yes, this is how you feel…" I barely mumbled, grateful for the moment of peace he offered me, but my words seemed to have the opposite effect, because as soon as I released them, he became maddened with urge.

"Baby, this feels fantastic," he spoke again, spreading his palm and pressing harder on my tummy to feel himself as the deepening trusts resurfaced, bringing back the speed he had tortured me with until then.

It was not enough for my prince though, who wanted to get the full experience, so he brought me back into position, gripping my hair in his other hand and forced my head to raise and take my body along with it, curving my spine.

"That's it, bend for me baby, show me how you take me in." He became possessed with his new discovery and forced my head to the point where I could not move, keeping my spine so arched that I feared he would snap it from the pressure. But he was right. It did feel phenomenal.

Being completely at his mercy, utterly his to do with me as he wished, take me with the force and strength he wanted brought unexpected jolts in my stomach. Those piercing thrusts, his need for me and this dependence gave me the best orgasm of my life.

I loved Ansgar.

I fucking loved Ansgar.

Ansgar

Chapter Nine

"Ten more minutes," Anwen's voice pleaded, her head nestling tighter to my chest. Neither of us knew what happened, how or why our lovemaking transformed into the savage dance we had performed for the past two hours, until our bodies became sated, until they absorbed enough pleasure to allow our surrender.

I had taken Anwen many times from behind, slow and deep, rough and hard, but I never before had her completely surrender to me. I must confess, I loved it. Though I did make my tongue apologise for the damage other parts had done, allowing my mate to finally relax and enjoy the pleasure she received, without being forced to release it in unforgiving gasps.

"I do not have ten more minutes, fahrenor. We have a meeting with the siren queen," I reminded her, but it did not have the desired effect. Instead of allowing me to rise from bed, Anwen threw herself over me and used me as her pillow, her body covering my chest and hips to trap me under her.

"No, you are mine," she protested with a deep groan.

I recognised that sound, I had heard it so many times before during our nightly conversations. Her voice turned slightly raspier when sleep threatened to overcome her and most of the time, she did not remember saying the things she spoke right before falling asleep.

"Always, fahrenor," I pressed a kiss on her forehead and caressed long lines down her back, allowing her to relax fully into me. "I'll come back soon, I promise," I forced the words out, even though the truth did not resemble my dreams.

If the queen allowed Amara and I access into their palace, it meant that our rooms would be guarded, or maybe even separated from one another, making moments like this impossible to achieve. "Jag vaedrum teim," I murmured into her, the promise I would keep for the rest of my existence.

I allowed myself a few more minutes in the company of my mate, giving my nostrils a chance to bask in her scent, my hands to caress her soft skin and my lips to plant kisses on her forehead, her cheeks and the part of her shoulder that I could reach, without having to let her go. But the time did arrive and with it, a knock on the door, which I assumed was Marreth. Ready to embrace his role and take my mate away.

I zipped my pants and hurried to open. My shirt had remained discarded on the other side of the bed, so I had to head back and grab it, along with the pretentious tunic Amara wanted me to wear.

The chance allowed it, so I shared another kiss with my sleeping mate before I went back to meet Marreth.

"Did the bed do something to offend you or...?" Marreth asked with a frown, after glancing in Anwen's direction, who remained asleep and wrapped in a white bedsheet, the only cover I could find for her. I realised we had left an absolute mess, the varied sized pillows either ripped to shreds or thrown through the room in our desperation to find each other. The mattress had been pushed to the side and remained trapped in between the metal bars of the bed frame.

"I trust my wife is well?" I changed the subject, my chest heavy with what I had to do. Punishing me for leaving my mate behind.

"She's not passed out," Marreth tilted his head as if to say he wanted nothing more than to achieve the same effect.

"Take care of her," I pinned him with a gaze, which he immediately waved off, rolling his eyes to show annoyance. I would feel the same if I had to leave my naked lover wandering around with a husband.

"I'll see you soon, prince," the commander patted my shoulder in encouragement and shoved me out into the hallway, making enough space to push the door behind me.

Rhylan's pacing gave the corridor a demanding clink, which forced my eyes in his direction. As soon as he spotted me, Fear Gorta stopped and hurried to my side.

"What in the god's name are you thinking, imbeciles?" he swore, those swirls of darkness I had come to know thanks to Anwen's gentle caresses coming into view. Though not for the same reason my mate had used them. The fire king's eyes looked bloodshot, tiny capillary veins pumping with rage, one that would soon be sent into my direction.

"We needed that. We all did," I simply said, uncaring whether he believed it or not. I needed to be with Anwen one final time, for both our sakes and for my own sanity. We truly did not know what we were getting ourselves into, we were in unknown terrain, at the mercy of beings that renowned themselves for killing males.

"Tread lightly, prince," Fear Gorta must have read the truth in my words. We hadn't played a ruse, we did not change the plan or left him out of decision making. We simply needed one final push to be able to fight what was coming.

"My wife is expecting me, King. If that is all?" I straightened my back and tensed my shoulders, preparing myself for the role I was meant to play.

"Have a pleasant evening," Rhylan half-grinned and stepped to the side, allowing me to walk to the door behind which Amara waited. I knocked twice and she made an appearance, wrapped in the bedsheet, just like I had left Anwen.

"Is it time?" she asked, taking a deep breath to encourage herself and as soon as I nodded, she removed the cover and stepped out the door, holding only the key Eidothea had gifted her.

I maintained my gaze pierced to her face, her hair, her forehead, any part of her head that came within sight, silently assuring her that I would not take advantage of her exposed figure until the time came. Until I had to.

We did not have to wait long, probably five to ten minutes until one of the mermaids that had gone through the change stopped in front of us. I would not, for the life of me, get used to naked females walking the hallways.

"Are you the prince and princess of Wind?" she spoke softly, her long dark hair falling down her back with tight curls. Some of them stopped just below her midsection to hug her breasts.

"We are," Amara smiled and nodded gently. This was a female ruled kingdom, so we had agreed that she would do most of the talking and negotiations, lest we wanted to offend the sirens and remain trapped till the end of our days.

When the mermaid asked us to follow her, I offered Amara my hand and did not say a word, content to walk next to the two and listen to the conversation they had started while trying to gather more information about the parts we had been allowed to see.

We walked hand in hand, marching through the hallways that started to become darker and more strained, the only light available coming from the shine of pearl strings, adorned on the side of the walls to look like a bead of candelabras.

Amara and I barely saw one another anymore, but luckily, our guide kept talking and telling Amara about how she remembered the first visit of the princess and complimenting some of the windling traditions she knew about. My wife must have been terrified, because her hand kept squeezing mine, so I followed suit and did the same, finding the length of her arm to place some encouraging caresses, which seemed to calm her down slightly.

The princess kept true to our plan and spoke with cheer and excitement, asking random questions about the city below and the position of the air dome, which I knew were exclusively for my benefit.

"The queen will see you now," the siren stopped abruptly and spread her arms to point our attention towards a massive marble statue, situated in the very centre of a wide glass room.

"Thank you, we are delighted to be here," Amara took the lead once more and bowed slowly to the female. That was all she needed, because the siren instantly vanished, leaving us on our own in a crystal bubble with only a statue to keep us company.

"How are we supposed to meet the queen?" I frowned and turned to Amara for the first time, trying not to gaze at inappropriate places while pointing my question.

"It's true," she snickered and pushed my shoulder gently, playfully. "Males have such a narrow view of the world," she added.

"It's not narrow, it is quite wide, if I might add, *wife*," I playfully mocked our connection, then felt the need to explain myself. "Circular ring of air, statue in the middle, no corners. It is wide," I allowed myself to giggle.

"You are too much," she wrapped her arm around my waist and pressed herself to my chest, resting her head close to my shoulder. "But that is why I love you," she breathed slowly, dispersing the words in the air.

I had no idea what was going on, but this was not Amara. This was not the windling princess I befriended, the one who offered me the deepest secret of her kingdom. But I trusted her and if she decided to behave like this, she must have her reasons. And I would follow.

Planting the image of Anwen in my mind instead of Amara's for an easier transition, I took a breath before I spoke again, following suit.

"I love you too, my darling. Were we not on official business, I would have you right here and now. You know what your naked body does to me..." I released the words with one or two octaves lower than my normal voice, but it would suffice.

"Mmhm...hasn't my prince had enough?" Amara lifted her chin to me and pressed her mouth on my neck, lifting herself on her toes to do it.

"Of you?" I asked while allowing my hands to trail down her back, taking in the soft skin that came alive under my touch and rested them on either side of her hips, grabbing a part of her ass as I did so. My eyes widened just slightly, afraid to overstep, but Amara smiled in approval. "Never," I added, tilting my head to come closer to her lips.

"My apologies for the intrusion," a voice stopped me on my way to a pretend kiss. Whatever test this was, we passed it. Amara's smile told me so.

My wife removed herself from my arms, pushing me away gently with the palm of her hand, as if to mimic that she was ashamed of being caught in a loving embrace. Very well played, I glanced at her with pride one final time before turning towards the statue.

Which had converted into a throne, displaying a female at its very centre. The Queen.

"My Queen," Amara and I bowed low in greeting, averting our eyes from the queen of the sirens, until summoned back.

"Please, dear guests, rise and come closer," her voice invited, allowing us to retake our stance and to look at her.

I offered my arm to Amara, who stepped close to me again and we walked the distance to the throne, while allowing our eyes to gaze on the Mother of Sirens.

She looked taller than her sister, long adamant hair covering her breasts and pelvis as she sat cross-legged on the marble throne. Adorned in pearls, her legs were long, and the skin looked brand new, untouched by the sun or any kind of harmful effects.

Simply put, *she* looked brand new.

"Queen Thelssha, it is an honour to see you again," Amara greeted the siren queen first and let go of my arm to curtsy low in front of the queen. I took my queue and bent at the waist to do the same.

"It is wonderful to see you again, Princess Amara," the queen spoke with strands of gold pouring down her lips, the song of her words filling the room with wonder. Instinct forced me to drop to my knees, the perfection of that sound affecting my brain in such a way that I knew nothing this pure would ever come out of this life again.

"Prince Ansgar," she addressed me. *Me.* I stretched my neck enough to allow my eyes to gaze at her, instant tears pouring down my cheeks. Sight became useless after her departure, because my eyes did not have a purpose anymore. Not after they'd seen her. I started shaking, muscles wanting to unhook from my bones from the purity of the being in front of me. There was nothing I could ever do that was worthy of living after this very moment. After being in her presence.

"My apologies," she smiled, and goddess mine, give her your essence. Take whatever you placed in me and offer it to *her*.

"Ansgar! Ansgar, open your mouth," a hand forced my eyes away from the heaven in front of me, shoving something into my mouth, then pressed my nostrils together and covered my lips. I did not know what it was, but the pressure forced me to swallow and fight the fear of the unknown, the necessity of drawing air too great to ignore.

As soon as I swallowed, everything calmed. The shaking, the tears, the ringing in my ears. I found myself kneeling on the floor, panting desperately in front of the siren queen.

"My apologies, prince," the siren spoke, only her voice did not spit strands of gold anymore. It was a pleasant tone, a melodious ring, but not one that would damage the very essence of my being. "Generally, a male does not feel the effects in the presence of the one he loves," the queen pointed while I struggled to retake my stance.

"He's always been one to fall in love easily," Amara tried to divert the affirmation. "So many sirens, too much beauty, a male can only take so much..." she slapped my shoulder admonishingly, then rewrapped her arms around my biceps.

"Please accept my apologies, my queen. We did not have time to rest, I—"

My attempt to defend myself was cut out short.

"Yes, I can sense how the rest time offered to you was spent," the siren queen smiled knowingly. Offering me a route for a request that was not planned yet deserved a mention.

"You have to understand, Your Highness, my body is weak. My mind follows," I admitted. "To see the female I love strolling around completely naked, to see her make the same gestures she performs on a daily bases with the added sensuality of those hips rolling…it…it blocks my brain, my Queen. It fills me with urges I cannot contain." I stopped to swallow a lump in my throat and to settle the need for another erection, because images of Anwen's naked body decided to stroll through my mind right then.

"I will speak to the sisters. We, of course, want your comfort, prince," the queen smiled, visibly pleased with the torture they had infringed on me.

"I am thankful, Your Highness," I bowed again, tilting my head to Amara to spot her reaction, but she remained statuesque.

"I will not declare it a bother, but your visit on a solstice merits the question. Why are you here? And why did you arrive accompanied by the Fire royals?"

That was it. What we came for. No more playing around with cordiality.

"Fire wants an alliance," Amara took the lead. "They are trying to make us think they are willing to change, yet we both know how that would work. My husband and I are following their plans in order to get an audience with Your Highness. We would like to discuss politics, when the time is favourable."

The siren queen stopped for a second, dissecting the offer she had received and pointing her full attention to Amara. To then shift it to me.

"What does Earth think of this?"

"I am a representative of the Wind Kingdom, my Queen, though my ties to Earth remain as strong as they ever were. They support our discussion," I bowed again, slowly, reverently, doing my best to demonstrate the truth in my words.

Queen Thelssha took a long minute of analysis before her following words became released.

"Fire and Water do not mix…" she stopped a breath before adding a smile. "Wind however, can do wonders for the mother of creation. I am inclined to hear your proposal. Until then, you will be my personal guests. And your guests, in turn, will receive the same treatment."

"Thank you, Your Highness," Amara and I bowed in synchrony.

"You are invited to dine with my sisters and I tomorrow evening. Until then, please enjoy the solstice celebrations.

Anwen

Chapter Ten

"I cannot stop thinking about Amara's nakedness. And your mate is there to enjoy the gifts," Marreth sighed. I didn't know how long I slept for, but the clock on the wall showed quarter past six. Nice touch from the mermaids to give us something to look at while drowning in our anxiety.

When I woke up, I found Marreth sitting in the corner, watching me sleep. There wasn't much else to do, truth be told, the white room only contained a bed and a bathroom door with a toilet, sink and shower. No mirrors or cosmetic products, nothing to keep one entertained. It felt as if these rooms had been specifically designed with the sole purpose of sex.

The mermaids definitely knew what they were doing.

I blinked the sleep away and grabbed a pillow to rest my back against, while wrapping myself in the bedsheet Ansgar had pulled for me. Thank you baby, this was super awkward already, the last thing I needed was Marreth seeing my hooha while I napped.

"I think he feels the same," I responded, allowing my fingers to rub at my eyes and take the sleep away. My body felt heavy, tired and aching, as if I'd been in a car accident or a gym training session that lasted for a week.

"I would assume so, since he made a point to leave you paralysed before he left," Marreth chuckled and looked at me knowingly, causing my arms to wrap the sheet tighter around my chest.

"It's not a critique," he immediately said, sensing my reaction. And it was true, his colours showed no sign of anger, only a dash of yellow floated around him to show that he was sad. "I struggled to keep my possessive thoughts on the princess as well," he confessed. It made sense now, why Ansgar had been so rough, why he needed to spill all that anger and raw domination. It affected them all.

"It's strange, you know? Every time I think I got to know him, something else resurfaces. There's always a new part of him to discover, a new experience that we go through that deepens our connection." I don't know why I was confessing things to Marreth, indirectly letting him know that I had enjoyed the rough sex more than I should have. Part of me wanted to know if it happened to them as well, to see the male perspective.

Look at me seeking relationship advice from fae warriors, I internally huffed.

"Amara is an entirely different person."

Well, well, I'm not alone in wanting to talk relationship.

"How so?" I jumped at the opportunity.

"I knew her since she was a youngling, frolicking through that massive plateau. I watched her grow and turn into a beautiful female. And the caring feelings I pushed towards her shifted, grew into something I did not allow myself to admit. Or to exercise." He stopped for a long while, his eyes trapped in memories and I kept silent, waiting for his following words.

"She made the first step. She walked into the soldier's quarters in a see-through veil dress, playing the temptress. She offered her mouth to me," Marreth snickered in delight, clearly enjoying the sweetness of the memory.

"The goddess hadn't even blessed her yet, she must have been seventeen or eighteen and believe me, Anwen, the goddess herself struggled to keep me courteous. Or well, as courteous as one can be while devouring the mouth of his future ruler," he shrugged.

"What happened?" I had to ask, I had to know. This was new information, Marreth had never been this honest before, hadn't allowed himself to delve this deep into memories.

"I was sent to war. The princess came to see me that morning, alongside the queen. To wish us good luck in battle. She could not speak the words, but her eyes said it all. She gave me her scarf, for protection. It was dipped in her perfume. I kept it inside my helmet, her sweet scent helped keep away the stench of death."

"That is very sweet," I smiled, imagining a young Amara passing the fabric in secret to a full armoured Marreth. Knowing how he looked, mounted on a horse and with his full armour, I had to admire her courage. It was intimidating.

"That's how I got the scar," Marreth pointed to the deep cut down his neck, the first thing I noticed about him. He did try to cover most of it with his dark hair and part of his beard, but it still remained prominent. "They tried to take it from me, so I turned my head to protect it. Some fighter...exposing my neck to protect a piece of fabric," he shook his head as if to admonish himself.

"You protected what was important to you. I find it admirable," I responded. I would not be one to criticise silly decisions, when I had made my fair share too.

"She is changed now. She's rougher, polished for hardship. A true queen," his sigh came interrupted by a knock.

I looked at him in question, but the commander prompted me to go and open the door, since the key had been handed to me. I assumed it was similar to the magicked doors they had back in the Fire Kingdom, which he and I had experience with.

"Hello," I opened to find a naked woman, of course, holding a piece of blue veil and a few golden pins.

"As per the Wind prince's request," she handed me the items with a soft nod and walked away.

I closed the door and leaned against it, holding the items to my chest.

"Thank you, baby," I giggled and walked to the bathroom to get dressed.

To say they gave me a dress was overstretching it. Basically, they offered me a long piece of veil and a few decorative pins, leaving the rest to my imagination.

"Doesn't look very regal," Marreth observed when I got back into the bedroom. I had wrapped the fabric around my body, using the corners to cover my breasts and tried to make some kind of sari with the rest.

"Beats being naked," I replied, slightly annoyed that he had the nerve to mock me when he wore pants, shoes and a shirt. "Better something like this than having your princess walking around naked, don't you think?"

"If you put it like that..." Marreth tilted his head to agree.

Only Amara did not receive a piece of veil, but a proper dress. Light turquoise satin covered her breasts and offered a generous cleavage, while a parade of veils created a long skirt with a train, making it look as if waves followed her steps. It reminded me of a very pompous version of Victorian gowns.

"You look amazing," I said the words on Marreth's behalf and earned a grateful smile from them.

"You do too, it's great to have clothes again, isn't it? Ansgar convinced the queen," Amara explained. "My poor husband said he could not focus on anything but the hips of the woman he loves," she snickered and looked at me knowingly.

I averted my gaze to Ansgar and displayed a small grin, before turning my full attention to Amara. We could do this; we could communicate like this.

It was only for a few days after all.

"Hello again," Eidothea's voice shifted our attention to the golden door, which opened to let her and Vikram pass. "I hope you are all having a pleasant stay?" the second siren queen smiled, but my eyes travelled to Vikram.

He looked absolutely exhausted, sickly even, the colour of his beautiful adamant skin turned into a shade of faded brown and the thick voluminous hair had lost its shine, looking like tangled pieces of silk. Even his eyes seemed tired, the way he blinked as if his eyelids became heavy.

"Brother?" Ansgar disregarded the siren and headed straight to Vikram, concern leaning in his step.

"I'm fine," Vikram nodded a few times, and I could not help but notice how his muscles strained, how he forced those tendons to stretch to allow such a small gesture. "I'll be fine, brother," Vikram reiterated when my mate's hand reached his shoulder.

"I will take him back as soon as I escort you through the gates," Eidothea replied. "He will recover in a few hours," she spoke again. Maybe my imagination played tricks on me, but the siren looked sad. Mourning the impending departure of her lover.

I did wonder how Vikram could survive a mermaid's kiss. After all, we had my brother's example to follow. I did not believe it at first and had to do a lot of research to understand that Rhylan's words spoke true that day, that a mermaid's kiss had the power to end one's life. And here Vikram was, a prince of a fae kingdom, a strong male, barely able to stand after a few hours with a siren.

"Let's go, then," Rhylan and Cressida appeared through their door, the perfect picture of elegance. Cressi had received a dark grey veil and did wonders with it, making it look like a De la Renta garment, with such an intricate design that would have taken someone else days to put together. How she'd managed to pull it off in such a short time, I had absolutely no idea.

We all gathered close to the siren in an attempt to urge her to move faster, all of us concerned about Vikram. Even Rhylan pointed his full attention to the prince and focused on the effects that being close to the siren had inflicted on him.

I didn't pay attention to the way there. We passed through pompous halls that looked worthy of a royal palace, I spotted some pearl and diamond ornaments at some point and my feet felt glad to step on soft carpets rather than the cold glass. We had three warriors in our band, who I knew were taking mental notes of all the exits, guards, directions and such, so I allowed myself to focus on more important things.

On the way Vikram's symptoms looked so similar to my brother's. The loss of colours, the dizziness he seemed to experience, because he started walking slower and leaning into the siren for balance, the tightness in the muscles and the way his eyes looked glassy.

Same as Erik's before he had to be rushed to hospital.

I didn't have to look at him to know that his chest was in pain, that his heart had to work overtime to pulsate through the strain and that, should he continue whatever activities brought him to this point, he would fade. Just like Erik had.

"Can you please just take him already?" I heard myself shout, unable to contain the anxiety. I couldn't see Vikram like this, I couldn't bear another second of his pain, of that agony he experienced with every step.

Eidothea stopped and turned to me, knowing perfectly well what I was referring to and not appreciating one bit that I was raising my voice at her. In her own home. Inside her kingdom.

"The celebration is through those doors," she pointed at yet another set of gold adorned doors. We had passed so many already that I became immune to their grandeur.

"Have a great evening," she wished us before she turned, taking Vikram with her.

"Brother," Ansgar called after him, but Vikram turned quickly, half of his body weight now sustained by Eidothea. "I'll be fine. I've been doing this for a decade, little one. I know my limits," he waved a finger in the air as if he was one of those footballers after scoring a goal.

"Let us go," Rhylan ordered and stepped close to the golden set of massive doors, making them open to allow us in.

Marreth and I followed suit, leaving a worried Ansgar and Amara behind. I spotted with the corner of my eye how Amara embraced my mate and caressed his shoulders slowly to reassure him. I knew he was worried and wanted nothing more than to go and hug him, to calm him down, but Marreth's hand remained a firm bracelet on my upper arm. The message clear, we were being watched.

As soon as we stepped inside, music rolled in our ears and an array of naked females started dancing. We had entered a ballroom, with huge glass candelabras that illuminated the high ceilings, with chairs and tables filled with food and drink and hundreds of mermaids, dancing and swaying their hips to the rhythm of the music.

It looked like a mediaeval orgy.

"This is what I call a party," Rhylan smirked and true to his name, and all the expectations connected to it, started swaying his body with excitement, reaching for Cressida and inviting her to a dance. The couple was easily distinguishable through the crowd of skin, but they did not seem to care and enjoyed the party as if they had lived through this a million times before.

"Should we follow suit?" Marreth asked, allowing me one final glance at Ansgar and letting me see that he was settled and had adopted his regal stance again, entering the room hand in hand with his wife.

"Of course," I replied and plastered a fake smile, allowing the commander to invite me to dance.

Awkward is a poor word for what followed, because some of the dances had to be performed in a group, which meant that everywhere I looked and touched, there would be a naked woman. I had to gulp a few glasses of champagne to be able to cope.

I was living through a fairy tale, the drunk part of my body constantly reminded me and urged me to partake in the dancing and the celebration, because who can honestly say they'd been to a mermaid solstice celebration?

But the other part filled with hatred. I could not understand how they could celebrate like this when they enjoyed killing innocent young men in their spare time as if it was just another common pastime. I wondered if she was here, in this very room, if she maybe had the nerve to come and dance with me, touch me or even come close to me without expecting any kind of punishment.

My brother's murderer.

"It's time! It's time!" Many of the women stopped their dancing and rushed to the high glass walls, where the moonlight started peeking through, creating a sort of reflection in the outside waters, as if a water stage had been created outside the ballroom.

The candle lights and pearlescent luminescence they harnessed around the palace dimmed, veiling the room in cosy darkness, with only the speckles of moon shining through the glass wall.

Everyone grew quiet, a sudden blanket of expectation grouping the mermaids into smaller huddles, all of their gazes pinned to the window.

"Happy solstice!" One of them, who looked to be higher rank than the others cheered, making the same exclamation rumble in the air. "Let us enjoy the offering and thank the goddess for yet another blessed solstice!" she spoke, then everyone went still.

The entire ballroom remained covered in moonlight, forcing us all to step closer to the walls and look at the water, instinctively knowing that something would be happening soon.

"This would be a good moment to retire," Rhylan appeared from behind me, touching my shoulder in a silent invitation.

"No, I want to see the celebration," Cressi insisted and shrugged her elbow to release herself from Rhylan's hold and to step closer to me.

"Anwen, let us go." It was Ansgar's voice that called me this time and I turned to see him right behind me, close enough to touch my waist if he wanted to, taking advantage of the darkness that covered us. "It's best to leave some things unseen," he whispered and just like Rhylan, he grabbed my arm in an attempt to take me away. Like Cressi, I shifted to escape his hold.

They knew what would be happening. They knew and did not want me to see it.

"No, I'm not going!" Cressi rustled away from Rhylan yet again, protesting at his forced hold. "Either you tell me what this is about, or I will stay here," she raised her voice just slightly, not enough to make a scene, but enough for her words to reach me.

"This will hurt you, fahrenor. Let us go," Ansgar pressed on either side of my hips, coming close to me from behind.

"What will I see?" I asked with a trembling voice, though part of me already knew. I had already guessed it.

"This is how they make new mermaids. They wrap the bodies in energy and in time, they will transform into what you see today," he tried to explain without using any triggering words.

The mermaids around us started cheering and I looked up at the tall walls to spot one of their sisters, flicking her tail around and coming close to the walls, swishing around with pride and trying to display something to the gathering crowd. My heart sank with the realisation, with the shape of the limp body she was carrying, but it was Cressida's voice that raised my terror.

"Is that a dead man?!?" she shouted through the darkness.

Ansgar

Chapter Eleven

We retired after the display of the tenth or eleventh body, after Rhylan forced Cressida from the room. The Fire Queen started screaming at the murders she witnessed, causing some of the mermaids to gather round and check on the disturbance.

Fear Gorta shifted to darkness, covering his queen and her cries, before they both left the room. Anwen took a few more minutes and I had to see how her body shook with what she saw, how every cheer of the mermaids chipped away at her heart, making her back muscles tremble from the soft cries my mate released.

"How long will they continue for?" a broken voice called me to her side, begging me to tell her a lie. But I could not.

"Until morning," I replied, before I grabbed her hands and made her turn her back to the tradition of atrocities the waterlings liked to celebrate every solstice and escorted her out of the room. Marreth and Amara had remained close, ready to jump back into action should the need arise.

"Let me take her," Marreth stepped next to me as soon as Anwen and I got into the hallway.

"No, I'll take care of her, I have to—"

"Prince, your wife is waiting for you," my friend pierced me with the command, reminding me that, even though most of the waterlings were gathered in that room, we could still be watched.

"Yes, of course, please care for your lover, Marreth," I responded, slightly louder than my normal tone of voice and passed the love of my life into his arms, watching how he situated a hand on Anwen's back and bent the other one to reach behind her knees before he lifted her and started walking away.

"Shall we, my love?" I turned back to Amara and offered her my arm, which she accepted with a tight smile.

I had no choice but to follow Marreth's steps as he continued walking the hallways with Anwen nestled in his arms. There was no sign of Rhylan and Cressida, not a speck of darkness to determine if they passed through these hallways or if Rhylan had decided to jump straight into their allocated room.

"Princess Amara, Prince Ansgar, already on the go?"

The last thing I needed right in that moment was to have a friendly conversation with Eidothea, who appeared through one of the side doors, probably returning from Mindanao after delivering my brother. The image of poor, shaken up Vikram had lingered at the back of my mind for the entirety of the celebration, unable to understand how my brother willingly subjected himself to the energy-eating vortex.

"I trust my brother is well?" I turned to her and plastered a hopeful smile on my lips, having to grind my teeth to refrain from saying something else.

"Prince Vikram is fully recovered," she spoke softly, then, probably reading the doubt on my features, offered further explanation. "As soon as we resurfaced, I fed him a healing pearl. They are blessed by the energy of the goddess, so they counter the effects of the offerings. You had one yourself during the meeting with my sister this afternoon, yes?" she smiled sweetly, forcing me to scroll through memories.

I remembered the pain, the shaking in my muscles, the desperation that now seemed to be so far away, the reasoning so out of mind. I could not remember why everything happened, only that it did. Until I became myself again.

"The queen offered me a pearl to feed to you, it counteracted your... state," Amara explained, confirming the truth in the siren's words. If it had such effect on me, then it must have healed my brother as well, I calmed my thoughts. After all, if Vikram had truly been doing this for a decade, as per his final words before leaving the kingdom, they must have had a system. Because the Vikram I knew at solstice was a completely different person from that sickly male I had seen, barely able to walk.

"I must admit, prince, that it is strange for one to react in such a way in front of my sister while accompanied by their loved one." she pointed, causing Amara and I to tense.

"We were very tired, we had barely arrived and —"

"And the fire princess was not in the room," the second siren queen stopped Amara's words. "And she will not be at dinner tomorrow either, how are you going to explain that?"

There was no point in hiding the truth, she already knew it.

"What would you have me do?" I asked, putting my life in the hands of a siren. If she uncovered our ruse so early after our arrival, we would all be punished, there was no doubt about that.

Eidothea sighed. "I do not like keeping secrets from my sister, however Vikram implored me, so I must put my mate's wishes before my own." She reached for the pin in her hair, adorned with pearls and beading and took one of the decorations. "Grind this into a powder and consume a little before meeting Thelssha," she handed it to me with long, shaky fingers.

"Now let me take you to your allocated room, the queen's guests do not reside at the entrance borders."

"I think I twisted a muscle," I complained while trying to stretch my back and put the tendons into their original position. My neck ached and the upper part of my body felt strained, as if I had been carrying a tonne during my sleep.

"That's because you are so stubborn," Amara reprimanded me from between the sheets, where she had spent the night in comfort. I wanted to give her as much space as I possibly could, so I offered to take the floor. The room we were escorted to was far greater than the original bedroom I shared with Anwen only a few hours back.

Eidothea offered us one of the royal chambers, where a massive wooden bed occupied the centre of the room, with walls painted in alabaster blue and decorated with shells and pearls. It looked grandiose, and I spent the better part of an hour admiring the intricate designs and paintings that surrounded us, finding it interesting to note how the sirens always preferred open space, or the idea of it. When they did not have it, they created their own illusion, in this case, building the royal chambers to be circular and completely avoid corners.

"It's the least I could do," I insisted, while placing my back next to the side of the bed and trying to push my muscles back in a weak attempt to stretch them.

"Come here," Amara sighed and shifted from between the sheets. In the following moment, I felt her hands on my shoulders, moving slowly towards my back and rubbing gently in circular motions. It felt divine. So much so that I allowed my head to rest back and started to release a slight moan.

"Goddess bless you," I closed my eyes and allowed her fingers to twist and turn, doing exactly what she needed to in order to take the pain away.

"So, so stubborn," she huffed again and continued the massage while I let myself drift away and note how the pain disappeared. Amara had insisted several times that we shared the bed the night before, but after everything she had been through, I wanted to offer her peace. I wanted to give her space, both for her thoughts and body. The last thing that mattered was my comfort.

"Next time I'll take one of your pillows," I groaned and opened my eyes to offer her a smile of thanks.

"Next time you're sleeping in bed. Goddess forbid we need to fight for some reason. How can I honestly trust you to defend me if you can't even raise your hand above your head? So, get off your high horse and sleep in the fucking bed. Trust me, our success is much more important than whatever jealousy your mate might experience," she scolded me.

Truth be told, I barely shut an eye worrying about Anwen all night long. I hadn't seen her since Marreth walked away with her and since we were in a different part of the palace, one where we could easily be spied on, I could not risk going after her. I had to place all my trust in Marreth and hope that he would be kind enough to help her through the night.

"It's not jealousy," I replied while stretching my back one last time to observe how everything was in its rightful place.

"I needed to be with her, last night more than ever. And I hate myself for just…being here," I forced a low huff while releasing the words.

"I'm sure you can survive a night without getting it wet," Amara rolled her eyes and shook her head from side to side as if to admonish me.

"You misunderstand. What Anwen saw last night broke a part of her that never mended, which neither I nor Rhylan, Cressida or any of her friends can fix. Love or magic cannot fix it," I explained, to which my wife tilted her head in surprise.

"What are you talking about?"

"Her brother," I admitted. "He found his death after a mermaid's kiss."

"A mortal? You are telling me that a mortal survived long enough to get to land and then perish?" her eyes went as wide as could be expected. The event was unheard of, humans instantly died at the contact with a mermaid's lips.

"Not a mortal. One of Fear Gorta's heirs," I reminded her of Anwen's status. "That is how we met," I could not help a sad smile at the memory, at the event that seemed to have happened decades ago. "She was seeking the truth about her brother but had a single clue: the Evigt forest. That's how she found me," I explained.

"It all makes sense now, Rhylan's determination. Anwen's trust in him. They seek revenge."

"They do," I confirmed. Anwen had confessed as much when she took me to her brother's room while we stayed in her parents' home. She showed me pictures of him, of the two of them, that adorned every corner of the bedroom. Anwen had loved him so much. They had both loved each other. And now only one remained, with the mission to bring justice for the other.

"And remember that the mermaids attempted at Anwen's life only months ago." I still couldn't understand how Rhylan had the audacity to bring her here, where she was in constant danger, but Anwen had insisted so many times that I had no choice but to stop protesting.

After a diverse breakfast filled with fruit, grains and cured meats, which Amara indulged in, we received the invitation to discover more of the palace grounds, if they could even be called that, so we took full advantage of the invitation.

My wife and I walked the corridors hand in hand with the pretence of admiring the view and trying to spy on the city underneath as much as the transparent walls allowed us. From time to time, one of the mermaids passed us and nodded in greeting, mostly to Amara, who had tried to keep part of herself uncovered to the benefit of our hosts and veiled only the distracting bits, as she called them before we left the room.

She looked as if she wore underwear with a little extra fabric, but true to her word, it offered the desired effect; the mermaids became friendlier towards her, and some even stopped to answer questions or to guide us on our journey.

We spent hours walking the hallways, until we were sure that we knew every entrance and all the doors that allowed the waterlings to grow legs and chase after us.

For lunch, we tasted some of the waterling delicacies, more to my taste than my wife's, who clearly enjoyed her carnivorous delights. This time, the table was covered in various types of mussels and clams, all raw and salty, ready to be eaten out of the shell, along with many assortments of algae salads. I must confess, some of these turned out to be delicious and I had a second serving, causing whispers around when my hand reached for a bit more salad. Amara rectified my mistake and reached for the food herself to place it on my plate. Apparently, males did not merit the right to reach for food in the Water Kingdom.

The long-awaited moment of dinner arrived with Eidothea again, who presented the invitation one more time and offered to escort us to the dining room.

She asked about our day as she led us through a different set of hallways, making Amara and me realise that we had been restricted to the outer parts of the palace and everything we had learnt proved to be of little consequence. It also reiterated the fact that we had been isolated from the others, with absolutely no way to return and remained completely dependent on the sirens to approve our release.

Basically, our plan had been demolished without even starting.

"Welcome back, it is great to gaze on you once more," Queen Thelssha smiled to us as soon as her sister invited us into the, of course, circular room.

She sat at a round table, carved in some sort of airy stone, along with various other sisters that chatted and drank away, completely ignoring our presence there.

The other siren queens, I reminded myself. Gathered together, in the same room. At the same table that Amara and I would be seated at. Which meant that this became a political dinner.

"It is wonderful to see you again as well, Queen Thelssha," I greeted before I pulled back the chair and invited Amara to take her place at the table. She did so slowly, unsure, her lack of political knowledge overpowering her stance. She was afraid and it became evident to all of us. I had to do something, and quickly.

"I know you miss your aunt, my love, but we will see her again soon," I said, the only observation that came to mind and would be easy to explain. "Let us enjoy some time alone in the meanwhile," I leaned towards her and placed a soft kiss on her cheek, making a show of my affection. She adopted her role of enamoured newlywed and caught my jaw with the palm of her hand and caressed me gently, as if wanting to keep me closer to her. I smiled back and placed yet another kiss, this time dangerously close to her lips.

"My apologies, my queens, the past few days proved very tiring," Amara shrugged slowly and accepted the glass of wine that one of the sirens offered.

"I assume so, but I am glad to see that your prince is fully recovered. It would have proved very dangerous for him to be in this room were his love for you untrue." The queen pointed a sharp gaze to me, some kind of test I passed in her eyes, and I thanked all the goddesses for the pearl Eidothea had offered.

"You don't have to worry about that," Amara jumped to my defence. "If I can say one thing about my husband, it is that his love is true and loyal. And it will always be so."

"I shall drink to your confidence, princess," the queen raised her glass. As soon as she did, all the other sirens followed, drinking in long and heavy sips without the need to stop for air. I had noticed that during the dinner celebrations the night before and in the lunch hall, mermaids needed very little air, if at all. I assumed they needed the oxygen and dryness to ease their conversion, but when it came to their lungs, no such necessities were displayed.

We ate the first course in silence, with a few mentions of solstice, some traditions and a few other sirens coming and going for various reasons, but the second course brought us right in the centre of an alliance invitation. Thelssha, Eidothea and to my surprise Branwyl, the mermaid that joined me for my keeper assignment trial started discussing their distaste concerning the humans and all the complaints they had gathered through the years.

"I simply cannot understand how your kingdom dedicated a good portion of your army to come to their protection. The only thing they know is destruction. The blessing of creation, our home, even yours, are riddled with plastic and dirt, the air is becoming unbreathable and trust me prince, that will not be such a problem for us, but to those defending their kind," Branwyl pleaded her case with eagerness in between bites.

"And this nonsense that Fear Gorta plans? An alliance? I don't think he remembers that he barely got out alive last time," one of the other sirens snickered.

"Remember? He wanted to be king! Ha!" some of them laughed through their teeth and others dropped their cutlery on the plates and started tugging at their bellies, barely able to keep their laughter in check.

"What happened last time?" I took advantage of the situation. Any information I could use against Rhylan could prove to be gold.

"It was a few years ago," the redhead siren to my left leaned over and started speaking. Her breath told me she had overly indulged in wine, but that only meant her words would be loose and unashamed.

I made myself the portrait of curiosity and leaned towards her and smirked.

"He came to our queen with this alliance nonsense, he wanted to open the fire tunnels and allow the water kingdom towards their lodgings. You know, they control everything down there, up until the centre of the earth? That's where Belgarath's body is," she whispered to me, pointing a finger as if urging me to keep the secret. "Anyway, he came to ask for help to dispose of their royals. The bastard even had the nerve to propose himself to be king, along with our beautiful queen! He wanted them both to rule the underworld together, just like Marrynah and his god had. Can you believe it?" she started laughing uncontrollably.

In truth, I did not, because it went against everything Rhylan fought for. If he allowed Water into the Fire kingdom, then the pathway to his god would remain shut forever and all his plans about resurfacing the deity would have been in vain. There must have been something else, and Fear Gorta had come here under false pretence. And got burned, apparently.

I continued to listen to the conversation, while also trying to hear some of the promises Thelssha had started whispering into Amara's ear. She appealed to an all-female alliance, the promises of what Water and Wind could do together, the idea that Earth could be persuaded through me.

My wife, to her benefit, kept mentioning my name and how we needed to discuss it as a couple, as the prince and princess of Wind, but that she was grateful for the consideration, and it would surely be a topic of long conversations between us. I wanted to interfere when the information I was not supposed to hear, one that affected my mate and possibly the rest of my life, reached my ears.

"Remember how his son squealed?" they continued laughing.

"You have to admit you had your fun with him first," another one disputed, forcing Branwyl to defend herself.

"How many of you can say they fucked Fear Gorta's children? It was an event," she snickered with pride, making me turn my full attention to her.

Branwyl, the siren that branded my destiny.

Branwyl, one of the siren queens.

Branwyl, the murderer of Anwen's brother.

Anwen

Chapter Twelve

Images of floating bodies kept me from sleep. The memory of those cheerful voices, the way they cheered as if they were at the super bowl made my stomach rustle. I had been sick four times already, but by the way the back of my throat announced that sour taste, I was far from done.

Marreth, to his credit, walked me back to the room I had shared with Ansgar on our arrival and placed me on the bed, then he rushed to the small bathroom and brought me a glass of water from the jug by the washing basin. I didn't remember much after we left that ballroom, where I had danced and allowed myself to celebrate with murderers. I recalled every second of the victim parade, I remembered Ansgar's words and the way he had wanted to take me away from it, and above all, I remembered Cressi's screams.

The rest became blurred, suddenly Ansgar was gone, and I was in Marreth's arms, having no idea where we were going. I couldn't focus, my eyes kept looking at the surrounding water in terror, scared that they would spot another dead body floating as an offering.

It lasted all night. They would be parading men's bodies every minute on the hour until sunrise. Which meant that they had killed at least three hundred men.

The logistics of it made my brain strain. How was it possible that every solstice, over three hundred men disappeared from the world, and no one noticed? How were they allowed to commit such atrocities year after year, season after season, without anyone stopping them? And how were the other faerie kingdoms putting up with this?

No one had shown surprise. It was Rhylan who first wanted us to go, so he clearly knew. Amara hadn't said a thing about this, so she probably considered it normal, Marreth carried me without showing any thoughts, so he clearly wasn't too disturbed and Ansgar had even sat by my side and explained the logistics of it all.

Everyone knew. And no one did a thing.

I felt vomit rise again and ran to the toilet, forcing Marreth to shift away to make room for me. He'd sat on the floor, crouched by the door for a long time until I convinced him to take half the bed, so his neck wouldn't rest in that weird way. Begrudgingly, he agreed to it a couple of hours later, when he started tilting his head and stretching his shoulders from the uncomfortable position he had sat in.

There was nothing to worry about, really. We were adults, we could share a bed. Unfortunately, that night, neither of us would do much sleeping because my panic attacks made me have a full-on vomiting session which didn't allow him to find any rest.

And to the commander's credit, after he gave me the privacy I needed to empty my stomach, he always stepped into the bathroom to bring me a glass of water and a clean piece of cloth. He was one of the good guys, Marreth was.

"How do they do it?" I finally decided to give my brain a break and ask. Maybe he knew.

"They mark the males they want. Hunt them for the upcoming solstice. Then make them disappear in turns. As far as I know the bodies can be preserved and brought out for the celebration," he explained.

That made more sense. There would be a long line of people disappearing during the course of three months around the world, which would not raise too much suspicion. After all, people disappeared every day, and there were many victims to choose from.

"And how do they pick?"

"I don't know. All I know is that they can't just pick anyone. The new mermaids need to have specific skills, so they select them according to the season's needs," the commander said. "I know it must have been difficult for you to see that. For you and the Queen."

I was surprised to hear him speak about Cressi using her title, but in all fairness, Marreth had always treated my sister with the utmost respect and always kept her in high regard. Calling her his queen made sense. Marreth was a soldier first, and he followed orders and rank.

"You know what pisses me off the most? That all of you knew. You fucking knew that we were coming here for solstice. And you also knew what kind of fucked up ceremony we would be attending. Yet none of you thought to tell us! None of you thought to say: Hey, you silly human girls, just so you know, they will be killing people

FYI," I snapped at Marreth, knowing he did not deserve it.

In fact, he was the least deserving of all, because I expected at least Ansgar to tell me something. I expected my mate, who knew my story to a T, whom I had taken into Erik's room, where no one entered apart from me and mom. I had shown him the deepest, most broken piece of me.

Rhylan, who planned this. Planned this! Who kept us training for weeks, who pushed me to find my powers and control them, for this very reason. And Amara, who tortured Cressi with so many lessons on how to curtsy, how to drink, how to lift her glass and so much bullshit, but never thought to share any of the important bits, like: hey, you'll be naked, hey, there's dead bodies and people cheering.

None of them had said a fucking thing.

"Babe, are you there?" I heard the voice through the door and jumped awake.

Cressi! Oh my god, Cressi!

"Yes, yes, I'm awake," I tried to shout from bed and immediately bolted to the door to open. I didn't realise I had actually fallen asleep at some point, and it seems that Marreth did too because in my rush to get to Cressi, I pushed against something hard. Which started groaning. I turned to find the commander sleeping with his back to me, trapping a pillow in between his legs.

"Hi hon," I opened the door and immediately stretched my arms to trap her in a hug. She didn't look too great either. Even though her gorgeous sunny locks covered part of her face, I spotted that she'd been crying. A lot, her eyes looking red and puffy, same as the tip of her nose.

"Come in babe," I shifted to the side and dragged her in, without letting go of the embrace. As soon as she saw Marreth, she stopped, her chest releasing a weird sound, half a sigh and half a hiccup.

"Rhylan needs you," she spoke with a broken voice, her words barely strong enough to come out.

"Thank you, my Queen," the commander instantly rose and stood straight in front of Cressi. He must have hated my guts, both literally and figuratively. He'd taken care of me while I'd been sick the night before and now, by the direct order in Cressi's tone, which looked to be coming more from Rhylan's lips, he'd surely have a busy day. After just a couple of hours of rest.

"Will you be well?" To my surprise, Marreth turned his attention to me, before he shifted to the side of the room, ensuring that Cressi had enough space to enter.

"We'll be fine," I pressed my lips together in a nod, silently thanking him.

"Very well, I'll be on my way. I hope you two have a pleasant day."

I huffed at the ridiculousness of the phrase, but Cressi dropped him a grateful smile and thanked him before he went out the door.

"He is a good one. Marreth." Cressi finally said. "You shouldn't be too harsh on him."

Anger rippled through my stomach once again, before I let my brain realize that what Cressi had just said was true. I was nothing to Marreth, really. I was someone who came into his life without caring whom or what I destroyed to get to my purpose. To get to Ansgar. But he was the one to always offer advice, to always tell me the truth, no matter what.

He'd told me about Amara before we went into the Wind Kingdom, he'd told me about Ansgar's condition before I went into the cell they had kept him in, he shared everything he knew with me. But this.

"Where is Rhylan dearest?" I changed the subject, patting my side of the bed to invite Cressi to take a seat.

"We had a fight this morning," she sighed and released some more tears, which she instantly wiped away with the back of her hand. Seeing Cressida cry opened a whole different line of shocking images. The last time I saw her crying was maybe at Erik's funeral? And before that, when she received the news about her parents.

She was such a strong woman for years, unbreakable even, that I created this impenetrable image of her in my mind. Cressi could not be broken, could not be ripped to shreds like me, she could not experience anxiety like any other human being. She was Cressi!

Then the image of her crying the morning we left to the Fire Kingdom came to memory. Because of Rhylan. And here she was, once more, shedding tears for the same reason.

"What happened?" I gently patted her knee and started rubbing her skin up and down in what I thought to be a soothing caress.

"I told him I wanted to leave this place. After last night, I just can't..." she shook her head, wiping away a new line of tears. "I begged him to go, to take us away from here and forget all this nonsense. At first, he said yes, he said that he would do anything I asked so we spent the night relatively calm. He tried to make me forget, I tried to make myself forget..." she sighed again.

I hadn't tried to banish trauma with sex, but it wasn't such a bad idea. Compared to shaking and vomiting my guts all night long...

"This morning however, it was like he woke up to be a different person. Everything he said during the night, all the promises... it's like they never happened. He is obstinate to fulfil his mission," she sniffled, using her fingers to wipe her nose. Then her eyes lifted, stopping to my own. "Did you know?"

I didn't need clarification; I knew what she meant.

"No," I instantly said. "But Ansgar and Rhylan tried to get me away last night, so they clearly had some idea." I couldn't help my angry tone, even though I knew it would affect Cressi even more. I was pissed off. Very pissed off.

"Where is Ansgar?"

"Hell if I know," it came my turn to sigh. "I haven't seen him since last night. Marreth carried me back, I couldn't really walk," I admitted. "He's probably living the life with Amara, singing fucking mermaid songs and cheering the death of people," I released a brutal answer, which I instantly regretted.

"You know very well he wouldn't do anything to hurt you. That man adores you," It was Cressi's time to console me.

"And Rhylan adores you too, Cressi. You know I hate him for choosing you, but you should have seen him before you guys met. He was an absolute bastard with no emotion and no regards towards whomever he might be hurting to achieve his goals. Now at least, he thinks about it before doing idiotic things," I snorted, causing Cressi to release a small smile.

"They brought lots of dresses in my room, we're allowed to go to parts of the kingdom now," she announced. "I came to get you. Rhylan will be away for the day so we can make our own plans."

"They're letting us into the palace?" I widened my eyes in surprise.

"Just a part of it, the one they deem safe, I presume. But still, if I'm going to be stuck in here, I could at least find out more about them. Maybe we could investigate a bit and see if there's any way to find out who those murderess bitches are," Cressi pressed her lips together, new determination shining in her eyes.

"And maybe we get to find who killed my brother."

Ansgar

Chapter Thirteen

"So very unlike you to invite me, prince," Rhylan's rumbling tone announced his presence before my eyes spotted him. Dressed in his usual black attire, the fire king looked tired, dare I say sad even, no doubt due to the events of the night before.

"My queen is expecting me in bed soon, so I hope whatever words will come out of your mouth are worth my trouble."

I absolutely despised the bastard. Even now, even when I was coming to his aid, when I set up a meeting to offer the information I received after dinner with the sirens, he had the nerve to mock me. Unfortunately for me, I needed him.

"Be it your way, Fear Gorta. If you don't want information, then I shall keep it to myself." I allowed a few seconds of silence, before I breathed deeply and adopted the same mocking tone. If he wanted to play, then he had found an opponent. "It must be difficult for you," I tilted my head and tsked, "to stay isolated from the action, your word or presence not counting…"

I felt him tense, his jaw becoming tighter. We did not have much time, both of us knew it, but somehow, we could not put our feelings aside and work together. Even in this late hour, gathered in a secluded corridor. Should someone spot us, our plans would be more than obvious, as well as the fact that I wanted to share official dinner conversation with the enemy. But I did not plan to release a single word of importance until I took care of what mattered most.

"I want to know about Anwen," I demanded, causing Fear Gorta to chuckle.

"Anwen..." By the way he said her name, I knew payback for my previous observation was going to come. And quickly. "Anwen is a twenty-seven-year-old woman. She has brown hair and hazel eyes, three tattoos, as far as I know..." he stopped to raise his brows to me in search of confirmation, "her last name is Odstar and she grew up in New York with her parents and brother."

"Rhylan, cut it out," I threatened. "How is she? Where is she?"

"She's fine, prince," Rhylan relaxed his shoulders, probably seeing how my rage started to grow. "According to Marreth, she did not sleep well last night, she was constantly sick, but he took care of her. This morning I sent Cressida there and they were spotted through the palace. They ate something in the library, where they spent most of the afternoon, before all of us gathered to have dinner in a small lounge with several sirens. Right now, she is with my queen, keeping my side of the bed warm and reading books they found in the library. She is fine," he reiterated to my benefit.

Very well, he gave me what I needed. My mate was fine. Probably hating me for not being truthful about all my knowledge regarding waterlings, something I knew I would have to pay dearly for that the next time I saw her. Which I hoped would come soon.

None of us expected to be invited to the solstice celebrations, and when we did, we thought it would be in some sort of private area. Anwen and Cressida enjoyed the celebration, the dancing, the food and even chatted away with some of the mermaids. Neither of us expected for the offerings to happen right in that hall.

I, for one, planned to take Anwen away to our allocated rooms and keep her and her knowledge safe. The last thing she needed was to spot humans that shared her brother's fate, paraded under the moonlight.

"What was your plan, Rhylan?" If I could get even more from him before I had to release any valuable information, I might very well take advantage of it. "During your last visit here?" I clarified. "Were you truly going to drown your kind?"

He stopped a breath, not expecting to hear the question drop from my lips. I didn't think he expected his name to be mentioned at all during dinner, by his reaction.

"What did they say?" I watched how his eyes turned into slits, raw anger lining his features.

"Not much," I admitted. I was not a fool. I would not tell him how they mocked his plan, how they made fun of his idiocy, as they called it many times. And especially, I was not going to tell him about Branwyl taking his son as punishment.

"I wanted the tear," he nodded, as if accepting that he had to tell me as much. "I proposed Thelssha an alliance, and believe me prince, the desperation I felt back then pushed me to savagery even

I considered great. But I was willing to do anything for liberation. I did not know they would seek punishment. I did not know they would go after my heir."

So he knew about Erik. "What happened?"

Rhylan sighed.

"While Thelssha kept me in her bed, she used the time to find out everything that was dear to me. And destroy it. She made me believe the plan I was forming alongside her would be put in place. I could come and go as I pleased, doing both the job I was assigned to by the Fire Kingdom and following my own plans. For years, I waited. For years, she asked me for patience. It was too late when I realised they were using me for amusement and information."

I watched how Rhylan leaned against the marble wall we met next to, as if the weight of his past decisions still tortured him.

"They are this strong because I helped them, I told them everything I knew. The Queen made a public show of mockery, wanting to teach me a lesson, for daring to even propose a king for their realm. I could not use my powers on the queen, no one can. If she dies, this whole thing crumbles," he pointed to the walls.
"And we all die in the process."

"How did they discover Erik?" I asked, causing Rhylan to sigh deeply.

"By following my blood. In thousands of directions. His murderer must have spotted him miles away, all they needed was a drop of my energy. They did in days what I struggled to do in a century. When I was released back into the Fire Kingdom, Thelssha gave me the news. That all my search could stop. That there was no one left of me. I tried to get as close to my son as I could in the time I had left and followed him around the world, hoping to find a cure. The time proved too short."

Pain became evident in his features, in the tight fist he kept pressing against the wall, in his dark eyes. Rhylan lived in constant regret. Rhylan returned to finish the job and punish the sirens for daring to attack his heir. And for once, I supported his reasons.

"The queen seeks an alliance with Wind. And by the way she keeps mentioning my ties to my kingdom, she thinks Earth will follow. They want to attack the firelings first and invade your territory. No doubt following your proposal."

"They would become the strongest kingdom," Rhylan voiced my concerns. If we allow Water to flow under the Earth, they would have all the power. Over all territories.

"I assume they plan to go after the humans afterwards, and crown themselves sole queens of the Realm," I replied.

"Which we cannot allow," Rhylan instantly responded, before I even had a chance to complete my sentence.

"What do you propose?"

As soon as I released the question, Rhylan shifted to one side, wanting to cover my shape with his tall frame. I heard determined steps coming straight to us. If we were caught, both of us would be put to justice and all the hard work Amara was doing right now, performing her adoration to the siren queen, would be for nothing.

"It's just me," Marreth inched closer to us, allowing Rhylan and I to breathe. "I checked the hallways, no one is nearby. All the mermaids are either in the great hall, continuing the solstice drinking or with the queens. And your wife," he pointed an admonishing look to me, no doubt questioning why I left Amara alone with the siren queens.

In truth, the princess was doing such a brilliant job at keeping the females company and enjoying her presence, that she sent me outside for a walk, giving me the perfect opportunity to meet Rhylan and making a show of how she needed me to stretch before we returned to our chambers, much to the delight of the ruling waterlings.

"There must be guards," I exclaimed, finding it difficult to believe that the mermaids would abandon their posts, especially since they had males in the palace lodgings. There must be yet another part of the palace which we hadn't seen yet.

"Should I...get lost tonight?" the commander asked, turning to Rhylan to receive confirmation.

"As long as you deem it safe," Rhylan replied, and I was surprised to hear it. The Rhylan I knew would risk anyone and anything to achieve his goals. Not when it came to friends, it seemed. Cressida had really played a part in melting away the prickness.

"Fake a fight," he continued. "Say how your princess is jealous of all the beauty and you are fed up with having to avert your eyes all the time. How you needed an escape. They will not question it," Rhylan advised, as if from experience.

"What about Anwen? You can't leave her alone while you run around all night," I pointed, causing Marreth to huff.

"But you can leave Amara to fend for herself, right?"

"Enough, the both of you. The princeling will return to his dinner promptly. He was only away for twenty minutes," Rhylan pressed a sharp gaze into Marreth to reprimand his outburst. "Anwen will sleep with Cressida tonight and I will guard the door. Everyone happy with that?" Fear Gorta shifted his gaze to us, waiting for our confirming nods.

"I'll be on my way then," Marreth dipped his chin again and walked away.

"There is no word of attack yet, nor how many troops they have at their disposal," I finished our conversation and took a step back, preparing to return to the siren dinner.

"We'll know more when he returns," Fear Gorta's gaze lingered to the spot where Marreth had stood seconds before. "Until then, I will care for my heir and my queen."

Anwen
Chapter Fourteen

Cressida looked gorgeous in anything, so I didn't even understand why she was trying. All she needed to do was flick her hair to give it that stunning volume and the soft curls she seemed to innately have and put a smile on her face.

I, on the other hand, had to work quite a lot to make myself at least half-presentable. Not that I cared really, but the last thing I wanted was to draw even more attention to me and looking barely alive after a late-night vomiting session wouldn't send the best image. Especially not from a princess. Urgh, I hated my new job title. Not only that I did not see myself as a princess, but because it came with all the primping and posing I had hated for most of my life.

Sure, I liked to wear dresses and play around with make up when I was a teenager, but as soon as I turned eighteen and my photograph could be legally taken, everything changed. Mom turned into this fashion-obsessed person who forced me to wear everything that looked to be on trend but had a horrendous effect on my body parts and kept mentioning how I could lose some weight to look better for photos.

She was flawless, of course, and so were Erik and dad, so that made me the black sheep of the family. I did not care and made a point to go out of my way to give them the ugliest poses they could ask for. Within a few years, they decided to stop photographing me because I did not present an interest. People already knew I did not fit.

And now I had to force myself into another mould, into more pompous dresses and tons of jewellery, just because faerie-daddy dearest fancied me to. Today, however, I planned to take advantage of my status and stride around the palace, getting into whatever rooms I could, to find information.

We did not have a plan, we faked getting bored in our rooms and wanted to go out and inspect the hallways, stumbling into this room or the other, with absolutely no higher purpose than our own entertainment. Hopefully we could find something, anything that would guide us in the right direction.

I did not look at the water creatures with the same fascination as the day before. A permanent expression of distaste plastered on my features, which Cressi made a point to note and ask me to calm down and put on a smile a few times, until I portrayed the feelings I was supposed to show. Unaffected. Bored. Maybe a little intrigued. After all, we were in a new kingdom, one in which we had supposedly arrived to form an alliance with.

I imagined a city break, one of the many Cressi and I used to take in our early twenties. Sometimes with Erik, sometimes with other friends, but so many times alone, allowing ourselves a girl's weekend. Looking at the person next to me, at my sister for so many years and the friend who'd always been there, I could not help but admire her.

Here she was, scared within an inch of her life but still managing to smile. I forced myself to do the same, hoping to make her proud. There we were, the queen and the princess of the Fire Kingdom, walking through hallways none of us had seen before and excitedly pointing at things or asking random questions to the mermaids as they walked past us.

"Is that so?" Cressi, a true queen, smiled sweetly to one of the mermaids who had stopped and asked if we had already seen the library. Apparently, that is where they kept all treasures.

I could not believe the nerve of these women. Mermaids. Sirens. Whatever. As long as they walked around naked, they were the enemy. But they did not see it like that, they made a point to care for their guests and proved to be much more hospitable than the day before.

When Cressi said she did not eat any kind of animal, including oysters, clams, and other types of marine life we had been served, they went above and beyond to cater for the queen, bringing her all sorts of fruit and sugary foods.

The more we walked, the more we realised that they saw us as equals, as sisters dare I say, and always welcomed us with a smile and advice, wanting to make sure that our stay was pleasant and that we did not need anything else.

Women caring for women. It was a nice feeling; I would not deny it. The friendship, the sisterhood. Were we in another world, we would have embraced and possibly even returned the feeling. But every time I looked at one, I wondered if it was she who killed my brother. If it was one of them that paraded dead men's bodies to the cheer of the crowd.

"We would very much like to see it, if you would be so kind," Cressi continued the conversation and suddenly, we found ourselves walking with a group of mermaids, all of them excited to lead us to the library and to show us the treasures of the kingdom. Lots of them mentioned Mama Tia and how we 'absolutely had to meet her.'

So, we went. Having no idea what we were getting ourselves into.

It turned out that the treasures they kept talking about with so much excitement were books. Thousands upon thousands, protected inside a marble dome filled with all sorts of shelves. Tall shelves, circular shelves, spinning shelves, they were all in there, guarding the leather-bound volumes.

Cressi and I stopped at the entrance door in wonder, unable to avert our eyes from so much beauty and all the wondrous colours tightly placed together, because every single piece of leather that protected a book had been carefully painted in various shades of blue, the titles marked with gold or silver lettering, making it seem that the waves of the sea had started to flow inside the huge library.

The mermaids that brought us there started giggling at our amazed expressions. After a minute of allowing us to stare, they bid us farewell and invited us in, asking us to go seek Mama Tia before they departed, each on her separate way.

I didn't know how to react, so I looked at the queen and my dearest friend for guidance. After all, she had more experience with awkward situations than I did, let alone connecting to people every single chance she got.

I slowly elbowed her, silently pushing her forwards and inviting her to enter the massive circular dome of the million books.

To her credit, she did so with her head high, even though her chest heaved a little with anticipation. We had no idea who Mama Tia was, but the sirens hadn't been so inviting about meeting their queen, or any of the queens for that matter, which meant this new person must have held high importance to them.

Or they sent us into some sort of monster's lair, though by the spotless look and feel of this place, I highly doubted it. This looked to be the tidiest, most upkept place and by the reaction of all those naked women who rushed us in here with pride and excitement, the most beloved too.

"It is my honour to welcome you, ladies," we heard a deep voice coming from behind one of the bookshelves, making Cressi and me jump and hold onto one another for dear life, like in one of those scary movies we used to watch together when we were teens.

"Hello," I spoke before my friend had a chance to, ready to summon my powers to keep us safe. "We...we're here to see Mama Tia," I announced and stepped in front of Cressi, ready to receive the blow, should one come in our direction.

Not that I was the bravest person on the planet, but amongst the two of us, I had a better chance of fighting back. And I'd taken more hits thanks to Rhylan's rigorous training. Bastard.

"As I said, it is my honour to welcome you," the voice repeated, this time stepping closer to us. I knew it was only the bookshelf separating us that kept us safe, kept us away. Even though her words sounded kind, the voice rasped different than anything we heard in the kingdom so far, raw and defined at the same time, perfectly placed into our ears.

God, they truly played a prank on us. They brought us in the kind of place where visitors are not allowed and this Mama Tia person was going to ask for something in exchange, or for punishment. What had we gotten ourselves into?

I turned back to Cressi to observe curiosity in her eyes rather than fear. Clearly my worries were my own, because my friend looked rather intrigued and ready to jump from behind me and circle the bookshelf just to get closer to that voice. But we did not have to, because during the time I took to look at my friend, it made its appearance in front of us.

"How can I be of help?"

I instantly turned to see the source of that rough, threatening voice. To find an old lady, probably in her late seventies, with her hair held in a high bun wearing woollen clothing.

Everything about her was crochet. Her jumper, her pants, even the socks and slippers she paddled around the library in. Mama Tia was short, much shorter than any mermaid we'd seen, her back slightly inched forward from old age and probably, spending decades of her life sitting somewhere with her nose in a book.

I wanted to laugh at my stupid instincts. I had been in such high alert throughout the day that I failed to recognise the voice of old age, the voice of this sweet old lady who smiled and whose hands slowly shook in front of us.

"Hi, I'm Cressida," Cressi shoved me to the side, huffing at the ridicule of the situation and rushed to shake the old lady's hand. "I am queen of the Fire Kingdom and this is my...daughter in law, Anwen. She is princess of the same realm," my friend said, making the air in my lungs stop and freeze.

Seconds died before I had a chance to show a reaction. Cressida had called me her daughter in law. Which made perfect sense, because under faerie law, my sister was married to my father. Which...god, I was Cressi's daughter in law. I wanted to laugh so hard, I wanted to stop and drop on the floor and roll and laugh. Laugh until my jaw cramped. I was Cressi's daughter in law.

My friend must have read the silliness on my face, because she quickly smacked my arm to bring me back to the present, pointing her gaze to the old lady's extended hand. Which I instantly inched closer and shook with joy.

"It is lovely to meet you, Mama Tia. Please accept my apologies, I am just...surprised," I admitted.

"It is no bother," she waved a few fingers at me as if it was nothing. "Not many have a chance to see an old siren," she spoke, her voice so much softer. I wondered if it was the echo of the room and her position behind the books that had made her sound so menacing only moments before. Because this old lady was as sweet as they can be.

"Come, my darlings, we can have tea," she pointed to a set of chairs and a table encased in between more bookshelves, where a small fireplace crackled.

Fire. Under water. That was something one did not see every day.

Cressi was the first to sit, but then she started fiddling around, insisting to help Mama Tia with the preparation of tea and did not give up until the old lady agreed to let her help and gave her the plates and cups to arrange on the table, along with a few assortments of biscuits and cookies.

I was happy to sit in wonder and look at everything around me. I could not believe how normal and homey this arrangement felt. An old lady, sipping tea by the fireplace, surrounded by books.

"So, what do you girls wish to know?" Mama Tia spoke as soon as she settled on her cushioned chair and enjoyed the first sip of tea. It was cherry blossom and smelled absolutely divine.

"Some of the other mermaids told us to come visit, but we must admit, they did not say much about you," Cressi explained, right after reaching for a chocolate cookie. It was surprising to see her like this, and especially, not checking the ingredients of everything she put in her mouth. I realised it was because she did not want to hurt the old woman's feelings. I admired my friend even more for that.

"I shall think not," the old lady smiled. "Most of them weren't even born when I started this project," she waved a hand in a circular motion, to make it clear she was referring to the library. "The Air Palace was created to store all our knowledge and energy, to protect it from damage. I volunteered to live the rest of my days as its keeper," Mama Tia smiled with pride.

Honestly, her job sounded amazing. Her entire purpose was dedicated to preserving, and I suspected reading, every single book there was, while enjoying the warmth and the crackle of the fire, sipping tea and eating cakes. And most importantly, being away from people and society's demands. Yep, it was a dream job.

"What are all these books?" Cressi looked around and silently admired the thousands of volumes around us, all of them placed at millimetric precision from the others in perfect synchrony.

"I make my own requests, but it is mostly our history. The traditions maintained and changed from ancient times, our logs, some of them are the daily shifts and other assignments, but I do have a few apprentices to help with the more mundane tasks," Mama Tia explained.

"What about all the offerings?" I hated myself for saying that word. "Is there a log for them as well?"

"Of course, we keep close attention to all of our seekers, and they report during their periodical visits. Generally, they come back for the full moon, so they will present their plans and any special requests," the old siren explained.

"What do the seekers do?" Cressi must have read the question in my mind and luckily, took the lead. We did not want to be too insistent on a specific subject and raise her suspicion.

"There are different assignments for each of our categories," Mama Tia sipped her tea and gave us each a smile before she continued. "We have healers, seekers, keepers, discoverers, architects, you name it. For every job, we have a specifically riped mermaid. It is why the kingdom runs to such perfection. The seekers are the one in charge of finding and bringing in new offerings."

"So, they kiss the humans?" I faked even more excitement, causing her to smile wider.

"Oh yes, they like to have fun, those girls," she spoke with endearment, as if what they were doing was such a fun job.

"How can you keep track of everything? It must be such tedious work and you must be able to remember so much. I forget what I did yesterday, let alone remember what thousands of your sisters are doing," Cressi spoke with amazement. "You are a hero," she giggled.

"Oh no, my sweet, not at all. We have a dedicated section for each seeker, along with every single offer they brought. That is how they gain their rewards, you see?" Mama Tia explained.

"Wow, that must take a lot of space," I made a point to look impressed, making Mama Tia point to the section where the seeker logs were kept. My heart jumped a beat when I spotted that they were catalogued by years.

Cressi asked some other questions and offered information about the Fire Kingdom and the Realm, answering Mama Tia's question with incredible excitement and longing. She spoke about her wedding, and I laughed out loud yet again at the dreadful experience she had in a church of Elvis. She and Erik had always joked about wanting to get married in Vegas and I admired that she kept her promise. And dragged Rhylan with her.

The teacups emptied and the cookies disappeared before we observed how long it had been and apologised for keeping the old siren talking for so long, especially since she was so busy, but Mama Tia invited us to visit whenever we wanted to, telling us how much she had enjoyed our company and how she would love to continue our discussions on another occasion.

"That would be wonderful," Cressi replied and I realised that she truly had fun with this old lady. She had enjoyed chatting away and sipping tea, passing the hours by the fire while inconspicuously spying on the enemy. A true fireling, I smiled to myself. But the cherry on top came with her next words.

"Mama Tia, we don't want to be a bother, but our males are away for most of the day and our rooms get so lonely sometimes," she added a pout to her expression. "Could we maybe borrow a few books to keep us company?"

"Of course, my darling. Take what you will," Mama Tia returned Cressi's sweet smile.

Ansgar

Chapter Fifteen

"Do you want to wake up late today?" I turned to Amara as soon as her eyes opened. In truth, I had twisted and turned so many times that the bed we shared jolted and the princess had to wake up.

"What time is it?" Amara mumbled from between dreams.

"Half four," I replied, having looked at the clock many times over.

"Of course I plan to wake up late. At least later than four in the morning," Amara snarled at me and tried to turn her back to me, but I placed a firm hand on her shoulder to stop the movement.

"Can you cover for me?"

She took a second. Another one. Three. Four, then inhaled deeply. "What do you need? And is it going to cost me my sleep?" her brows arched.

"Not at all, I need you to sleep and get out of this room as late as you possibly can. Give me as much time as possible," I insisted, tightening the tension on her shoulder just slightly, enough to make sure I had her attention.

"And what will you do?" Her judgemental frown deepened, telling me that she already knew what my plans were.

"I'm going to see Anwen."

"Ansgar..." she sighed, managing to reprimand me at the same time.

"I need to, Amara. I need to see her and make sure she is alright. That she doesn't hate me." My stomach knotted at the thought, the remote possibility that Anwen might indeed, have hateful feelings towards me. "Please," I added, finding her dark blue eyes and begging them with my own.

"I'll go to breakfast at ten," Amara finally said. "Make sure you are back by then." Without another word and without caring about my mouthed thank you, the princess turned and wrapped the blanket around her shoulders and over her head, as if to block my departure or any noise I made on my way out.

During my meeting with Rhylan, I made sure to ask about their new location, which Fear Gorta had gladly shared, assuring me he would take care of my mate. Part of me believed him, Anwen held some of Rhylan's power, therefore Belgarath's, and if this obsession with bringing back the god meant something to him, then Anwen's energy could not be lost. Which in turn, meant she was safe. The other part remembered how many times he used Anwen for his own goals, how he disregarded her feelings every chance he got, put her in danger's way and used her as bait.

I had to make sure she was safe, that she was protected. And I would only believe it when I saw it with my own eyes.

Getting through the corridors unnoticed turned out to be more difficult than expected. Compared to the night of solstice, when the mermaids drank their full and looked only towards enjoyment, this night they had tightened the guard duty. The celebrations were over, and the mermaids swam past the corridors with precision, glancing inside to spot anything out of the ordinary. I waited a long time to establish their swim schedule and the places they seemed to pay most attention to, the marble walls and entrance doors, so I made up a timed movement that allowed me to stop behind the open corridor entrance doors seconds before they came to survey.

To my shame, I must have lost more than an hour to cross the ten hallways that separated our dormitory from the guest ones the firelings had been allocated, but I managed to knock on both doors and shift to the side right before another mermaid threw a glance in my direction.

"What is it?" Cressida's head popped out, looking dishevelled and half wet. Sweat, I understood, unable to contain a grin. Rhylan had most definitely kept his queen busy.

"It's me," I whispered from the side of the wall, making her tilt her head to follow my voice.

"What happened?" her voice triggered an internal alarm.

"Can you open Anwen's door for me please?" I whispered, trying not to use more decibels than the precise number to reach her ears. "Quick, we have less than twenty seconds."

"What are you talking about?" she frowned and tried to step out into the hallway to find me.

"Cressida no!" I whispered. "There are guards. Close your door right now, count to ten and open it again."

"What? What are you—"

"Cressida, now!" I ordered and made myself disappear into the shadow before another waterling swam close to the transparent outer walls, peeking inside.

Just like I had asked her, the door opened seven seconds after the mermaid's view shifted from our position.

"She's upset with you," Cressi came out and walked the few steps that separated her bedroom from the next door," stopping to look at me before she twisted the knob.

"I know, that's why I'm here," I lowered my gaze, trying to tell her that I would accept my punishment, whatever it might be.

"And I assume Marreth will need a place to crash?" she raised her brows at me expectantly.

"If it is at all in your capacity," I replied with hope.

She huffed. "Just fucking say yes. It's five o'clock in the morning, quit the fancy talk for once," she groaned and opened the other bedroom door, shoving both of us in before another minute passed.

Cressida walked to the bed and pulled one of the veils that adorned the canopy, allowing me to spot Marreth, twisted to one side.

"Wake up," she kicked his leg, having no consideration for kindness when waking someone so early. Which, I assumed, I hadn't had either when it came to her.

"What is it?" Marreth's eyes opened, widening at Cressi's presence in front of him.

"You have to come to our bedroom. These two want privacy," she shifted to allow Marreth to spot me behind his queen.

Before he had a chance to protest or swear at me, I jumped into action. "Our bedroom is twelve corridors away, take the first eight straight, then turn left and walk another three, third door to the right. There are guards patrolling on the minute, but you can make it running and hide behind the doors, try the western part, it's wider. This is the key," I pressed the key to our bedroom into his hand, which luckily, hadn't been spelled against a male using it like the rest.

"Have fun, prince," he said and jumped from bed. Marreth snatched the key with excitement and escorted a grumpy Cressida out of the room, leaving me alone with my sleeping mate.

Palpitations rose in my chest, the excitement finally filling that hole she left the last time we saw each other. My eyes focused on her shoulder, the way her hair spread like the roots of a Cloutie tree and I felt overcome by a rush of jealousy towards the bed sheet that covered my mate's body.

My excitement to wake her up was instant, but so was her evident need to rest. There were books spread around her side of the bed, on the nightstand and adorning the wall to create a small tower made of piles of books. How she'd managed to carry all of them inside, I did not know.

Impatience pushed me to let myself be dominated by instinct, so I stretched on the side of the bed Marreth had occupied only minutes ago, allowing myself to do what the respectful commander had not, inch closer to my mate. The warmth of her body overpowered my senses, raising shivers down my back and waking gooseflesh on my arms, my chest and lower abdomen. Along with the sinking sensation I felt every time she was near. It felt as if I knew I would die if I didn't touch her.

I allowed my fingers to gently brush her hair, taking in that dark earthy colour. It always reminded me of the cinnamon pressed on top of seed cakes, there to embellish the pastry, but demanding attention. So were her wild locks, never once bouncing without purpose, without capturing the eye and begging full attention. Leaning down, I placed my head on her pillow, catching a part of her hair under my cheek and trapping the wild chestnut river. Hundreds of memories invaded my mind. Of the thousand kisses I had placed in her hair, of the many hours I spent in bed, my nose nestled into that scent while holding her in my arms. Her hair smelled of freedom, of the happy times we spent together, bringing me to past, quieter times.

The bare skin of her shoulder tempted my fingers to reach, to touch, to rejoice in more memories. Her skin was so soft, like a long-awaited caress. Warm and fearless, as addictive as fresh rain.

I allowed my fingers to trail down her shoulder, to inch closer to her neck and the velvety part behind the shell of her ear until my movement was forced to a halt, a smack across my face pushing me away from my claimed treasure.

"I will fucking kill you if you touch me!" a savage, wide-eyed Anwen turned to me, her chest heaving with the sudden loss of sleep.

She blinked at me through alert lashes, analysing what was in front of her, or better said, *who* was in front of her. I spotted the exact moment she recognised me, her shoulders instantly relaxing, her chest becoming feather light.

"I thought you were Marreth," she explained.

"Clearly," I did not hide a proud smile at her reaction to being touched by another male. *That's my Anwen.*

"Not that you don't deserve it too, so…keep it," she huffed with a frown and turned her back to me, suddenly deciding to punish me with her silence.

"Fahrenor…" I leaned into her, caressing the shell of her ear, with my words. "I haven't seen you in two days, we don't have much time…" I tried to appease her, to explain myself.

"Then leave," she retorted from under the covers.

"Never, my love," I replied softly and leaned further into her, trying to touch her shoulder. She shrugged away from me.

"I'm mad at you," Anwen spoke, her voice filled with the burden of unshed tears. "You lied to me," her voice broke and I hated myself for causing her suffering.

"Please…my love…" I begged. "Forgive me. Anwen, please, look at me," I tried to caress her shoulder again and, to my relief, she did not shift away. "Forgive me, baby," I pleaded with her while forming small circles on her shoulder. Waiting. Waiting for something to happen. For her to hit me again, to move away from me, to kick me out of her room.

Almost a minute wilted between us before Anwen turned to me, allowing me to gaze at her beautiful, hazel eyes.

"You didn't trust me," an accusatory sharpness sprouted in them while Anwen sat straighter in bed, the bed sheet wrapped around her chest. "Not enough to tell me."

"I wanted to spare you suffering, fahrenor. I did not want you to see that, when I knew what it can do to you," I admitted. "Seeing you force those tears back...it kills me." I did not want to mention it, I did not want to bring up the fragile state of mind she had been in the past couple years, since her brother passed. What terrified me most was that she would give up fighting, that she would simply give up.

"You didn't trust me..." I watched as a tear escaped through her eyelashes and rolled ostentatiously down her cheek. Showing me her pain. And above all, claiming my role in all this.

"I am sorry," I said again. "I am sorry, fahrenor. I am so, so sorry." Damn her struggle to keep me away, if she wanted to remove me from her sight, she had enough energy to do so and knowledge on how to use it. Without waiting for an invitation, I wrapped my arms around her and forced her to my chest, pressing her into me.

Anwen struggled for a few seconds, trying to get away, trying to free herself, but I held her close, tightening the forced embrace a little stronger every time she wrestled against me. I allowed her to shed that wrath, to expel those tears and to hit each side of my ribs in the process, until she finally calmed down.

Until she released a final sigh, one that seemed to take the world away, and relaxed into my hold, allowing me to bask in her warmth. We spent long minutes like that, taking each other in, breathing and sharing the same air, letting our lungs find a steady rhythm that our chests wanted to follow.

At one point, Anwen's arms wrapped around me, her palm lying flat on my shoulders, returning the embrace I had forcefully offered.

"Thank you," I whispered, grateful for the silent forgiveness I was not deserving of, but somehow received.

"Don't keep things from me again, you hear me?" my mate murmured from between unshed tears, breaking yet another piece of my soul.

Goddess, I beg of you, allow me to be truthful to my mate. The same plea I had begun to utter so often, it had turned into a daily affirmation. And I tried. I tried saying the words without feeling my energy break, I tried to speak them without ripping my heart out. To no avail.

"The tear is in the palace," she grabbed me from thoughts, and I had to lean back to meet her eyes.

"What?" I barely whispered, forcing Anwen to repeat.

"The tear is in the Air Palace, I'm sure of it. The lady I met today said they built this to protect their knowledge and energy. I already saw where they store the knowledge, so there must be a place where they store the energy," she nodded a few times, as if wanting to convince herself of the truth of her words.

"Fahrenor that's…thank you." She had managed to gather more information in a day, on a tour of the palace than any of us had in all the court meetings. I had to tell her, I had to tell her about my findings as well. I had to tell her about Branwyl. I had to.

"Who else is aware?" I asked instead, unable to shatter that radiance in her eyes. I hadn't seen it in such a long time.

"Cressi was with me, but we didn't talk about it, so I'm not sure if she knows or not. If she does, then she definitely told Rhylan."

I dipped my chin at the clear reasoning of her remark.

"Anwen, I also need to tell you something. About the other tear."

Goddess, I beg of you, allow me to be truthful to my mate.

Nothing.

Once again, nothing.

"I have Zaleen's tear with me," I said instead, releasing the information that would not hurt me.

My mate's eyes widened, forcing her to blink once, as if her brain needed the extra beat to understand the information.

"Where is it?" She frowned, looking like she was going to give me a good scolding for not keeping such a treasure safe. Without waiting, I grabbed her hand and placed it on my left biceps, where I had buried the energy source inside the deep tissue.

"It's here," I replied, causing her to chuckle and slap my chest admonishingly.

"Stop joking like that," she huffed.

"Anwen, it truly is here. It's near my bone." I shifted my arm slightly for emphasis.

"What are you talking about?" her brows formed a deep V.

"It's small, like a crystal, so when I got it, when Amara brought me to a secret room to grab it, I made a cut into my muscle and shoved it inside. I didn't want to have it on me physically, so this seemed like a better option at the time.

She swallowed hard, then cleared her throat.

"Who knows about this?"

"Amara, she was present during the whole thing. I'm not sure if she told Marreth."

"If she did, then Marreth told Rhylan."

"Anwen," I said again.

Goddess, allow me to be truthful to my mate for the love of everything sacred.

I couldn't.

I could not speak.

I could not say it.

"Catalina's tear is also with me," I said the only part that I could confess.

Goddess? Respectfully, fuck you!

"You have both?" I looked at my mate to find her barely breathing.

"I do, and Rhylan does not know about this one," I pressed my words. "No one knows about this one."

"Ansgar..." her hands draped across my shoulders, caressing my skin with worry. "Are you safe?"

"Do not worry about me, fahrenor. I am perfectly safe." I stopped a beat. If I could take advantage, if we had a couple of hours left, why wouldn't I? There was so much more to tell her, so much more to plan, but, to my own cowardice, I chose to spend the time putting a smile on my mate's face rather than ripping her heart out.

"Though...there is something that might help," I smiled sheepishly.

"What?" she instantly asked. "Anything."

I didn't find the words to name it, for what would I ask? Her closeness, a kiss, a long line of them? The way her body trembled against mine? Moving in unison through a sea of desire to produce ripples of pleasure until both of us turned mad?

Instead, I inched closer and allowed my lips to feel what they had been longing for, to taste that rosy mouth, filled with honey and delights.

"Hm..." Anwen snickered, allowing a smile to curl her lips. "I can do you one better, prince," my mate smirked as her hands wrapped around my shoulders and pulled me tighter into her.

Goddess mine, her closeness, the scent of her arousal, the way her fingernails dug into my skin while her tongue furiously danced with my own in that long awaited kiss. It drove me mad. If I allowed myself, I would drown in this passion and gladly seek my end within the arms of my mate.

"Anwen, I need to tell you something..." I released between pants, my chest heaving with the desperation to possess her, urging me to start doing so. Everything called for her, my skin, my heart, my energy, that need for connection overpowering everything else.

"I don't care right now," my mate replied, using her knees to jump on me and press me into the mattress, therefore making me her captive.

I gazed at her then, observing in wonder how strong she had become. How different Anwen was from the young female I had met in the forest, so afraid to claim her own thoughts and share her passions.

The female in front of me, however, was a queen. Claiming the offering that was rightfully hers.

"Anwen, trust me, I wouldn't do this if it weren't important. Please, you need to listen," I tried to catch her shoulders to shift her from the position of power she had settled herself in, but I found my arms stopping midway through.

Trapped.

Held by something, keeping me away.

I looked to discover how a line of darkness wrapped around my forearm and forced it to stop at the exact moment I had tried to shift it. I did it again. And again, moving my forearms inches away, to observe how each time, that speck of night trapped me and halted my motion. With unimaginable gentleness, which did not take a toll on the firmness of the action.

Meanwhile, Anwen sat comfortably on my pelvis, crossing her hands over her chest with pride.

"How do you like me now, prince?"

"You are the air, the moon and every light that crosses the earth," I instantly spoke, amazed by her. She was my mate. This beautiful, gorgeous, intelligent, and strong female had been made just for me.

Yet, my answer caused her to frown. "Not the sun?" she giggled slightly.

"The sun is too harsh, my love. Only the moon is adequate for such a skilled temptress," I rasped, aware that my hardness started poking through my pants and that she had placed herself in the perfect position to torture me.

"Then please, allow me to perform my role," Anwen moved her hands theatrically and slid down my length, allowing me to feel her wetness through the veil that barely covered her centre.

"Anwen, please," I tried to stop her because I was seconds away to give in and forget about everything and everyone but the need to possess my mate.

"I think it's best if the public is silent for the act," Anwen smirked and before I knew it, my hands were firmly planted above my head, along with a band of night that became a silk thread which covered my mouth.

I couldn't speak, I couldn't move, I remained strictly at her mercy.

The sensation of her power over my skin made be turn ravenous. The thought that she had me defenceless, to do with me as she pleased arose gooseflesh down my back and a jolt in my stomach.

I wanted her. I needed her thoroughly and completely and was ready to abandon my whole being to her will.

"Amhwn," I tried speaking her name to no avail.

Damn it baby, don't do this to me now, don't torture me like this.

The plea echoed strictly in my mind, since my mouth could not pronounce the words, but each attempt proved fruitless.

My mate shifted from on top of me just enough to undo and pull my pants down, allowing my hardness to spring free and show my readiness. She smiled with excitement and kicked my knees to the side, forcing me to spread my legs and make enough room for her to squeeze through.

Before I had a chance to even breathe, Anwen's warm tongue started drawing lazy circles on my tip, making me go mad with sensation. She must have known what her actions caused me to feel, because she did not stop and slowly tortured me with tongue and teeth, up and down and in circular motions until I ended up begging for her. Until I wanted nothing more than the back of her throat.

I shifted my hips in desperation, trying to show her my need, urging her to please, please, please have mercy on me, but she continued. Ruthlessly tasting me, painting along my veins with the tip of her tongue and pumping me in her hand, making me so crazed and desperate that I never thought I'd see the end of my days.

When I was on my way to passing out from overwhelming sensations, Anwen finally took mercy on my poor self and pushed her mouth to take me in fully, to let me feel her tongue caressing downward while the soft muscle on the inside of her cheek grazed me with its slickness.

And, just like I'd mentally begged so many times over, my mate allowed me to feel the back of her throat. To push past that point where I had to bend a little for her to take me all the way in and it felt divine. The way she squeezed me, the way my length prodded in the tight space and how she released me slowly only to bring me back deeper, sucking her way down.

"Uhhk beehm," I tried to speak, to summarise into words what my mind lived in sensation, completely forgetting about the band of darkness that demanded my silence.

Without paying any attention to my words, or the sounds I tried to release, Anwen's fingernails started digging into the side of my hip and down my pelvis. That was it, the sign of my undoing, the limit of my patience, the release of my leash. I could not stop. I could not control it. My hips started moving on their own accord, thrusting forwards, pressing my length deeper down Anwen's throat, forcing her mouth to open wider and take me all in.

Her head bobbed a few times in surprise, struggling with the new sensation until she wrapped her hand underneath my hip to find extra support.

An invitation for me to continue. A sign that she was enjoying it.

Goddess, how I love this female, I thought as I forced myself further down her jaw, making her throat expand to take more of me in.

Anwen

Chapter Sixteen

"I love it when you come for me, baby," Ansgar barely managed to whisper in between pants and through the pressure of impaling myself into him until I could feel the tip of his cock piercing into my lower belly.

After torturing him to the point where his hips started shaking, I allowed him to do whatever he wanted with my mouth and find his pleasure down my throat. Only when he remained crazed with the sensation, his chest heaving to press deep inhales, I released him.

I wondered if he could taste himself in the kiss I offered, and that question made me liquid. I barely allowed the prince a minute to regain his breath until I started pumping him once again, my fist tight and determined until his hardness responded to my claims.

I did not care for foreplay, I just wanted to feel him inside me, I needed to have him and feel those unforgiving thrusts he had released into the back of my mouth.

He was more than happy to show his excitement and the need for me that kept growing, even as I struggled to take him deeper and deeper.

"Please, fahrenor, I need to touch you," Ansgar reminded me of the lines of darkness I had placed around his arms.

It did not feel right. I did not want that power to disappear, not now, when it came my turn to enjoy it. Instead, I kept my lines of darkness around us, using them as suggestions to my specific wants. Pushing my prince's mouth towards my breasts, for example, or lifting his palms and directing them to cup my ass. And squeeze tight.

I loved feeling this powerful, this savage. This strong.

And I took him with me. Release after release, we enjoyed one another in different ways, sometimes making love and whispering sweet things or downright fucking like savages. It never ceased to amaze me how quickly we could shift from one to the other.

"People can hear you fucking, you know?"

The door opened with Vikram, whose expression dropped when he saw his brother slamming into me from behind, my face pressed on the mattress, my hair wrapped around Ansgar's fist, pulled tightly to force my spine stiff. We had confessed how much we enjoyed that raw encounter and wanted to recreate it. The release dripping down my thighs was a witness of that.

"You've been at it since five in the morning?" Vikram asked but his words cut at the realisation that Ansgar kept pumping into me, completely oblivious to the fact that someone was in the room with us.

My mate did not plan to stop.

I shifted my neck just enough to spot him, savagely taking me, his head dipped back, jaw tight and if I had to guess, his eyes pressed shut.

He must have heard Vikram, he must have. He was so weary of our surroundings, always checking for safety threats, always counting exits, guards and such. But he did not seem to care that there was a person in the room, too obsessed with finding his pleasure.

In fairness, I came several times, and he deserved it, because the sex had been mind-blowing. Not that it wasn't super good every time, but Ansgar had gone out of his way to do everything I asked or suggested via my arms of night.

Aware that things were quickly becoming awkward, I summoned my powers again and veiled both of us in a cloud of night, taking us away from the amused gaze of the middle prince.

For a few more seconds, I allowed myself to go back, to feel my mate's hardness, stretching at that point that drove me absolutely mad. I felt how my body parted to receive his every thrust, how he pulsated inside of me and how his fingers dipped into my hips, bringing me closer to him, closing in that whiff of space that separated my skin from his.

God, he felt so good. He felt so good that he made my core prepare itself to harness new sensation, the built up already begging for release.

I couldn't do that, I wasn't going to cum in front of Vikram, I would never hear the end of it. To help Ansgar, I lifted my ass just slightly, giving him better access to me and spread my thighs wider to allow his length to penetrate to my very centre. A few seconds later my mate's groan announced his release. A few more thrusts and he let himself to fall on the bed, taking me along with him to trap me in his arms.

I gripped the bedsheet and covered us before allowing the darkness to slowly fade. It revealed a very amused Vikram, smirking wider than I had probably ever seen him do, sitting on a chair next to the door and inspecting the darkness intently.

"Well, well, well, someone likes to play dirty," he grinned, as if to scold us for daring to take another minute to ourselves.

"Next time, learn to knock, you prick," Ansgar replied, answering my unspoken question. He did know Vikram was in the room. He knew and did not care one bit.

"Dear brother," Vikram crossed his legs and leaned back in the chair, stretching his shoulders, "I thought it important to tell you that your wife is becoming a bit…hm…how should I call it? Desperate? Annoyed?" Vikram pouted theatrically.

"She knows where I am," Ansgar said but instantly shifted. "I told her I would be back by ten and she was fine to wait."

"Sure, sure…" Vikram's eyes sparkled. "Though I would suggest you get dressed and make a run for it, seeing how it's half eleven."

Ansgar turned so quickly, I thought he would break his neck in the process, searching the walls for a clock. I followed his gaze and checked the truth in Vikram's words.

"Shit." Ansgar released a breath and jumped from bed, displaying his bare ass to his brother on his way to search for his pants.

"Chill, chill," Vikram started laughing hysterically, the image of Ansgar bouncing up and down while his length still struggled to relax caused his brother to drop tears as he pressed his hands on his stomach. "Marreth's keeping her company, they are going to lunch together posing as old friends and the commander is telling everyone about his tragic past and so on. You have time." Vikram stopped, realising he needed to calm Ansgar down before he had a heart attack. "But you should get going. And be very careful when you get out of here."

"I'm sorry, baby, I need to go. We still need to talk, but—"

"It's fine," I caught his forearm and squeezed gently. "I'll be fine, I need to have a chat with Vikram anyway. Be careful and maybe I'll see you at lunch," I smiled softly, knowing that would most definitely be the case. After all, I had to go pick up my fake boyfriend.

"Jag vaedrum teim," my prince pressed his lips on mine one more time, before shoving his brother out of the chair and opening the door to peek outside. Five seconds later, he was gone.

"If you want sex advice, boo boo dear, you need only ask," Vikram grinned at me, making a point to display his perfectly white teeth, "but by the look of it, you seem to be doing just fine."

His comment caused me to roll my eyes. "Do you have a few minutes?"

"For you, always," Vikram replied with interest, his grin dropping only slightly, a dash of worry appearing on his face.

"How do I get to the seekers?"

"Do what?" Vikram frowned, having no idea what I was talking about.

"The mermaids that scour the world for men to kill, according to their skills and to whatever the kingdom might need?" I pressed my words, mimicking his expression.

The prince rose from his seat and took the few steps that separated us, planting himself on the bed, next to me. Never mind that I was naked underneath that flimsy bedsheet, never mind I probably smelled of sex and of his brother. Or sex with his brother. After all, this wasn't the first time Vikram had seen me naked, or partly naked, thanks to that nasty habit of not knocking he kept.

"Anwen, this is not something you want to get into." Hm...so no more nicknames when it came to serious business, I noted. "You can get hurt. Or cause something that can't be repaired." I noted how his commander instinct suddenly awoke, the need to protect his kingdom and his people. I had to admire that about him.

"I don't plan on doing anything stupid, Vikram. I'm not an idiot. I just want to know," I replied, gripping the bed sheet a little tighter since one of my boobs threatened to escape.

"Know what, Anwen?" the prince pressed, his gaze suddenly aware of all the books that surrounded me. Some of them had been on the bed, by my side, but Ansgar made sure to kick them on the floor during our time together. I didn't have a chance to add a bookmark or make a note of the one I was reading, but I wasn't too worried, because none of these books proved useful. None of them mentioned anything about my brother.

"Who killed Erik," I said what I already thought would have been obvious. Noticing how his brows furrowed, I continued.

"You've been to my home, Vikram. You met my parents. You saw how broken the family is. I need to know," I insisted.

"And what do you plan to do? Wait at the entrance and ask them individually?" he huffed at the ridicule of what he thought to be my plan.

"I just need to know. I have no idea what I will do or how I will react, but I need to know her name. I just need to know," I said again.

"Anwen, we don't know the standing of our kingdom yet, let alone yours." He must have realised what he said, and I appreciated how he rushed to correct it. "The one you represent, I mean. The one Rhylan gave you power over. I heard the queen doesn't even want to see him, she only speaks to my brother and to Amara. They haven't even prompted an apology regarding the threat on your life. The plan is working so far, Thelssha thinks she is charming the windling princess, Amara and Ansgar have free rein in the castle, evidently," he pointed at the dishevelled bed.

"I also have some access. I went to the library yesterday and saw all the seeker's logs."

His eyes scanned the room with the sudden understanding. Of what I planned. Of what I had been doing.

"What did my brother say about this? Since you are here talking to me, I doubt he agreed to it."

His reply pissed me off, making me move from bed and put distance in between us, taking the bed sheet with me. I don't think I wanted to move away from Vikram, rather, to give myself more space to be angry. And to point at things while I spoke.

"First off, pretty boy," I lifted my finger in the air, and by the way he tried to hide a smile, I knew I had amused him. "Your brother is not the boss of me. He may be my mate, but I do what I want. As I proved many times, sometimes not in the best ways," I pressed my lips together. I hadn't started this speech well.

"Second," I drew in more air and continued, "if it weren't for Erik, I wouldn't even be here. Ansgar and I wouldn't have met, none of this would have happened. So, in a way, we owe it to Erik. And thirdly, he was my brother."

My heart trembled a little at the use of past tense, when it came to referring to Erik. "As I'm sure you know, one would do anything for their brothers. I need to do this. This is what started everything, I have to finish. With or without help."

It took Vikram a long moment of silence, before he finally nodded.

"I'll see what I can find out," he nodded again, making my chest suddenly lighter. "All I know is that they return at full moon, similar to our keepers. They are assigned to posts, they do the work, then come home for celebrations."

"Why the full moon?" I had to ask, finding it bizarre how they all needed to connect it to important events.

"For a long time, our ancestors thought the full moon was the goddess, calling us home. They worshipped it. No fae is complete without a full moon, it is the most beloved time. The air feels lighter, it's easier to smile when the light shines down on us," Vikram said but it was his brother's words that sounded in my mind.

You are the air, the moon and every light that crosses the earth.

"They generally arrive after sunset," Vikram continued, banishing the storm of butterflies that invaded my stomach. "I'll ask Eidothea, see if she knows anything."

"Thank you, Vikram." I walked to him and took his hand in mine, squeezing it slightly.

"Anwen, please don't do anything stupid," he sighed, unconvinced.

Ansgar

Chapter Seventeen

Amara was going to kill me. And I had no reason to defend myself because I deserved it. Here I was, running through the hallways to get to my supposed wife, with yesterday's clothing and filled with mating scent. From another female. She was going to kill me.

Unless... I had to stop and take a few breaths to realise that my eyes showed me the truth. Because there Amara was, at the table with various mermaids, chatting away and gesturing while holding a crystal glass. Only she did not use a chair to make herself comfortable, but Marreth's lap. Who was also holding a crystal glass in one hand, while resting the other on my wife's hips.

"What am I missing?" I stepped into the room, causing them to shift their attention to my sudden entrance.

"A shower," Marreth smirked.

"A comb," Amara followed and giggled, her eyes scanning my hair, which must had looked disastrous after being filled with so much sweat and gripped by my mate for dear life on various occasions.

"Apart from that," I clarified. "How is this happening?" I flicked my finger to point from the commander to the princess.

"Eidothea is in charge today, this is her harem," Amara extended her palm to summarise the entire room.

"We are amongst friends," Marreth added as well and for emphasis, he leaned in and caught Amara's chin with a finger, twisting it gently to steal a kiss.

"You might want to go back to our room and change, lunch is at half twelve and Eidothea wants to see us," my wife said. Then, thinking that I might use the extra incentive to get cleaned up, she added. "Anwen will be there too, so you should look the part," she giggled at whatever thoughts crossed her mind and by the way she scanned me up and down, I knew they were not the most innocent ones.

"Thank you, I will do. Are you alright to remain here?" I needed to make sure, not wanting her to feel abandoned yet again.

"She'll be more than fine, prince," Marreth snapped. "Also, your brother came by about an hour ago, looking for you. We told him where you were so I'm sure you probably already saw him."

"I did," I nodded and turned, leaving the two in a sea of laughter and joy.

I returned within the hour, freshly showered and adorned, dressed in a green shirt and sleeveless dark grey tunic and very comfortable trousers. I had been walking in the ceremonial garments for a couple of days and started to absolutely despise the small cape Amara had insisted to add on my shoulders, which made movement uncomfortable and made me feel like I was constantly watched, the motion of the fabric behind me making me look back hundreds of times a day.

Since today proved to be a casual encounter, I opted for comfort, leaving my hair fall unadorned on my shoulders and grabbed only a small dagger which rested on a belt strap, hoping to enjoy its idle state for the rest of the day.

True to what Amara had said, the room remained filled with happy mermaids, enjoying delicacies and wine, with Amara not moving from Marreth's lap and with new visitors. Cressida and Rhylan sat on the other side of the circular table, their backs to me, but I instantly recognised her golden locks and his wide shoulders.

"Where is Anwen?" I asked instead of a greeting.

"So eager, prince," Rhylan turned just enough to let me see his profile. "Have you no compassion towards the poor girl? Keeping her awake since the crack of dawn and now coming back for more?" he admonished, slowly shaking his head from side to side.

"Clearly, there are no secrets in this realm," Cressida turned and displayed one of her welcoming smiles. I needed it, I needed to see the joy return to her face.

The last time I had seen the new fire queen, her screams had remained trapped in my mind, that anguish and shock she had been in making me drown in guilt. I needed to know she was once again her happy self. I was impressed by the sudden realisation of how much I had come to care for her in the short time we had known each other. Every single time she offered me kindness, a smile or advice, no matter the situation, no matter what she was doing in that moment or whatever I interrupted. She always made time to share a kind word with me, and the present posed no exception.

I returned her smile. "Clearly," I tilted my head.

"Hello, prince," the fire queen smiled again. "Anwen is with Eidothea and Vikram, they will be here shortly. Something they needed to talk about first," she raised her shoulders gently, giving it no importance. "Come, let's have breakfast. Or lunch, depending on what your tummy fancies," Cressida patted the empty chair next to her, inviting me to take a seat. Rhylan's groan came instantly, making me accept the invitation just to annoy Fear Gorta a little more.

Talk...something Anwen and I hadn't managed to do. Something I was too coward to push. We had to talk. Anwen and I had to talk, and I had to be truthful to my mate. I knew the information I had to give her would wreck her soul, but I was willing to see it through alongside her. Whatever she needed, I would offer. If she needed a shoulder to cry on, I would be there. If she needed apologies, I would do my best to arrange it and if she needed revenge, I would help with that too. As soon as the timing was adequate.

By Anwen's determination that day in her brother's room, I knew she would not let this go. I knew she needed to find out everything that happened to Erik, and if I had to tie Branwyl to a post and rip the information out, I would do it. Anwen needed to know. And I held no loyalties to the sirens.

I would help my mate through this.

"Thank you all for joining us, my apologies for the delay," Eidothea's voice clinked from the entry hall to announce her arrival. Along with Vikram. And my mate. I looked at Anwen hoping to find a smile, or at least an acknowledgement of what we had just shared, but her jaw was tight and full of tension, her eyes lost somewhere in thought.

She walked to the table, mechanically following the siren queen and my brother to the table and letting her body fall on the chair next to mine without a word. She acted as if there was no one else in the room, like nothing mattered except the thoughts that had clearly possessed her mind and clouded the brightness in her hazel eyes.

"Baby," I whispered to her, using the expression that had been so problematic in our relationship but that had recently become so important to us. Whenever one of us got too entrapped in planning and stepped away from reality, it became the other's mission to bring them back. I couldn't even remember the amount of times Anwen had cupped my cheeks and turned me to face her, whispering these words. And true to our tradition, my mate turned her attention to me, called by our unyielding connection.

"Are you alright?" I asked the question she had spoken so many times during the months of planning. During the exhausting training sessions. During the troubled nights.

She nodded.

Slowly.

Just once.

"I hope everyone is having a pleasant morning, and once again, thank you for giving up your time to join us today. My sister was called away on an inspection, so I thought this to be a perfect moment for us to have a truthful conversation," the siren queen forced my attention back to her.

I could not leave Anwen like this, something was not right, something was clearly not right because my mate struggled to keep her composure. Whatever she and the new couple talked about had brought her to this state and there was nothing I could do right then to rectify the situation. But let her know I was there. For whatever may come, for whatever she needed me to do. I was there.

Keeping my eyes on Eidothea, I shifted in my seat and leaned closer to Anwen, hoping she felt my presence. I placed my palm in her lap and caught her fingers in mine, trapping our hands together. My heart lifted a beat when I felt her fingers gently squeezing mine, her eyes shifting to me just enough to acknowledge my closeness. And to tell me it was helping.

"We don't have a lot of time to waste, some of us have other plans, so we'll get on with it quickly," Vikram spoke, casually leaning in his cushioned chair like he had sat at this very table a million times before and he had the same power as Eidothea.

"That is very thoughtful of you, prince," Rhylan noted, his voice dropping an octave. Fear Gorta did not like to be commanded and he especially struggled to cope with giving up his position of sole authority. In the past two months, all of us had done everything Rhylan wanted, listened to his plans, followed his meal and training routines and offered help whenever he requested it. Now, however, he found himself at the mercy of others, something he made a point to show his frustrations about.

"Of course, I'm a very thoughtful male," Vikram put more salt on the wound and smirked, extremely pleased with himself.

"Is this a safe environment to talk?" It might have sounded silly, since my brother was extremely comfortable with this arrangement, but my eyes darted across the room to spot all the mermaids gathered together, either serving more food or wine, casually resting on the sofas or other chairs or walking around the large dining room.

"They are my harem, thus sworn to serve me. I would die for my girls, and they would do the same for me," my brother's mate assured us.

"Very well," Cressida took the lead, and I guessed it was to spare some of Rhylan's ego, because Vikram looked to be on the verge of releasing another remark. "How can we help? Why are we all invited here?" the Fire Queen asked.

My eyes darted to Anwen, still trapped in her thoughts, barely present during a conversation that seemed to become important, so I squeezed her fingers a little tighter, forcing her to come back to me. To live the present and be here, to banish whatever thoughts kept her trapped.

She glanced at me again with pressed lips, as if wanting to hold something back, something that wanted to burst out and forced a soft and quick smile. Then turned to Eidothea.

"I do not want a war. I am not in support of such an action, and I disagree with my sister's judgement. Our kingdom has lived in peace for decades and I want to keep it that way. Thelssha, however, does not see reason. She has become obsessed with seeking justice and with finding revenge. We have had to move our cities lower and lower because of all the pollution, the water does not suit our needs as it used to because of all the spillage that we are forced to take in every single day."

"It is true, the Realm has become too large for its own good," Vikram confirmed. He should know best, he spent half of his time with the humans, but his words spoke true. I had a chance to see it for myself in the months I lived in their realm, when I visited Anwen's home. Humans were everywhere, by the thousands, living in the concrete buildings they loved so much, without the need for nature, crammed into tiny spaces where air was barely breathable.

"I agree," Cressi spoke again, and all our eyes averted to her. Suddenly aware of the attention, the Fire Queen shrugged. "What? It's true, the world has gone to shit. There's too many of us, not enough resources and we're killing the planet. And the worst part is that nobody cares. I may be human," she must have read our surprise for what it was, "but I take pride in my realism. Which is why I supported Rhy in his plans from the very beginning," her hand instinctively found her king's and relaxed into his touch.

"What do you stand to gain if the gods return?" Eidothea asked, veiling the room in sudden silence. All of us waited. Waited to hear Fear Gorta.

"I fulfil the promise my ancestors made to the god. And I give the world a chance to change. For the better or for the worse."

"And how will this work?" Vikram pressed.

"We join the tears of the goddesses. The energy will have a summoning effect, calling them back. They, in turn, will return my god. And together, they can decide what to do with the world, that will no longer be up to us."

"The goddesses will be the first to return?" Amara jumped with the question; her voice amazed.

Rhylan nodded. "Only they have the power to bring back Belgarath. We know his location, but do not have the power to awaken him."

"A thousand apologies, Queen Eidothea," Marreth spoke with such reverence that put all of us to shame. We had seen Eidothea as Vikram's mate, spoken to her as such, while forgetting she was the second queen of the Water Kingdom. That she held such high power. "I find myself confused by your sudden decision to go against your sister's wishes and wonder what might have brought you to such ideas."

That hit the mark. Marreth spoke what all of us had started to wonder. Why would Eidothea betray her sister? Why would she want to stop her kingdom from gaining power?

She must have known the question was coming, because the siren jumped at the opportunity. "We also have some information about the return of the goddesses, and as Fear Gorta said, the first step is uniting all the tears."

I felt Anwen's gaze slowly brush the side of my face with worry, but it was my turn to focus my attention elsewhere and only squeezed her fingers again. To tell her that I was safe as I allowed Eidothea's words to fall into my ears.

"The one who returns the goddess to the realm is also granted a reward. Legend is, they may ask for whatever they wish, it will be granted by the blessed energy of Marrynah."

"What is it that you wish?" Amara asked, absorbed in the siren's story.

"A life," she smiled sweetly. "The opportunity to walk the earth when I wish to, be with whom I want and not have to live terrified that too much of my touch can kill my mate."

"You want to be human?" Rhylan scoffed.

"I want to be fae," Eidothea replied, no word of reprimand in her tone. Her turquoise eyes shifted towards Vikram. "An earthling," she added, causing my brother to display a proud smile. My brother leaned into her touch and pressed his lips on hers, showing all of us that a siren's true love had the power to grant energy, rather than become a killing weapon.

"Sylvan Regnum is amazing," I was surprised to hear Anwen speak. She had kept silent for the duration of the conversation. "Queen Bathysia will love you, and they have this amazing garden overlooking the palace and you can see far up in the mountains. And the chocolate," she stopped to release a slow moan. "Girl, you haven't tasted deliciousness until you had earthling chocolate," my mate shifted in her seat with excitement.

Eidothea smiled, her chin dipping a little to show Anwen how grateful she was for this sudden burst of excitement. "I look forward to it."

"My queen, apologies," one of the mermaids rushed into the dining hall, interrupting the conversation. "The princess is waiting in the throne room, as requested."

Everyone froze. Eidothea froze. Anwen froze. Vikram froze, while the rest of us looked at one another, having no idea what was happening. Until Anwen let go of my hand, her stance statuesque and slowly raised from her seat. As if on cue, Cressida did the same, allowing tension to paint her features.

"Please excuse us," my mate said before leaving the room without further explanation, Cressida following silently after her.

Anwen

Chapter Eighteen

I knew where the throne room was. I'd been there less than an hour ago, accompanied by Eidothea and Vikram. That is where I found out who my brother's murderer was. That is where I had asked the siren queen to call her, and that is where I would meet her.

Seven hallways separated us.

Two straight, third one on the left, walk another three then left again.

Eidothea's instructions sounded in my mind on repeat, barely allowing me to hear a word from what was said at the table. I already knew. I had already asked the siren why she was offering me her help, why she was willing to betray one of their own.

I had already guessed she wanted a new life. Having a mate myself and being separated from him for a year had taught me that I would do anything — anything — in my power to get him back. And to keep him with me. I would betray, I would cheat, I would lie, and I would, probably, kill too.

When she mentioned her wish to become fae, I understood that I could count on her help. That I could trust her. And she had proven so, because less than an hour after our conversation, here I was, walking towards what I wanted most. My brother's killer.

I never thought Cressida would want to come with me, let alone volunteer to do it, but her presence had been the finalising drop in the deal Eidothea and I made. At first, the siren was reluctant to tell me the information.

She started second guessing giving me the opportunity to find the end to my quest, to the search I started three years ago.

Until Cressida appeared and started appeasing the situation. She had this gift about her, the diplomacy in her words and the softness of her tone, that she could make people do anything she wanted. As I watched her charm the second queen of the sirens, I wondered what my sister would have been like if she had been born one. How different the world would have been with Cressi as a siren queen, willing everyone to her command with that sweet melodious tone of hers and those soft but powerful smiles she used to charm the world.

Within a few minutes, Eidothea agreed to meet with the mermaid that had taken Erik as an offering, as long as Cressida accompanied me and was present for the entire conversation.

So, here she was, walking in silence beside me, her steps as determined and filled with rage as my own. I realised that I wasn't the only one seeking revenge. That I wasn't the only one that had come to this kingdom and forced into an underwater prison with an ulterior motive. That everything Cressi had done so far, probably since we arrived, guided us there.

In the throne room.

In front of a dark-haired woman.

My heart started pounding and I had to force air into my lungs while my stomach seemed to have dropped in my knees. She was there.

"Hello," she turned, having the nerve to look annoyed to see us there and took a long moment to gaze at both of us in turn and study us up and down, before she crossed her arms over her chest and shifted her weight on a hip.

"Hello," I heard a small trembling voice and looked to my left to realise it was Cressi who had released the greeting. "What is your name?" my friend continued.

"Excuse me?" the mermaid frowned, her chin raised and slightly tilted, looking at us in disbelief.

"What is your name?" Cressida repeated softly, her voice void of feeling. For the first time in my life, I heard her speak mechanically and I didn't even think breath entered her chest anymore.

"I am Branwyl, princess of the Water Kingdom," the mermaid raised her eyebrows, still not believing we had the nerve to ask her to introduce herself in her own kingdom. "And who might you be? The queen or the princess?"

We were taken aback by her correct assumption, so she clarified.

"Who else would even have the nerve to saunter around in those cheap fabrics? What female wouldn't be proud to display her gifts? Clearly, you two are as pathetic as your *king*," she pressed the last word with an extra sprinkle of ridicule.

"Are you referring to my husband? Rhylan Gordon, King of the Fire Kingdom? The male who lived for millennia, who raised and collapsed empires while you and your kind were barely tadpoles?" Cressi mimicked Branwyl's movement and tilted her head as well, as if needing more clarification. I barely held back a proud smile.

"I am referring to the sarcastic prick who had the nerve to dare call himself our king," Branwyl spat back. "Just because he is a king to an unknown and useless realm now, doesn't give him any right to return and flaunter that disgusting crown on your head."

"You were here?" I finally found my words, the push to come closer to the answer I wanted most. "When Rhylan first visited?"

Branwyl huffed, using a hand to brush the wet hair off one shoulder before she turned to me, proudly revealing her nakedness. "Of course, I was here, haven't you heard what I just said, girl? I am a princess of this kingdom."

"I am also a princess of mine," I cut her off. "Which means you and I have the same standing." I raised my chin to be perfectly parallel to my feet, just like I had been taught to do so many times. Hold my head high. Prepare for what she was about to say and keep my heart from exploding.

"Huh, so you are the replacement?" she groaned in disapproval. "Shame, your brother was so much better looking," the mermaid pressed her lips together and started draping her eyes on me, as if to take in all my flaws. The last thing I cared about were her intimidation tactics, so I did not respond to her evident critique. She had just admitted to knowing my brother. To seeing him.

"You knew him, then? You knew Erik?" My heart beat with such rage, I wondered how it did not rip through my torso.

"Knew him?" she huffed with uncontained pride. "I was the one who found him," she smirked at me with pride and stepped closer to me, as if to show me the possession in her eyes, to revel in everything she had done to my brother.

Cressida wasn't breathing next to me, and I had to check with the corner of my eye to see that she was on the point of passing out. We did it, we found my brother's murderer and she had almost confessed her crime. Yet, I needed more. Much, much more.

"And what did you do?" I asked, struggling to keep my tone even. I couldn't read the sirens, but her feelings must have burst out because a hint of fuchsia rolled out of her hair, along with drops of salmon. Pride. Pride and annoyance. The bitch looked back with pride at taking my brother's life. I felt the ripples of darkness tickle my skin, begging to come out, but I clenched my fists, trying to contain them. I needed her to say it.

"What did you do?" I asked again, tempting the mermaid to come closer to me, to say all the words I needed her to release.

"What I do with all men," she smirked with pride, letting those sweet lips purr venom. "But I must admit, I did have my fun with your brother. I took my long, sweet time and enjoyed him. I kissed him so many times that it's still a wonder how he managed to hang onto his energy after I was done with him."

"You are the reason he's dead?"

"The reason?" she smiled sweetly. "No, my darling, I am the cause," she spoke with pride.

I exploded.

Seeing her tempt me with her act, taking such pride in killing an innocent man and enjoying it, telling me how she tasted her victory and floundering around her achievement.

Darkness covered everything. I allowed the night to ignite, to blow out of me and into Branwyl, sending all the rage, all the pain, every single tear I ever shed because of her. Sending it all in Erik's memory.

Seconds passed, keeping the room veiled in adamant lines. Seconds during which I cried, I shouted, I released all my demons.

She was here. She was right in front of me, taking the blow of my power.

But it did not bring Erik back.

It did not take the pain away.

It did not sort anything.

When I finally summoned the night back, the first thing I saw was Cressida. Crying. Fallen on her knees.

I looked around to find Branwyl, but she must have disappeared, she must have ran away. There was no sign of the mermaid.

I looked back at Cressi, who lifted her teary blue eyes to me. "You killed her…" she murmured.

"No, I…" I stopped, my eyes spotting the smudges of blood on Cressida's face. In her hair. On her dress.

My face was wet too, but I thought it was tears. I looked down to see crimson and specks of something solid on my dress.

And on the floor, where Branwyl had been. Where she left behind a puddle of blood and remains of meat.

Where she found her final moment.

Ansgar

Chapter Nineteen

"Ansgar, don't," Eidothea's arm reached to stop me when I tried to rise from my seat and follow Anwen. She just left, without an explanation, without even a reassuring gaze.

She just left.

"Anwen and I have an agreement," the siren queen reassured me, inviting me to sit back down. "There is still much to talk."

"And what is your plan, my queen?" Marreth posed the question, demanding our attention. Parts of his dark ruffled hair lingered in between Amara's fingers, who did not cease curling the ends of his locks while mindlessly resting her forearm on his shoulder.

"I will speak with my sister on her return. Tell her that neither my part of the army or the other kingdoms are in support of her claim. And try to make her understand how her approach is damaging to the entire realm," the siren queen responded with determination.

"And how do you envision the development?" Rhylan pressed from his seat. He tried to remain nonchalant and uncaring, but I felt his unease. Just like me, he had absolutely no idea where his queen had gone. He too, remained abandoned.

"Almost impossible to shift, as all decisions my sister makes," Eidothea sighed, then continued. "But, I hope that she will come to see reason. Not instantly, not without fighting back and protesting, probably not without spilling her rage."

"Do you expect to see results?" it was the windling princess who asked, her fingers stopping their circular motion from between her lover's locks and trailing down the scar on his neck. Without even flinching.

I watched that scar intently several times over, Marreth and I had even made jokes about how the fireling females found it grotesque and he would have struggled to catch some enjoyment were it not for his commander's title.

Even though he always laughed about it, I knew it hurt him. To look like that, to make softer hearts flinch at the sight of him. But not Amara. Never Amara, who looked at him as if he would bring her the moon. I felt a sudden jolt of joy for the both of them, for my friend, who had finally found a purpose.

"Not instantly, no. But I expect to delay the war, at least. And I trust all of you agree with this plan?" The siren queen stopped to gaze at each of us in turn, following how we all nodded almost simultaneously.

This is what we wanted, this is what we had come for. To delay the war. To stop it from completely happening, if at all possible. And what Eidothea offered was a better chance than we had imagined. The petition for peace, coming directly from the second queen's mouth must be worth more than a thousand royal visitors making the same plea.

"Very well, we are in full support of your decision, Queen Eidothea," Rhylan took the lead. "May we linger for a few days before returning? We will not get in the way, you have my word."

"Of course, Fear Gorta," that won't be a problem. "I assume you have ulterior motives for your return, which involve some conversations with the mermaids that entrapped you and made an attempt on your daughter's life?" the siren queen did not hesitate to unveil Rhylan's unsuccessful past visit for all of us.

"Yes, as you can imagine —" Rhylan's stomach twisted, making him bend at the waist and catch himself on the edge of the table to prevent his body from completely falling. He looked as if he was in deep pain, his eyes wide and crimson, witnessing a vision none of us could follow. Fear Gorta remained petrified for a couple of seconds before regaining his composure and straightening his back with a deep inhale. "If you would excuse me, there is an urgent matter I must tend to." Without waiting for our reaction or offering any other explanation, he turned and left the dining hall in a hurry.

"What is up with him?" Amara frowned, directing the question at me, but I shook my head. Whatever it was, it gave me cause to worry.

"Well, now that we got rid of Rhylan so quickly, shall we go for a stroll, my sweet?" Vikram turned to Eidothea, offering her one of those smiles I knew so well.

"I would be delighted to," the siren queen returned my brother's smile and blinked sweetly before placing a small kiss on the corner of his mouth.

"That's our queue," Marreth pushed his chair back and shifted to offer his hand to Amara. As soon as she was up, the couple turned to me. "What are your plans?"

I struggled to hide my smile at the hidden meaning of their question. Both of them too polite to ask me to keep the hell away from the bedroom and give them some time together.

"I need to have a chat with baby brother, so he'll be with me for a few hours. You two enjoy," Vikram responded in my stead.

"We do?" I frowned in surprise, since Vikram and Eidothea had just expressed their desire to be alone. And I really needed to go find my mate. Something was definitely not right and Rhylan running out of the room made me even more concerned.

"Yes, we do," Vikram confirmed and walked up to me, then rested his arm on my shoulder and proceeded to lead me out, Eidothea trailing after us.

With no other choice but to follow my brother and his mate, I left Marreth and Amara in the company of the rest of the mermaids that remained in the dining room, though they would surely make their way to more private terrain. I made a mental note to show up to bed as late as I possibly could, or better yet, see if there was a way for me to spend the night with Anwen instead. It all depended on Queen Thelssha's return, which I assumed, would be the subject in question.

After guiding me through dark hallways, my brother's arm returned to his lover's waist and proceeded to walk ahead and guide me through the glass corridors, trapped in a hushed conversation, with my brother only turning in my direction from time to time to make sure I followed.

My steps trailed after theirs while I focused my gaze on the newly found corridors, the intricate twists and bends in the road to wherever we were going, which looked to be leading us deeper into the palace then I had been allowed before.

All the while Vikram kept insisting on something, trying to convince Eidothea.

By the way he kept looking back, I knew it had to do with me. The siren halted her steps several times, as if wanting to turn back, but my brother's hands and kisses convinced her to go on, every single time.

I wanted to take advantage of her stopping midway and ask more questions, tell them that, whatever this was, I had something to do as well. My worry only grew and the fact that we'd walked so much and hadn't heard any news or seen the firelings, made the seed of my worry flourish.

"Ansgar," Vikram finally stopped, Eidothea's hands still trapped in his and turned slowly towards me. "Tell Eidothea about Zaleen's tear. She needs to know where it is."

My eyes widened with surprise and concern. Why was Vikram suddenly mentioning this? And why would he want me to reveal such an important information in front of a stranger?

No, not a stranger, I reminded myself.

His mate.

His mate for over a decade, one that, by the looks of it, was willing to do anything in her power to be with my brother. And my brother, who'd sacrificed so much to have the freedom to spend the time amongst humans, so he could enjoy the illusion of an encounter with the female he loved.

I thought about the sacrifice he had to make, of renouncing a future with heirs for these stolen days and solstices, for the possibility to be in the arms of his lover and all the work and sacrifice he had to put into it on a daily basis. To maintain the charade of the unconquerable prince, to keep joking about his feelings and amusement, when all he wanted to do was to be with his mate. I had to trust that. I had to trust him.

"I have it with me. I've had it since the day after my wedding," I confessed, shifting my gaze through the hallways to ensure we were alone.

"Where is it?" Eidothea's turquoise eyes stopped on me.

"Inside me," I replied. "I made a cut into my body and shoved the crystal through muscle, then sealed the wound."

If she must have thought me a liar, as soon as I said the word 'crystal', her shoulders lost their tension. She believed me. And trusted me.

Which led me to think that Marrynah's tear was also a crystal.

"What about Catalina's?" she asked, causing Vikram to shift in discomfort. My brother looked at me as if to say it was my choice how much I revealed about our kingdom. About myself.

"It is also with me." I was aware that my reply would be considered curt, but I did not grant it importance.

"And if you have Marrynah's, what would you do? What is it that you desire most?"

I swallowed with surprise when the siren queen let go of my brother's hand and stepped to me to cup my face and force my gaze to hers, pinning me in place. Wanting to get into my head and read my thoughts.

"Make sure we're all safe," I replied. "Make sure that the world doesn't get destroyed in a useless battle for power."

"And if they return?" she spoke softly. "If the goddesses return?"

"Then I shall fall on my knees and ask Catalina to grant my mate permission to live with me," I replied truthfully, saying the first thing that popped into mind.

I hadn't allowed myself to think about the possibility of our success, much too concerned about the impending war we were trying to stop, about protecting Anwen, about protecting the kingdom and the realms.

Of course I wanted happiness, of course I wanted a long life with my mate, without dangers, where we could live in whatever kingdom she chose, surrounded by many heirs. I wanted to grow old with Anwen. I wanted to live every moment I had seen my parents share. I wanted to have children and grandchildren and perform rituals and praise the moon for their well-being.

I wanted it all.

"And if the tear demands a sacrifice? Would you suffer for it? Would you suffer to ensure your mate is safe? That your kingdom is safe? What would you give?" her fingers squeezed my jaw, making my head bob a little.

"My life."

Eidothea nodded, suddenly convinced. "Very well. You shall receive Marrynah's energy."

Anwen

Chapter Twenty

Anger slowly evaporated, leaving me veiled in blood and pieces of meat, having absolutely no idea what I'd done. How it had come to this. I only remembered her laughter, the mocking tone she used to speak about my brother, the pleasure she took in destroying his young life. He had so much to live for, so much to do, so much to accomplish and experience. All taken away by this miserable being.

I looked at my surroundings, the throne room that remained painted crimson, a masterpiece I did not mean to create, yet, now that I inspected, rose pride in my senses. The darkness made its way back into my veins and flowed with a slight rush, with a sense of accomplishment that made my heart beat just a little bit quicker.

It didn't help. It wouldn't bring him back, I knew this.

But that dark part of me, that feeling of retribution that became sentient was pleased with my work, with the knowledge that she would not be laughing anymore, just like Erik couldn't either.

"You killed her," Cressida murmured again, large tears pooling down her face and washing away the specks of blood that touched her skin. She tried to swallow, an audible gulp falling into her stomach. "You killed her," she said again.

"Yes," I simply said, acknowledging my action. "I did."

My friend was scared, terrified even. Of me.

I had become a person to raise terror. I had become a killer, just like Branwyl. I was no better than her, for what had I done? Let my impulses loose, take what I thought was mine to claim.

"I killed her," a new rush came through my body, this time pushing the bravery away. There was no pride left to guide me, no sense of accomplishment but…shame. Dread. Fear.

I just killed someone.

What would Erik think? Seeing his sister converted into a murderer, using the powers Ansgar had convinced me could do so much good, to claim vengeance.

Oh my god! Ansgar…

What would he say? What would he think?

"What in the god's name happened here?"

I couldn't look at the door, couldn't bring myself to look at Rhylan and stood straight, keeping my focus on the puddle of blood at my feet. I sensed him rush to Cressida, who remained on her knees, covered in specks of crimson, crying and shaking slightly.

"My love," I heard him speak. So softly, with so much care and love. "You are safe, I'm here," Rhylan said. Curiosity pushed me to turn my head just enough to see how he wrapped my sister in his arms, bringing her to safety.

I was glad. To know that she would be safe. To know that she was loved in such a way. Even if it was by him.

Another thought came to life, bringing back that hatred. Rhylan. He was the one responsible for this. He'd made the mermaids seek revenge against his kin, he'd chased my brother and told him the truth, he'd come to Evigt and turned my life upside down.

He too deserved to be punished.

Night flourished in my veins, pushing those tendrils towards their own maker. He too deserved to become blood and bone. Nothing else.

Rhylan was responsible for Erik's death, for Ansgar's suffering, for so many of my tears.

"Don't even dare, sprout," something pushed me back, something wrapped around my neck and squeezed.

My darkness instantly vanished while my hands were forced to wrap around that tightness, to fight for my right to bring air into my lungs. I blinked in terror to see that Rhylan had been the one to send it. A line of darkness, a line of night.

A line of death.

Claiming me. Punishing me for daring to send it against its master.

My vision started to blur, my tongue to swell and saliva became dust in my mouth. I could not breathe. I would die. This would be my last memory.

No.

I was on the floor, fallen over the puddle of mermaid, gasping for air, tears struggling to make their way down my cheeks.

My hands struggled to press on my chest, to remove my clothes and anything that might come in between my breathing while the tendril of blackness slowly thumped around me.

Between tears, I looked back at Rhylan. Who still held a shaking Cressida in his arms.

I had just tried to attack him while he held my friend. I could have hurt her...

"Listen to me very carefully, sprout," Rhylan spoke, his eyes crimson coloured, filled with the rage and fury. "You just made your first kill, you just tasted raw power. And your body is demanding more."

I took another breath and looked back at him, forcing the words to come to mind. Allowing him into my brain.

Don't listen to your fury. Don't listen to your rage. Don't listen to the calling, Rhylan's voice dug deeper.

You need to calm down.

Breathe and calm down.

I allowed him to guide me, I let Rhylan's voice invade my thoughts, trying to follow the calm in his tone and watching how his hands traced soothing caresses on Cressida's arm.

Minutes passed by, finding their end in between us, just like Branwyl had.

Minutes during which Rhylan used his power to calm us down, until Cressida recovered her will to live and I pulled back the urge to kill.

Finally, Rhylan's voice caught life back into my ears. "Are both of you alright to walk?"

"Yes," I replied with a raspy voice while Cressi nodded, her head not leaving its resting place on his chest.

"Let's go, then."

It was all the push I needed to summon strength and stand on my own two legs, ignoring the way blood dripped down my knees and calves. I sat in Branwyl's blood for so long, my dress had absorbed most of the liquid and I was now forced to carry the weight of my murder with me.

"Let's go to Ansgar's room," I suggested, the sudden need to be with my mate overtaking me. I didn't know how he would react; I didn't even know if he would want to see me again or not, but he needed to know. I needed to tell him what I'd done and prepare him for what was to come.

Because I did not just kill the mermaid who took my brother's life. I killed a princess of the Water Kingdom.

"We're getting the fuck out of here," Rhylan replied and pushed on his knees, forcing them straight and keeping Cressida in his arms. One of his hands stood wrapped around her waist while the other caught the back of her knees, lifting her in his arms. Cressi did not seem to react or notice the change, she simply shifted her arms around Rhylan's neck and continued to gaze into his chest, looking utterly lost.

"But I need to tell Ansgar. He needs to know," I tried to protest when one of Rhylan's lines of darkness wrapped around my mouth, forcing me quiet.

"What do you think will happen?" Rhylan rasped, his eyes filled with rage and worry. "When they discover this? It's only you or I that can summon this kind of power, sprout, so there's not much option for an accident to happen."

"I will take my chances; this is my doing—"

"WHAT ABOUT CRESSIDA?" his lungs split with the shout, making me shiver. "You proved you can defend yourself, but she is human. How do you expect her to protect herself in case you or I fall?"

"I…" I stopped. Because I had no answer. Because I didn't even think about what this could mean to my friend.

"Exactly. If there is a life right now that matters most, it is hers. And I will do my all to save it. So, you either come on your own volition or I strangle you until you pass out and carry you out myself."

I stopped. A breath. Two. Three.

I nodded. "Let's go."

I mechanically followed Rhylan across corridors, all the while hoping to bump into Ansgar. Into Vikram. Into someone. Anyone that would deliver a message. But I never protested, not once. Because Rhylan was right.

I had behaved stupidly, recklessly and put my friend in danger too many times already. This was the final straw. I would not hurt Cressi, I would not hurt the person who's been there for me all my life. My sister, my friend and my ally.

If Rhylan said we needed to get out so she would be safe, then we needed to get out. If there was one thing I solely trusted him with, that was my friend. His queen.

He had proven his love for her time and time again.

I followed and let tears flow down my cheeks, feeling how they dripped down my neck and fell into my cleavage. I cried for myself, I cried for Erik, I cried for Cressi and even for Rhylan, who had to give up everything he had worked for because of me, I cried for Ansgar who would hate me for doing this.

I had sealed all our fates in one stupid minute. And took a life.

"Well, well, well, if it's not just the person I was hoping to see," I heard Rhylan adopt his court tone again and shifted from behind him to spot Eidothea pulling something to her chest.

"What are you doing here? Who told you I would be here?" The siren tensed, her cheeks crimson, her hands shaking, still gripped tightly over her chest.

"Does it matter?" Rhylan smirked, obviously pleased with something I could not yet understand.

"What do you want from me, Fear Gorta?" Eidothea's eyes started scanning him, Cressida, me, and instantly widened at the sight of blood.

"I want you to get me out of here," Rhylan snarled, then sent a line of darkness around the siren's waist, pulling her closer to him. "And I want that tear you're holding."

Ansgar

Chapter Twenty-One

"I do not want to sound offensive towards your mate, but I can't wait to get out of here," I told my brother, causing him to chuckle.

"Tell me about it," he grinned with pride. With hope. It had been such a long time since I saw Vikram so carefree, so happy and excited about his future. He was always the funny one in the family, always making everyone around him chuckle, always with a smile on his lips. But now, he looked to be blossoming, a fresh seed enjoying a spring ray of sunshine.

"What do you think mother is going to say?"

She would most likely faint, I thought to myself. The son she had protected most, the only one who could further her powers through heirs, renouncing it all and bringing none other than the second siren queen into the kingdom a decade later. Our mother would need heart healing serums. Definitely.

"Hey, when I initially mated, Anwen was a human," I shrugged, trying to reassure him. "If they could accept that, a siren queen should be a piece of seed cake," I elbowed him, joking.

"We're lucky Damaris is saving our asses with that second youth. Mother and father will be too preoccupied with their grandson to pay us much attention. I hope…" my brother leaned against one of the marble columns we sat by.

After convincing Eidothea that I would not use the tear for any evil purposes, she agreed to hand it over, on the condition that both of us had to wait for her to return. She did not trust us enough to take us to their treasure hall, which we assumed, was buried in the castle.

After all, if they had a library, they must have built this place to guard other treasures and keep them from water damage. It made so much sense for the tear to be inside, especially since neither of us had been granted access to venture this far through the hallways.

They were so intricate that neither Vikram nor I had any idea where we were, which made it very easy for Eidothea to ask us to wait right where we stood. The only clue that we had gone to a deeper level came from the colour of the water surrounding the circular tunnels, allowing us to observe its tumult through the glass.

"She'll be fine, Vikram. You will both be," I patted my brother's shoulder encouragingly. "If she turns fae she will not be dangerous, you will not look as if you are half-way through denouncing your energy and dine with the goddess, which will make mother happy. And she is a queen, there will be no training involved or issues about comporting herself," I mentally tried to create a list which might have laid out his worries. "You will finally spend more time home, I assume, which in turn, will make mother happy, father will be delighted to hold dinner conversations with another royal," I continued. "Damaris…well, Dam is Dam so you'll have to deal with that."

"Thank the goddess for his mate," Vikram agreed with a smile.

"Yes," I chuckled again, "Takara is a blessing sent by the goddess to help us tolerate our own blood."

We loved our brother, of course, but he had always been distant and hadn't shown any interest in our lives until we grew up. He did enjoy engaging with Vikram to play pranks on me, a tradition that seemed to have continued into our adulthood without me having any option to stop it, but our older brother was always kept separate from us.

He had his own chambers since he was a babe, growing used to solitude and finding solace in books, training and discovering knowledge at a very young age. He had been groomed for the crown, for taking over the kingdom, and when Vikram and I appeared into his life, his duties had always come first.

When he turned into a proper male, he didn't speak to either of us for two full solstices, until mother found out and enforced the rule of family dinners. Which had continued until the present day. Whoever was in the kingdom, had to be present at dinner. Very few exceptions ensued, like when Damaris or I asked for our mate's hands in marriage, when father had been sick that dreadful week or when the babe was born, though I only knew that from my brother's stories.

"Does Anwen like her?"

I scanned my brother, observing the slight worry he released with the question before returning to his composure. It was endearing that he worried so much. Wanting to make Eidothea fit in with the family, making sure everyone was comfortable and enjoyed each other's presence.

"Trust me, brother," I felt the need to pat his shoulder again, "a week after you bring her, you will be forgotten. Same as me and Damaris." I didn't give him a chance to frown and added, "Anwen and Takara are going to corrupt your mate to the point where they will abandon us for late night sessions of wine and chocolate tastings."

We both smiled, remembering the last time Anwen and Takara went to buy some wine. They had returned home in one of the seller's carriages, at his insistence, so drunk that they could barely stand. They had so much fun that they wanted to continue with the family and Takara made a potion to help them slightly sober up, so they could start drinking again. Two cases of wine disappeared that day, but a memory that would last forever had been created.

"I hope so brother, I know I should not have reason, but I feel anxious to introduce her to the king and queen," my brother confessed.

"Damaris was too. And I was pissing myself, remember? It's a rite of passage," I tried to calm him down.

Vikram continued smiling. Until a scream pierced through the corridors.

My brother and I instantly tensed and gazed at one another in surprise. We'd never heard anything out of place in the Water Kingdom so far, and the sound seemed to be coming from beneath, some sort of echo dragging it.

Then Vikram said the words I feared most. "Eidothea."

He started running. Through intricate corridors, down flights of stairs that seemed to only be leaning downwards before shifting into plain surface, I followed my brother, gripping the only dagger I had with me.

This was not siren work. They were not violent creatures, at least not like that. A waterling always preferred a smooth approach, a silent kill without witnesses or pain. This was something else, something another kingdom would do.

I continued to follow my brother in his desperate attempt to reach his mate, but that single scream did not pose a direction, so after a while we realised we were running blind through the palace, with no idea of how to get back or to reach the siren queen.

My brother broke, falling to his knees, looking utterly defeated and terrified.

"What do I do? What do I do?" his hands gripped at his hair, pulling at it in a sign of desperation. I didn't know if the question was directed at me or at himself, at our inability to find his mate.

"Let's go back," I urged him. There was no point in us running like headless creatures around the corridors. The water started getting darker and the magic that illuminated the hallways as we passed did not work with our powers, leaving us in the dark, barely able to distinguish one another.

I looked around one more time, hoping to find something, hoping…"Vikram! There!" I pointed but then realised Vikram couldn't see my hand, so I felt around me until I found his full figure and turned his head to the direction I wanted him to pay attention to.

The other side of the glass, where a small light flickered. It could only be Eidothea. At the sight of it, Vikram caught wings and started running as if his life depended on it. Until he suddenly stopped and fell on his knees.

This time, holding his mate.

I had never seen a siren cry before, I did not even think they had the ability to do so. They were always presented to us as these frivolous, heartless creatures who enjoyed toying with the affection of males and beings around them, sucking on their energies to gain their own satisfaction. But looking at the siren queen, seeing her heartbroken to the point of shaking pain instantly changed my opinion.

"My love," Vikram kept repeating, his hands touching every part of her body while the siren's arms wrapped around his neck. Her head leaned on his shoulder, filling it with dripping tears. As soon as my brother's hands calmed, I realised she was not injured. And felt thankful for it.

We allowed her a few moments to calm down, but as she lifted her head to look at her mate, I saw it. The damage around her neck. The bruises pierced through her skin and spread around like disease. She had been strangled. And somehow, managed to stay alive and scream for help.

"Who did this?" I asked, unaware if my brother had noticed it already. "Who?"

Instinctively, I grabbed her arm and squeezed it in mine. To demand an answer. To reassure her.

"Fear Gorta," she finally released the words, then more tears dropped down her cheeks. The siren turned to Vikram, her eyes pinned on his. "Forgive me…"

"No," my brother shook his head, not accepting her words. Completely ignoring them. "No," he said again, pressing her tighter to his chest, offering her the protection she lacked. The safety she clearly needed.

"I'll go check on Anwen," the words came out before my brain had a chance to process them, the urge to find my mate overpowering the rest of my senses. If Rhylan was on the verge of committing crimes, I had to keep her as far away from him as possible.

"Go, I'll bring her back as soon as she calms down," my brother urged, nodding in encouragement. He too understood how dangerous this had become.

"Ansgar…" I heard the broken voice call after me and turned to see Eidothea slowly shifting in my brother's protective arms. "She is gone."

My world broke. My heart stopped. My knees bent, forcing me to adopt the same terror my brother had experienced before. As if understanding that the air was blocked in my lungs, Vikram asked on my behalf.

"What do you mean?"

Eidothea wiped away a few more tears and let herself fall to the ground, hugging her knees to her chest as if to protect herself. My brother's hand instantly reached her back to place soothing caresses, to let her know she was safe. By the way his jaw tensed, ready to rip through his teeth, I realised he had just then seen the marks on her neck.

"I was coming back from collecting the tear…" the siren started speaking, taking long breaks in between her sentences, as if trying to sort through the memory, or whatever parts of her mind had remained unaffected by the attack.

"Fear Gorta intercepted me. He was covered in blood, carrying his queen. I don't know if she was dead or injured, I don't know…" she shook her head. "All I remember is that she did not move. And he had to carry her."

"And Anwen?" I asked.

"She was with them too. She was walking alongside Fear Gorta, she too was covered in blood, her face was caked with it. And her dress…" Eidothea moved her turquoise eyes up and down as if envisioning my mate.

I barely found the courage to ask. "Was she hurt?" I felt a punch to my chest from the dread running through my veins.

"She looked to be safe. Shaken up, there were tears everywhere, wiping away the blood on her face, but she was alive," the siren queen pressed her lips together and stopped for a moment, allowing me to take in the information.

"I can't understand how he knew. He must have felt the tear, he must have guessed somehow. He forced me to give it to him, but I would not. I would not," her voice trailed until it became a whisper.

"Where is he?" my brother asked.

Eidothea sighed with defeat. "He's gone. They are all gone," she shook her head. "He threw darkness at my throat and kept me trapped, forcing me to lead them to the exit. They wanted to leave the kingdom. Return to the realm," she explained.

"All of them?" my voice sounded broken.

"Before he left, he forced me to give him the tear. Said he would kill all the sisters if I didn't. I gave it to her while I opened the portal. I couldn't give it to him, I just couldn't," she shook her head.

"Gave it to who?" my brother asked.

She turned to me, her eyes pleading forgiveness.

"I gave it to her. I gave it to your mate."

Anwen

Chapter Twenty-Two

I was flying. My body was not my own, my chest heaved with a new pressure that I did not allow yet was forced into me. The back of my throat became rasp, as if I'd shouted to the point of destroying my vocal cords. Had I? I could not remember.

My back hurt, the muscles connecting my neck to my shoulders and my ears buzzed with the accumulated pressure that felt as if it would break through my brain.

My head pounded, an irregular pulsation forcing blood into my scalp and...out of it? Did I have a head injury? I did not know.

God, I felt like I'd been hit by a train. By many, many trains. Over and over. How was I still alive? That freaking pressure in my left ear pounded so hard I wanted to smash my own head against the closest wall and just faint. Get it over with. Just get rid of this god damned pain.

I couldn't see, either my eyes wouldn't open or everything was dark around me, a cover of night that felt slightly cold but familiar. Had I been here before? Or was I slowly dying, and this was my last memory?

No, it couldn't be. My life wasn't flashing before my eyes.

I didn't see my mom and dad, I didn't see Erik or Cressi, I didn't see my friends. And, more specifically, I didn't see him. Ansgar. I couldn't die before seeing him again. Those beautiful stormy eyes. Gosh they were beautiful.

How I wished he were here, to grab me in those strong arms of his, to caress my hair the way he knew I liked it most, creating all those knots I struggled for half an hour to remove every morning.

I loved him raw, I loved him passionate, I loved him careless sometimes.

How could I have been so lucky to be his first? First human, first girlfriend, first lover.

But what if that was all that I would be? The first one. What if I was dying, what if in years or months he would find someone else? And that was all I would remain to him. His first.

"I need to live," I forced the words out, forced my tongue to spit away a gag of blood and guts, dried vomit and whatever other putrid things stayed there.

I forced new air into my chest, ripping away the pain that stroke through my neck and down my shoulders, into my back and my spine.

"You will live, sprout, this is not the end of you."

Rhylan. His voice had become so familiar, I could recognise it anywhere.

A sudden sense of awareness caught me by surprise. The pressure in my chest was caused by his shoulder, pushing into me. I wasn't sitting upright, which made all the blood pump into my head.

Into my neck and shoulder and throat. Rhylan was carrying me over his shoulder.

"I can walk."

"No, you cannot."

"Please put me down, my head hurts. It hurts so much," I complained, feeling how my voice squealed like it belonged to a wounded animal.

He stopped. Sighed. "Fine."

The soles of my feet touched something hard, something raw and wet and I struggled to keep enough pressure in my knees to support my own weight. Barely. I touched his chest or his arm, something to keep me upright for long enough to regain my composure.

I couldn't see. It was pitch black all around.

"Where are we?" I asked, fumbling to grip the ground and stabilise my own body.

"Home," Rhylan replied, not feeling the need to offer further explanation. "Can you walk?" he asked, softly, with worry.

"Yeah, I think so," I replied. "I just need to find my balance."

"Here, grab my hand," Rhylan said and before I knew it, the palm of his hand reached mine and trapped it in a tight grip. Then slowly, delicately, it started pulling me, forcing my legs to follow and take the first step. Then another. And one more.

We walked in darkness for what felt like hours, that tight grip he had on me never loosening. Rhylan never stopped advancing, he only decreased the speed of his steps when he felt that I was on the point of crumbling down or falling into the uneven terrain. I had no idea where we were, and if I had to guess, I would say it would be some sort of cave because my bare feet felt pieces of rock piercing through my toes.

"Keep thinking about him, sprout. Keep thinking about your boy," Rhylan finally spoke, probably sensing that I was at the end of my will to live.

Whether he planted an image in my mind or my need to return to Ansgar was so great, his face popped into my mind. The way he threw me those hungry smiles at the dinner table, letting me know what would happen as soon as we were alone. Those beautiful eyes that only shone for me, those glimpses of a shrewd smile when he spoke about things that only I would understand, that only I knew of.

I loved him with the kind of passion that can only be found in books, with such a deep need that I thought I would combust just thinking about him, with a conviction that scared me. There was nothing else but him. I wanted nothing but my mate. Needed only Ansgar.

But he wasn't here. Once again, we got separated. Once again, I had abandoned him.

A veil wrapped my mind, my memories, keeping them tightly pressed against a wall of forgotten lands. I knew the present, I knew the past and had all my wishes still, I knew what my heart felt and whom it loved, but I did not remember anything else.

Why I was here. What we had done to get to this dark never-ending lane of dampness and destruction. Why Rhylan kept dragging me forwards.

Something...something I had to remember. Something that pressed against the back of my mind, not letting me face reality.

Something I'd done.

"Where is Cressi?" I heard my voice crumple against the night around us.

"Still asleep," Rhylan's voice echoed through the walls, falling back towards me.

"Here? Is she here?" I insisted, concerned about my friend's fate. I did not know why, I could not remember why, just that I had to be.

"I'm carrying her, just like I did you."

"Don't," I heard myself say. "Don't let her head fall back. She'll have a massive headache," I tried to tell him, since I had barely lived through the effects of blood pooling through my brain.

"I won't," Rhylan replied and stopped for just a second to let go of my hand. I assumed it was to rearrange Cressi in his arms. I had no idea how he'd done it, how he'd carried both of us on his shoulders, how he'd been able to walk with us. Trying to make things easy for him, I touched around in the darkness until I felt his back, then shifted my fingers to grab his shoulder and trailed down to his arm.

"Just keep her comfortable, I'll follow you," I reassured him, pressing my fingers into his biceps for emphasis. It wasn't the most comfortable position, but it would do.

And hopefully this road to nowhere would be done soon. After all, how long could we walk for? We needed food, we needed shelter, we needed to stop and clean the wounds both of us surely had, judging by the bursts of pain that pulsated across my body.

But what mattered to me most, right then and there, was for Cressi to be safe. It started to be my biggest motivation, my highest and most important goal. I did not know why, but I knew that I would agree to anything as long as Cressi was safe.

"Thank you," Rhylan murmured and continued walking, dragging me along with him. His steps became smaller, as if he wanted to make sure that I could keep up, offering me this kindness.

"Thank you as well," I said, not knowing what else to reply.

I had no idea how long we walked for, but I followed him blindly and did as promised. I kept thinking about Ansgar, letting memories invade my mind and take me away from the pain in my feet that had started to become unbearable. I focused on the images, so sharp that I could touch them.

That day I found him naked in a tree. Gosh, the laughs we had about that, it made such a good story of how we met.

Our first kiss.

Our first dance.

The day he proposed.

That evening he took me to the mountains to show me the stars. How he held my hand and never let go, no matter where we were or who we were with. Claiming me unashamedly, telling everyone that I was his and he was mine.

"Anwen," I heard Rhylan's voice, pulling me back to reality.

"My feet really hurt," I cried out. "I can't take more of this," I suddenly became aware of the wounds on my feet. I was definitely bleeding. Maybe the terrain had changed and was more spiked, or maybe we walked for so long my bones started cracking under the pressure. I did not know. All I wanted to do was stop.

"We're almost there," Rhylan announced. "I need you to stay with Cressida. I need to go get help."

"What? You're gonna leave us alone in the darkness? Are you crazy?" I shouted into the adamant abyss, not knowing in which direction to push my protest towards.

"Anwen," fingers cupped my face, pressing my cheeks into my jaw. "It's only a few minutes. Take care of Cressida."

Immediately, one of my hands was grabbed and placed over hair. A lot of it. I immediately felt around and reached a shoulder. Top of a head. A face. I felt my friend's face to find it wet.

"Is she hurt?"

"Yes, I need to go get her help. Just stay here, ok?" A firm hand pressed my cheek before vanishing.

"Rhylan?"

"Rhylan?"

"Are you gone?"

Nothing. No answer. We were alone, cold and wounded in the dark and Rhylan had just abandoned us.

"Cressi…" I fumbled around to find her torso, then wrapped my hands below her shoulders and dragged her closer to me. I felt her limp in my arms, unaware and completely gone.

"Cressi, are you awake?" I tried to no avail. I felt her face for injuries, but she seemed to be fine. My fingers didn't catch anything oozing or any deep cuts, just her face, that might have been damp or full of blood, I did not know. I did the same to her hair, feel around her scalp to make sure she didn't have any head wounds. Then I lowered my fingers to her shoulders, each arm and her torso, along with her back.

She was fine. Passed out, but fine.

"Cressi, what the hell have we gotten ourselves into?" I cried out, allowing tears to freely flow on my face.

This was my fault. It was my fault that Cressi was here.

I brought Rhylan to my home, I introduced him to Cressida, I was the one to ignite the fire between these two. I'd been an idiot.

Knowing what Rhylan was capable of, knowing what he did to Ansgar, I brought him to my house, to meet my family and had offered my best friend to him on a silver platter. And he took it all. Made her his queen. And brought her with him everywhere he went.

He brought her here. And he abandoned us.

"Cressi, it will be fine, we'll be okay," I tried to caress her face, or what I could find of it. "We'll be fine, I promise."

"Of course you will be fine," Rhylan's voice permeated through the darkness, coming so close to us I thought I could reach for him.

And indeed, here he was.

"Sprout, I need you to close your eyes," he ordered.

"What for? I can't see anything, anyway," I protested, suddenly aware of his hands touching Cressi, wanting to take her back.

"Because I'm going to turn on the lights and I don't want your pretty eyes to be in pain."

I nodded, though I wasn't sure if he saw it or not. I assumed Rhylan could see something through the heavy curtain of darkness because he'd been the one to guide us through it. I did as he asked, closed my eyes and covered them with my palms as well.

"Ready?" I heard him ask.

"Uh-huh," I instantly replied, dipping my chin and getting ready for the blow of light that caught life around me. I felt it everywhere, on my skin, crawling between my fingers and forcing my attention, so I slowly removed my hands and allowed the red dots underneath my eyelids to get used to the strength of the sun.

But it was not the sun, I observed when I finally let the light in and blinked a few times to banish the remains of darkness.

It was a tunnel, filled with torches, fire hanging from huge ceiling candelabras.

I'd been there before, I knew these halls, I recognised this space.

The Fire Kingdom.

"Welcome home," I heard Rhylan say.

Ansgar

Chapter Twenty-Three

Anwen was gone. Along with the tear. That's all my mind could focus on.

"How did this happen?" I barely found the strength to ask, to breathe, to not collapse and fall into the earth.

"She went to meet Branwyl," my brother started speaking. "She begged Eidothea to arrange the meeting, she needed to hear the princess confess."

I saw red. Fury and rage lifted to my fists, sending them in Vikram's direction, who took the blow without questioning it.

"How could you let this happen!?! How did you even think to put Anwen in a room with her brother's assassin and hide it from me?"

"She begged us, Ansgar. She wanted to do this on her own," the siren queen confessed.

"We need to speak to Branwyl then, if she was meeting Anwen when it all started, then she must have the information," I let reason back through the gates of my mind. Maybe the mermaid heard something useful, maybe she was present when this betrayal happened, when Rhylan shifted sides and decided to steal my mate.

Of course he fucking did. Why in the goddess's name had I expected things to be different? This wasn't the first time I had put my trust in Fear Gorta, only this time, it was not my life that was in danger. It was my mate's.

"Prince," the siren queen called my attention again. "They were covered in blood. All three of them. There's no knowing if Branwyl is still alive."

"Tell us how it happened, my sweet." Through some kind of miracle Vikram managed to ignore my rage and the punishing blow I had discharged into him and turned to his mate, doing the only logical thing that would help us all. Find out everything that happened.

"I came back with the pearl, and they intercepted me. And when Rhylan forced me to open the portal to take them back, I couldn't give it to him. I wouldn't betray my kingdom in such a way. I may be weak, but I would not completely give in. So, I hoped," she said, turning her gaze back to me. "I hoped that everything you told me applies to her as well. That she would make the same sacrifice to save you. I turned the tear into energy and pressed it into Anwen's chest."

"Can it be recovered?" It was the most important question, could the energy be extracted out of my mate?

"It can be extracted and turned back into a pearl," Eidothea confessed and lifted a heaviness off my chest. "Only if it is freely given by the bearer."

"So as long as Anwen has the tear, Fear Gorta can't complete his work," Vikram noted.

"That is what I hope. That she will fight this. For you," Eidothea spoke, scanning me once more. "For all of us."

The second siren queen took us to the throne room in the hope to find Branwyl, but we all understood we'd arrived too late. The only thing that remained from the mermaid were pieces of meat and strands of hair, along with a lump of blood which had been smeared across the floor. We found handprints as well, female ones and steps that led out of the room. No other information to help us decipher what had happened.

"An explosion of energy was used to create this kind of damage, and that can only come from the Fear Gorta. He must have summoned his powers to kill our sister," Eidothea explained. I had seen Rhylan do that with the windling soldiers, sending a whiff of darkness across the room and turning them all into nothing, but this seemed a little different. When he'd done it in front of me, the energy was tasked with sucking life from its bearers, a very precise motion, since Queen Jyanna had remained untouched. This was something else, this was a brutal pulsation of rage, this was new and uncontrolled power.

This might have been Anwen. Trying to defend herself, trying to keep her friend safe.

"Did you say Cressida was unconscious?"

Eidothea nodded. "Rhylan held her, she wasn't aware."

"He attacked here," I started putting the pieces together. "He must have found Anwen and Branwyl fighting, he must have done something to separate them, or tried to take Cressida away. Anwen panicked and tried to defend herself and her friend."

"Anwen...did this?" Vikram looked at me with surprise and when I confirmed, he started examining the room with newly found interest.

"Not intentionally," I added to Eidothea's benefit. Branwyl was a cruel wicked being and must have deserved such an abrupt ending, but the last thing I wanted was for my mate to be judged for treason. "I know her power, I've seen it many times. It's soft and gentle, nothing of this magnitude. Something happened to make her explode like this."

"I am horrified and relieved," my brother added. "At least Rhylan won't get to her that easy if boo boo can wreak this much havoc."

"That is to be seen," I replied, unconvinced.

An erratic schedule followed. After Eidothea recovered her composure, she summoned Thelssha back for an urgent meeting. My brother did not leave her side, though he started to put a little more distance in between them, the effects of being in her company for the entire day starting to show.

I returned to the bedroom and slammed on the door, forcing a panting and sweaty Amara to open and look at me in surprise.

"Anwen is gone. Rhylan betrayed us all and stole the tear. Thelssha is coming back for a meeting and situation assessment. She'll be here in an hour." I released all the information at once, feeling a part of me break as I had to give the announcement.

Anwen is gone.

"What in the goddess…" Amara opened the door wider to allow me in, letting me spot a concerned commander who let his body fall into bed.

I performed the same action on a nearby chair.

"How did this happen?" Marreth asked.

"He attacked Eidothea. Who was returning to us with Marrynah's tear. Forced her to open the portal. The siren passed the tear to Anwen before Rhylan took them away." Somehow, I could only form thoughts in short sentences.

"Rhylan left?" he exclaimed in disbelief. "He just left us here? Took the tear and vanished?"

"And my mate," I heard my voice break.

"Is everyone else safe?" I felt Amara stepping closer and reaching for me, her hand finding rest on my shoulder.

"Eidothea is alright. Shaken up. Branwyl is dead. We don't know how Cressida is faring, she was unconscious when the siren saw them last."

Marreth started booming with rage and interweaving a crown of curses in Rhylan's direction, talking about loyalty and decades of servitude, but I could not listen. My mind couldn't focus on the present, on his frustrations.

Anwen was gone, my mate was gone and nothing else mattered but bringing her back. Taking her away from that monster's hold.

I remained still, trapped in thought while Amara and Marreth talked in the background and asked questions I did not have answers to.

When Vikram came to get us, I barely found the strength to rise from my seat. My hands started shaking and the pain in my chest triggered rushed breaths. My mind started spinning, invoking thoughts that did not have a place in my future.

What if he hurt her?

What if he forced her to give him the tear through torture?

What if he took her life to recover the energy?

I didn't feel the tears dripping down my cheek until Amara placed a handkerchief in my hand, making me aware of the drops that kept falling.

"We're going to get her back, brother," it was Vikram's turn to pat my shoulder encouragingly before dragging me out of the bedroom, along with the windling lovers to meet the queen.

We walked the glass corridors slowly, in silence, defeated, until we reached a throne room that laid filled with angry mermaids.

"Let me make sure I understand. You tried to betray me, you lost our kingdom's energy, and now you want my armies to claim it back?" Thelssha addressed her sister, who remained kneeling in front of the marble throne.

"Yes, my queen," Eidothea's defeated voice barely replied. "We need your help."

"And why should I give it? Why should I allow you to live?" Thelssha's portrait of rage reminded us all of the terrible ruling laws of the waterlings, unforgiving with the weak.

The queen sat on her throne, still speckled with the blood of their princess and looked at Eidothea, the most beautiful siren amongst them all. Her crown was forgotten, no need for displaying rank when the second queen remained kneeling, her head bowed so low that her spine formed a perfect half-moon shape.

"Because Earth is behind her claim," my brother's voice resounded through the room, demanding the attention of the mermaids closest to us. His back straightened as he walked into the throne room, forcing his steps to come closer to his mate. We weren't allowed weapons in the presence of the first queen, but my hand instinctively shot to my waist in search for a dagger.

The way these waterlings looked at my brother was unforgiving, and it was only a matter of seconds for one of them to place a life-claiming touch on him.

Ruled by the connection of our childhood, I followed in his steps, suddenly very aware of the hundreds of hungry mouths around us. It was enough for only one of them to break rank, to make an attempt to claim revenge on the life of the lost princess and we would be done. A single brush of their lips was all they needed.

My brother's courage did not falter, nor did his urgency to be close to his loved one, to offer her the protection of his presence and, should it come to it, his own life. I knew the feeling all too well, the urgency to protect, to make oneself a human shield.

"How can you support your claim, prince?" Thelssha spat, looking in disgust with the corner of her eye at my brother, not even deigning him with her full attention.

"We will travel to Sylvan Regnum and gather the armies to fight against our common enemy, under a single claim," I added, finding my stance behind my brother. One look at him and I knew his thoughts, if we needed to perish to protect our mates, then so be it.

"When?" Thelssha groaned in annoyance.

"Immediately, my queen," Vikram and I bowed in unison.

"And what business does the windling prince have with the theft? How are you involved past the evident support of your blood?"

I had to come clean. I had to confess and make her understand how important this was to me. How I would do anything for my mate. The confession dropped, ripping any alliance we could have built with the Water Kingdom.

"The fire princess is my mate. And she was taken from me."

At the release of my words, a few gasps followed, then the room shifted to complete silence. The siren queen gifted me her full attention this time, looking at me with intrigue and a dash of surprise.

"And the windling princess?" she asked, her gaze searching the room. For Amara, I realised.

"She is my wife, by law only," I admitted.

"You do not love her..." Thelssha's words came out as a realisation. "You've been taking pearl powder..."

"I do love her, my queen," I added, not wanting to say anything that would put Amara's life in peril, "though only as my friend. We have become close since our marriage."

"And does she support your claim? Will the Wind armies offer their alliance too?"

The queen was taking advantage of this situation, an act evident to us all. I looked at Vikram, who used most of his body to shield his mate from view, his features becoming more taut, the colour in his cheeks slowly vanishing. He needed to get away and soon.

"I do, my queen," Amara's voice came from behind us, making me turn to find her in between the sea of naked females. Standing next to a visibly angry Marreth.

"Very well, Earth and Wind armies shall meet us in three days at the entrance into the Fire Kingdom. We shall see then where your loyalties lie."

"My queen," Eidothea's shaking voice called to her sister. "Please don't use the humans," her chin shook slightly. "Please give us a chance to do this without bloodshed."

A cruel smile caught life on the siren queen's lips. "Since you like humans so much, sister, maybe you should try living like one."

Anwen

Chapter Twenty-Four

I stretched my neck until I heard a crack, instantly finding the relief I needed in my shoulders. I didn't sleep on tall pillows; they made my neck fill with pressure and made me have to twist and crack my bones for the rest of the day to feel like myself again.

I didn't like sleeping with a bra on either, it made my torso feel tight and uncomfortable, but here I was, scratching at the marks under my breasts. This sleeping arrangement sucked.

After I cracked my neck a few more times, I finally allowed my eyes to open and take in the reality I could no longer postpone. I was back in the fire kingdom, in the same room Ansgar and I have lived in for a few weeks. Only this time, I was not its captive. Or at least, I hoped so. The new title of princess of the Fire Kingdom must be good for something.

As soon as we arrived, Rhylan took Cressida to his room and called the medic. Various soldiers patrolled through the hallways and asked me if I needed anything, all bowing while they spoke and trying to make sure I was comfortable, while I came in and out of the room.

The doctor spent hours by Cressi's bedside, only stopping his fixated attention on her long enough to bark orders at his helpers to prepare potions for him, bring ingredients, water and cloth and many other things, while Rhylan and I paced the room up and down until we moulded it to the shape of our feet.

"Get some rest, I'll stay with her," a hand shook my shoulder, making me wake up and lift my face from where it had been resting on the table. "I'll stay with her," Rhylan insisted, his arms wrapping around my own tighter, not giving me a chance to protest.

"What if she needs anything?" I used my other hand to wipe away some liquid that casually made its way out of my mouth while I rested on the hard surface.

"Then I'll summon you immediately," he nodded. "You're only a door away," Rhylan tilted his head as if to remind me of the living arrangements we had shared.

"Okay, thanks," I replied and opened the door to head back to my own room, surprised that no one was there to stop me, that no one asked to follow me or needed to know my intentions.

I turned the knob to find the copy of the sitting room back in Evigt, the sofa Ansgar had slept on during that week when we were too stubborn to communicate, I looked at the remains of all the dried roses he had grown for me, wilted dreams across the room.

My stomach begged for food, but I did not want to eat, part of me feeling undeserving while Cressi was struggling in bed, unable to wake up. I wouldn't eat until she could do it too, until we'd be able to have breakfast together and gossip about the kingdom and all the wonderful things I was sure Rhylan had prepared for his queen.

I forced that pressure down into my guts, urging them to wait. Also, I wasn't sure that rummaging through the fridge would be the best idea. If the roses hadn't been cleaned, I doubted the kitchen would be either, so I did not want to risk food poisoning.

Tired, barely able to stand and dragging my feet, I opened the bedroom door where the scent of orange and rain invaded my nostrils, making me release a sigh. Tears started dripping down my cheeks, summoned by the loss of my love. I did not have the strength to open the wardrobe, where I knew his clothes would be resting next to mine.

Instead, I threw myself in bed and grabbed the pillow that, I hoped, held some of Ansgar's scent, pressing it tight to my chest before I closed my eyes.

I don't remember dreaming, I don't remember waking or calling for my mate. I must have passed out as soon as my head hit the pillow, and by the way those bra lines looked and the tightness in my neck pressed into me, I must have slept for a long while.

Having no idea what time it was, I rushed to the hallway and knocked on Rhylan's door as gently as I could, needing to know if Cressi had woken up. I waited about a minute until a ruffled and shirtless Rhylan opened the door, his eyes glazed with sleep blinked at me. God damn, he looked hot like this.

"Hi sweetness," I joked. "Just checking on Cressi."

"I thought you were dead," he replied, eyes scanning me up and down, probably noticing how I didn't bother to change. "You've been passed out for two days."

That explained all the pains I started to experience. "So, Cressi?"

"She's asleep, it's three in the morning," Rhylan grunted, then he must have realised that the last time I saw her, she was surrounded by doctors and potions and he looked so worried that I was sure he would have killed whoever stood in his way just to release some of that tension.

"She woke up yesterday, ate an entire chocolate cake, made some comments about not needing sunscreen and made a full list of items she requires, then had my ass for bringing you here."

"Fair enough," I nodded, knowing fully well he wasn't lying because what he said sounded just like Cressi. I really needed to talk to her, but I knew this massive sexy gargoyle wouldn't let me wake her up, so I did the next logical thing, told him I would wait till morning.

"Breakfast is at seven," he grumbled before slamming the door in my face.

Okay then, back to my room it is.

I struggled to contain my stomach. It started to demand food and I knew that I would be close to fainting by breakfast, but this was not a time to upset Rhylan.

I did visit the kitchen in the hope to find some food, but as soon as I opened the fridge, the putrid smell made me gag. Water was still running, fortunately, so I drank three full glasses, tricking my tummy into thinking it was full, at least momentarily.

I then removed what remained of my clothes and underwear and stepped into the shower, allowing my skin to drop all the blood and memories it hung on to. Recent events started to return to me, along with the increasing pressure in my chest.

Did I really have Marrynah's tear? Had Eidothea actually given it to me? She must have, because I remembered a pressure that touched my torso before a cascade of bright light enveloped me, taking away my stance, my strength, and my mind.

The next thing I remembered was darkness and Rhylan carrying me. I assumed the same thing happened to Cressi, though she took longer to recover.

It made sense in a way, I was now part fae…I thought. I wasn't exactly sure what Rhylan's energy did to my body but it changed it somehow. I could read people's feelings, I had powers of my own, I recovered quicker and I…killed.

The distaste on Branwyl's expression appeared before my eyes. The flash of anger that sent me into momentary madness. Two days had passed.

They must have found her remains by now, they must have figured it out.

Which meant that Ansgar knew. Ansgar knew I was a murderer, that I was no better than the mermaid whom I spend months despising. I was no better than her.

I had told Ansgar once that whoever did this to my brother wasn't deserving of love. Which meant that I could not claim retribution either. I couldn't ask him to love a murderer and part of me knew he wouldn't. That no matter how deep his love for me was, how endless and limitless, he would not allow himself to continue being with me. Not when my prince was such a noble and loyal man.

Defeated and feeling utterly alone, I got out of the shower and dried myself up, then forced my hands to open the wardrobe and let my nostrils be inundated by the aroma of fresh clothes.

I am a true fireling now.

I too had done what I blamed these people for, I too had killed for what I thought to be just.

Not wanting to appear in the corridors as if I had any claim over this kingdom, I chose a pair of jeans and some trainers. If Rhylan wasn't forcing me into those dreadful dresses again, then I would go for comfort.

I also grabbed one of Ansgar's shirts. It was too big for me, of course, I had to fold the sleeves three times and it looked more like a nightgown over my jeans, almost reaching my knees. But I also found a belt and wrapped it around my waist to give it some sort of form.

With my hair undone and slightly wavy, I looked like a pirate. I only missed one of those massive swords.

This look could come in handy if we ever have to attend a costume party and we're totally unprepared for it. I allowed a smile until reality sunk in again. There wouldn't be any parties. There probably wouldn't be any Ansgar either.

I spent the remaining time cleaning the room, removing all the empty vases and dried flowers, making my bed and drinking a few more glasses of water until the clock I found hidden between some books showed ten to seven. Finally, time for breakfast.

I opened my door to find two guards stationed at the entrance, bowing low at the sight of me.

"Princess Anwen," they greeted in unison.

"Good morning," I replied awkwardly, not really knowing what the procedure was.

"We are here to escort you to breakfast, whenever you are ready," one of them smiled. Smiled. For the very first time in my life, I saw a fireling display a genuine smile.

"I am ready," I replied and nodded, as if my words weren't enough. Instantly, the two of them turned on their heels and started marching down the corridor.

I walked slowly behind them, giving myself time to take in all the changes. Everything looked brighter, warmer. More light on the corridors, beige carpets rather than the dark ones I remembered, paintings on the walls?

Even the soldiers looked more cheerful, their uniforms adorned and silver, rather than the dark grey they had been wearing when I initially visited. Forcefully visited...

Every time we passed a new entrance, the other guards greeted me with joy and kept the doors open wide for me to pass and even some of the people I found in the hallways stopped and shook my hand, happy to have me back. Their words, not mine.

What in the hell was happening here?

"Ah, finally," Cressi's cheer removed the surprised frown I had displayed during my walk to the breakfast room. A private room, I sighed with relief, where Cressi and Rhylan shared a table, with another empty chair for me, I assumed.

"Morning, sexy," I greeted her, truly happy to see that she had recovered. Unlike me, Cressi went for a full regalia. Her hair was adorned in a fancy updo allowing strands of golden hair to fall on the side of her left shoulder, like one of those Victorian movies we used to watch when we were younger. A tall diamond crown found permanent residence on top of her head. My friend wore a black velvet opera dress, which lifted her breasts nicely.

One look at Rhylan told me he was thinking the same. The new king dressed in his usual black Boss suit and black shirt, tailored to perfection.

"You two look…" I stopped, trying to find my words.

"Like we give a damn?" Rhylan decided to add his two cents to the conversation. "Unlike you?" he lifted a brow as if to ask what the hell was I thinking.

"Hush you," Cressi gently nudged him, "I think it's cute. That's Ansgar's shirt, I imagine."

"He never got to wear it, but yes…I suppose it is," I added. Then, without waiting for any invitation, I stepped closer to the empty chair.

As soon as I showed my intention, one of the guards that served breakfast pulled it for me, helping me take a seat. Then, he circled my chair and apologised, before placing one of the fabric napkins into my lap. The same guard then asked me if I wanted coffee and when I confirmed, he grabbed a French pot and started serving me.

"It's like a fancy hotel, isn't it?" Cressi smiled with excitement, then took a generous bite from her avo toast.

"Is everything here vegan?" I asked in surprise and newly found appreciation towards Rhylan, who clearly made the effort.

"I'm trying to convince Rhy to give it a go, he's moaning a bit but taking it like a big boy," she winked at him with pride, causing me to chuckle.

"I'm sure he is," I turned to him with a smile, but the expression I found told me that I would be dead long before the information left my mouth, if I ever decide to share it.

"How are you feeling?" my friend asked, this time struggling to cut a piece of bacon. Pardon. Vegan bacon. "I came in to check on you a few times but didn't manage to wake you. Rhy said you needed the rest and that…that thing may take a lot of your energy until it settles," she pointed to my chest.

Okay, so we landed straight into the big topics.

"How is this going to work?" I turned to Rhylan while spreading my fingers over my chest, expecting to feel something. Nothing but skin and bone.

"Now that you are awake, it means the energy is settled. It will probably need a few more hours to combine with Belgarath's powers that already reside inside of you, but it should be ready to extract by sundown or tomorrow morning."

"What do you mean, to extract?" Thank goodness for Cressi who was asking all the hard questions today.

"I need to have it, don't I?" Rhylan frowned at his queen in surprise.

"But you don't have the others, so what's the point?"

"I don't, but the princeling does, and we have what he wants most," Rhylan pressed a tight smile and tilted his head, returning his attention to something on his plate that looked like tofu.

I allowed him to settle and took a few sips of my coffee, taking advantage to check that Cressi was fully recovered before I made enough courage to open the conversation.

"I need to talk to Ansgar," I let the words and my request to float through the room. Even though the table was relatively small, and Rhylan was situated to my right, I still allowed enough time for my words to circle the room twice over before I released new ones. "Can you take me back? Can he come here? Is there a place where I can meet him?"

"Is there a day in my life where you don't piss me off with your stupidity?" Rhylan used the same tone to add.

"Carefl hw yuw tewk tw ew dawher," Cressi tried to admonish him through a huge mouthful, causing me to straighten my back with impertinence and Rhylan to sigh. This stepmother thing started to work wonders for me. I had no control over Rhylan, but I could ask Cressi things and when it came to who was really wearing the pants at this breakfast table, the queen won it all.

"My apologies," he released a breath and I almost bawled. "Since we have committed a murder, then theft, and ran away without a trace or a word to our associates, how do you envision a meeting taking place?"

"I go to Ansgar and talk?" I replied, though I knew what he meant.

"And where will you find him, sprout? Have you thought that your prince may be in chains? Paying for your deed?" he spat, causing Cressi to point her fork at him and shout an admonishing "hey!"

I stopped. I hadn't even thought about that. I haven't even thought that the mermaids might go against the people we left behind.

"In that case I really need to go!" I responded with determination and stood. Long enough to spot the top of their heads, because the next thing I knew, my legs and waist were wrapped in darkness and pressed against the chair.

"I would advise you to sit down and eat. You are not nearly recovered and will go nowhere until I can guarantee your safety and that of the energy you are carrying inside you." Rhylan didn't even look at me, suddenly too concerned with some sort of meat he struggled to cut into tiny pieces.

"But I need to—"

"I have already sent scouts to assess the situation. We will know more when they report," he replied as an attempt to calm me down. Then he turned, very slowly, allowing me to see every muscle contorting with the motion. His voice echoed heavy, like a hammer against hot iron. "Now sit down and eat. You need to recover your strength. The last thing I need is to rip your heart out by mistake when I take that tear out of you."

Ansgar

Chapter Twenty-Five

"I still think I should come with you," I told Amara, inching closer to help her regain balance after the long jump. After Queen Thelssha agreed to our proposal of raising the kingdom's armies and consolidating them, she allowed us an hour to band together and make the plan, while permitting Eidothea to say her goodbyes to her harem, before her banishment.

"And I still think you need to come home," Vikram insisted, stepping closer to us, not wanting to feel left out with Eidothea sighing in his arms.

"You already have a lot on your plate," the princess pressed her lips together and shared a quick smile to Vikram, who struggled to remain calm with a brand-new human in his arms.

"Send word if you need anything," I insisted, shifting my gaze from her to Marreth and back again. The commander offered to take my place and escort the princess back to their home, ensuring me of her safety. Truthfully, amongst us all, Marreth was the one who would be most trusted when it came to Amara's security. All of us knew he would give his life for his lover, if it came to it.

I did not know if the return would be pleasant for either of them, since Amara and I left with the pretence of a wedding celebration and alliance visit, but now she would return alone and claim an army for war. All of it, in my support.

"It is time that the kingdom found out about Marreth's return," she spoke softly, "as well as the waterling's plans. I am confident my aunt's ears will not remain idle for long."

I nodded, admiring her confidence, the strength the princess had summoned in the past few months, sure of herself and her right to rule.

"Very well, may the goddess bless your journey," I responded, wishing them farewell until the set time of the reunion. We only had three days to travel to our kingdoms and bring the armies together. A task that sounded almost impossible.

"Can my husband and I bid our farewell privately, if it does not prove an inconvenience to you all?" the windling princess smiled sweetly, scanning a lazy gaze around. It was not a request, we all came to realise, but a demand. Instantly, Vikram and Marreth stepped back, finding something else to do, leaving me in the full blow of whatever was to come.

"So?" she crossed her arms, the universal you-are-in-deep-trouble gesture all females instinctively did. I had my fair share of this stance, having to learn its effects the hard way. First from my mother, then from some of my tutors and lately, from Anwen.

I pursed my lips, probably looking like an idiot, but for the life of me, I didn't know what I did wrong. Except abandoning her multiple times and not keeping my word to return when promised, getting her in trouble with the siren queen and of course, forcing her claim for support from the Wind Kingdom since my life looked to be in danger. As well as placing my mate's importance over hers on every single occasion.

"You married an idiot," I stated the obvious, causing her to release a bitter chuckle.

"That's not news. What are you going to do now?"

"I...don't follow," I admitted, causing her to roll her eyes with annoyance.

"What are you going to do when you get Anwen back?" she pressed, and I almost wanted to hug her for such positivity.

"I will bring her home and keep her away from that bastard for the rest of her life. I hope?" Cressida popped into mind, if she chose to remain with Rhylan there was nothing I could do to stop Anwen from seeing her friend. Though I was sure special visits could be arranged.

"So...you plan to bring her to Sylvan Regnum? And live there together?" her words fell like a knife to my chest, the reality sinking in.

"I would have to return to the Wind Kingdom," I nodded, a sudden knot in my stomach. There was no possibility of Anwen and I having a life together after all of this was over, because I was a married male. Sworn into a marriage of alliance, with a kingdom to rule.

"Do you *have to*? Is this what you want?" the princess asked, causing me to stop and read the plea in her eyes. Far different from one of a wife claiming her husband back.

"Maybe I don't have to?" I tried to read her expression and as soon as the words landed, I saw the liberation in her chest. On her face. In her smile. "No, I don't have to," I said it again, tasting the words, the freedom they offered.

"I was thinking," Amara grabbed my shoulder with newly found interest, suddenly realising her plan had a new ally, "if what the sirens are saying is true, if the goddesses return and we can ask them a favour... that maybe..." she stopped and took a moment as if to find the courage to express her thoughts, "maybe we can ask them to dissolve our marriage?"

I drew in a sharp breath, which caused her to immediately explain her reasoning. "It's not a real marriage anyway, we haven't consummated it, so if this were any other marriage, it would be disbanded in a year."

If our marriage hadn't been for alliance purposes, either of us could claim a disband after the year was through, according to the laws. But since this arrangement took place in a royal family, the common laws did not apply. Unfortunately for us.

"I see..." I barely spoke, barely allowed myself to hope for freedom. Freedom to be with my mate.

"Of course, this is only if both of us agree, if it is your dream to rule a kingdom then we would have to find an alternative solution..."

"Amara, all I want is to be with my mate. I do not care about rank, kingdoms or where we live," I confessed, not caring about the curtness of my words.

"And I want to become a queen," she spoke softly, as if allowing herself to say it out loud for the first time. "With Marreth by my side," she added.

"I think it is a most wonderful idea," I explained and, unable to help myself, I caught her in my arms and spun her once or twice, squeezing her tightly. She had become a dear friend and I was beyond grateful for her support. For her patience. For her trust.

"I'll see you in three days, future ex-husband," she giggled.

"I'll see you in three days, future ex-wife," I said and planted a quick kiss on her cheek before stepping away and signalling to Marreth that our conversation was done. The commander smiled as he approached, definitely aware of the conversation Amara wanted to have.

I walked back to my brother, my eyes remaining on the new couple who hugged and disappeared in a gust of wind.

"What are you so happy about?" Vikram asked me with a frown, visibly worried for Eidothea, who hadn't said a word since we left her kingdom. Since she was forcefully removed alongside us.

"I won't have a wife soon," I smirked and placed my hands on my brother's shoulders, locking his mate in between us before making the jump.

"Ansgar, what in the goddess' name?"

I chuckled at my brother's reaction, barely able to contain a grin at the sight of Damaris. Fallen on the sofa, drowning in the cushions, his face the portrait of confusion. On the other side, we had Takara, holding baby Ansgar who hadn't stopped cooing since meeting the siren queen.

"I was as surprised as you are, brother, believe me," I spoke softly, aware that my voice could travel through the walls and that Vikram and I shared the same floor. My brother and his mate had remained with our parents, discussing recent events and giving them the steps of their decade-long relationship.

Understanding their need for privacy, the prince and princess had invited themselves into my rooms, both determined to receive all the details they needed.

"So, all the sneaking around, all the lovers he got, were actually her?" Takara shook her head slowly, as if she could not believe it. I must admit, I found it hard to understand it as well, the dedication, the sacrifice, the constant lying and hiding, the double life my brother had to uphold, while keeping his true love a secret.

"How is it possible for a fae to mate a siren?" my brother asked, not expecting an answer, then he started to show a smile. "I guessed it, you know?" he turned to his mate and leaned back on the sofa, stretching his back and letting his chest swell with pride. "This impossible, unbelievable thing that's happening to my brother, I guessed it," he nodded again to himself.

"Of course you did, my love," Takara replied with a mocking grin, focusing her attention on the babe rather than her husband. I also wanted to laugh when the memory resurfaced. My keeper assignment ceremony. After we returned to my room, right before the parchment became ready to reveal my destination. We drank and cheered, making fun of one another, as we always did.

You're still in love with Eidothea, Damaris had accused. I couldn't remember Vikram's reply, but he remained shaken for half a second. Enough for us to ignore it back then. Enough for me to remember and put the pieces together.

"He did," I confirmed, shifting curiously to Damaris, who nodded again, proud that at least someone paid him attention.

"So how is this going to work? Now that she is human?" the healer asked, shifting the babe into a sitting position, which made his wide eyes blink at me with curiosity, as if he too wanted to know what would happen next.

"We have until the full moon to return the tear. Or the goddess. Whichever comes first." Thelssha had been very clear in her demand before forcing the portal open and cursing her sister with a mortal life. The transformation would only last until the full moon and should the stars predict our failure, Eidothea was to be returned to the sea and spend the rest of her life in solitude, locked away in a cell.

If we did succeed, she was free to choose. Either remain with my brother or seek her own life back into the kingdom, the decision was up to her. I liked to think that I knew what she would choose and wanted to see my brother happy beyond anything.

But at the moment, the former siren queen was in pain. My brother was obstinate to carry her to the castle as soon as we landed in the forest, but after a while she insisted on trying to walk. Eidothea's feet didn't last more than a minute, the hard ground and grass under her soles so different from the smooth terrain she was used to in the glass palace.

As soon as she complained of pain, my brother grabbed her in his arms again and walked her to the castle.

We must have been a sight, both of us walking, returning grim and unannounced, one without a mate and the other carrying a naked female wrapped in a shirt. Vikram did not help the situation either, as soon as he saw mother and father at the palace gates, as per the welcoming rituals our family always liked to follow, he decided to cut his intranquility from the root and tell them everything in a single mouthful.

"I'm mated to a siren, she's now a human. Ansgar lost his mate again. We're going to war in three days."

As predicted, mother almost fainted and father had to take a seat when he found out who the siren passing through his gates was. The three of us decided to make ourselves scarce after that, telling the king and queen that we would join them for dinner.

"It's funny to think that all three of us are mated," Damaris spoke, a sudden joy in his voice. Until he looked at me and spotted my sombre face.

"It would be nicer if all three were with us," I replied, my throat suddenly becoming dry.

"You will get her back, Ansgar," Takara's voice came out sweeter, more thoughtful than ever. "Anwen and you have a way of finding each other. Especially now that the two of you hold the power of creation."

"I suggest that you take your mate back," Damaris inched closer to his wife and son, leaning to offer each of them a kiss before he continued, "keep all these energies and make a babe. Surely it will be a god or a goddess with all that power going around," he half-joked, but I could not appreciate the attempt.

"Let's get her back first," I replied, still buried in thoughts.

"Right, we'll let you prepare for dinner, Ansgar here needs to be fed anyway," Takara, bless her, sensed my need for privacy. She passed the babe to his father and reached me to place a kiss on my temple, before they retired, telling me that I had time to bathe and change before dinner.

I listened to the advice and filled a bathtub with hot water and submerged myself, letting my thoughts fly to Anwen, imagining what she might be doing, where she might be and forming plans to get her back. Bring her to her rightful place. In my arms.

The siren looked spectacular, even in her human shape. The few hours we had to prepare for dinner had been used to arrange her hair and adorn her with a dress that perfectly matched her eyes. My first thought was that she looked like one of the goddesses while my eyes had to scan her a few more times to try and understand which of the three.

"I know she is stunning, but you have to stop gawking," Vikram expressed his annoyance, though it seemed to be only on his behalf, since Eidothea did not mind the attention. Instead, she scanned all of us sitting at the table, making me realise I wasn't the only one staring, and smiled in turn.

"It seems that the energy replicated into my human body," her voice clinked with reassurance, as if *she* wanted to make us feel better about staring.

"We never had the pleasure to dine with a siren queen, forgive our audacity," the king spoke, his shaken-up voice making all of us simultaneously return our gazes back to our plates.

"Not at all, King Farryn, I am beyond grateful for your hospitality," the siren replied.

She was so different from Anwen. I couldn't help it, the thought popped into mind, the memory of Anwen's first visit, how shy she had been, her hands shaking in my own when I introduced her to my parents. She felt like a stranger in our realm, and I tried to do my best to make her feel welcomed. Eidothea, on the other hand, claimed her right from the first instant, so used to the reverence and commanding presence she raised around, speaking with her chin up, even in these moments of dread. A queen till the end.

"Eidothea explained her punishment to us and the repercussions of her help, even if given unwillingly," mother started speaking, drawing our attention.

"So, Anwen has the tear now," she clinked her voice against my ears, making the information ring in my mind.

"She does," I released the truth in a low sigh.

"Which means that Fear Gorta will not allow her to return so easily," mother added, as if wanting to put the information in my thoughts. Making me realise how dangerous the situation had become.

"Anwen can stand her own," I said without a doubt, but my throat felt raspy, so I grabbed one of the wine glasses from the table and downed it. My action did not help my case as much as I wanted it to, probably making me doubt my mate more than believe in her.

"We all made mistakes," Eidothea spoke again. "Anwen should not have been left alone, even if she wanted to face her brother's offering reaper."

Offering reaper, I internally huffed. The siren code for murderer. Then I blinked, realising this was new information for Damaris and Takara. I wasn't sure if mother and father knew about it either.

"Anwen obliterated the princess, her brother's murderer," I released the words slowly, allowing the room to take the information and react however they pleased.

I, for one, did so with pride. My mate had finally embraced her powers and claimed the revenge she had wanted for such a long time. A true princess in herself. I did not know how the events leaked into being or why she felt the need to burst her power in such a raw way, but she stood her ground.

Anwen fought back. Which meant that she could do it whenever she needed to from now on. Including with Rhylan.

"There was blood and chunks of meat everywhere," Vikram felt the need to add, motioning with his hands as he explained what he saw. "The throne room was filled with drips of dried blood, everywhere you looked. And there was this small puddle that contained a few more remains. Anwen fought hard," he added.

"Are you sure it was her power and not Fear Gorta's?" Takara enquired. "How evident was the energy trace after they left?"

"I'm sure it was Anwen. I know her power," I nodded with determination. I would not let them think of her as a weak former human. I knew what my mate could do. I had seen it, felt it. She was slowly embracing her powers, accepting her new self.

"And that was before the tear?" mother asked.

All of us nodded, making the queen copy our gesture, sudden understanding lining her features. It meant that, if Anwen could defend herself before receiving the new energy, she would become unstoppable now. Able to not only defend herself but fight back. Against anyone.

"How are the armies going to progress? What is the strategy?" Damaris posed the question.

"Amara will meet us in Goa with her armies and the sirens have promised to stay away from humans as long as we return the tear of their goddess."

"Is Wind going to be an ally on the battlefield?" the prince and our future king wanted to ensure.

"There will be no battlefield," Vikram pointed. "We're only going there to impose threat, but there will be no fighting. Not if we can help it."

"Explain," the king demanded, so I took the lead, speaking the plan Vikram and I had already formed on our walk to the palace gates.

"Firelings will probably be released as an intimidation tactic, but our armies will be stationed at the entry points, clearing them as they come out. We only need a few soldiers for that, the exit is heavy terrain, and no more than a handful of beings can access it at once. We will be ready for that."

"But why is all the army coming?" Takara enquired.

"We're taking only a quarter; Wind will do the same. The kingdoms need to be barricaded should the sirens try to take advantage of our departure and launch a surprise attack," Vikram explained, his gaze softening at the sight of Eidothea, sitting next to him and struggling to chew on the food. My stomach dropped at the sight of them, at Eidothea occupying Anwen's seat.

"We need another chair when Anwen is back."

The thought escaped my lips without me wanting to release it, but as soon as they floated in the air, I realised it was too late. Mother and Takara looked at me with pity, their lips pressed in that universal he-needs-a-hug sentiment.

"I am sorry, son, we did not think…" the king turned to me and reached across the table to press his hand over mine. "With the chaos of your return, we did not have space to plan."

"No problem at all," I shook my head, banishing away a tear that wanted to escape, "it was a suggestion for future arrangements," I swallowed hard, the gulp audible in the entire room.

"Of course, my son," my mother added, and thank the goddess Damaris changed the subject back to battle plans.

"So, tower guards, city defence, close the commerce and merchant routes, guard the borders," he made a list of upcoming duties.

"I'll take the Realm Defence, the rest of the army can remain here," Vikram pointed with determination.

"But that is only a few thousands," mother protested. "I cannot allow you to face the firelings undefended, while the entire city is under lock and key. Neither of you," she shifted her gaze to me.

"And I will not sit here and leave the fate of my mate in the hands of a traitorous bastard, while the siren queen might try to take away our home," my brother's voice rose to the ceiling, making Eidothea flinch. He realised and settled down, apologising. Before the situation escalated even further, I intervened.

"Vikram and I will travel through the kingdom, find Anwen, recover the tear and leave," I spoke our plan quickly. "I know the ins and outs of the Fire Kingdom and I might still find some loyalty there. Marreth will also join, he was first commander of the firelings for the past decade. The three of us, together, can find Anwen."

"And when you do?" Takara's voice was barely a whisper.

"We hope the legends are true and bring Catalina back to her rightful place," I smiled.

Anwen

Chapter Twenty-Six

I need Ansgar. I need to get back to Ansgar.

Just keep walking, keep walking, keep walking, I encouraged myself when I reached the dark corridors. I had no idea where I was going, all I remembered was darkness, but I hoped that if I kept going, I would eventually find some sort of exit. Find an earthling and ask for their help, just like we did before.

Rhylan acted crazy all day long, constantly checking on me, touching my chest and poking into me as if I was a rotisserie chicken and he wanted to know if I was cooked through.

It became uncomfortable as hell.

Cressi did not help much either, trying to guard the both of us and make sure Rhylan didn't do anything stupid. No matter how many times I tried to explain that her presence agitated him rather than calm him down, she kept insisting that we all needed to calm down and sit together to come up with a plan. Something that neither Rhylan nor I agreed to.

Whatever spies he sent did not come back. Or if they did, Cressi and me were not made aware. All I noticed was that his tension grew by the hour.

I had seen him like this before, that day when he came to claim payment for the Cloutie root I used, ready to harm whomever, without caring about anything but his goals. I had also seen him desperate, that day when he passed me some of his power, then wrapped me in a ball of flames and kicked me through a wall. Cressi hadn't seen the bad side of her husband, but I knew him. And I knew what he was capable of.

"Just let me talk to Ansgar, let me write him a letter or something, try going into his mind, use a pigeon, anything, just let me send him a message. He needs to know what happened," I kept insisting to no avail. It was as if my words bounced back from Rhylan's ears.

Also, what he said at the breakfast table did anything but calm me down. If Ansgar was truly trapped in the Water Kingdom, if he was punished for what I had done, I would never forgive myself.

The image of his wounds came back to me, that day I washed him and had to remove caked blood and pus from his shoulder blades... I never wanted to see him like that again, I would not allow it. They needed to know what happened, needed to know that it was me who killed the princess, me who deserved to be punished. No one else.

Not Rhylan, not Cressida and especially, not Ansgar.

"Please, just let me go back," I begged again, this time at dinner, causing Rhylan to smack his fist against the table, making it crack in half and taking the food, glasses and plates along with it.

Cressi remained paralysed, still holding her fork, reactionless. Her husband, however, finally turned to me. Finally spoke.

"What part of *no* does your tiny brain prevent you from understanding?"

His eyes turned crimson, abandoning that cold adamant I had gotten so used to, that I even found endearing.

"Neither you nor Cressida will leave this place until I can guarantee my queen's safety. And because you had to go and explode fucking mermaids in your spare time, we are all trapped in here."

His words brought a new realisation, and by the way Cressi started shaking in her chair, I knew she understood it too. All of this was my fault. Rhylan did not want to flee, he did not want to have to trap us back here, but I had forced his hand. By putting Cressida in danger.

And he would do anything to keep her with him, to keep her safe.

"I'm sorry..." Cressi's words barely escaped, her body entrapped in a permanent state of shivers. "It's my fault all of this is happening," she barely spoke, her eyes lifting so slowly, barely noticeable, towards Rhylan.

"No, sunshine," Fear Gorta fell on his knees in front of his wife in the next second, cupping her face and forcing her eyes to find his. To find unconditional love in them. "We will get through this..." Rhylan spoke softly, with so much gentleness that my heart crumbled. Then he turned to me, his gaze shifting from a soft understanding to unrelenting determination.

"Go to your room and stay there," he ordered, not wasting another second on me.

So, I left. But not to my room. I asked one of the guards to show me around to take me to the various rooms I had not been privy to visiting before and when we reached one filled with jewellery and gold ornaments, no doubt belonging to the late queen, I faked interest and asked him to return within the hour and give me time to pick what I wanted to bring with me.

As soon as he was gone, I vanished and started running through the corridors, having no idea where I was going, where I wanted to go. Until I found the dark passageway and shoved my body through the obsidian doors.

I hadn't stopped in what felt like hours, pushing my legs to move and feeling beyond grateful for the divine inspiration to wear trainers, jeans and a shirt today. Even if the cotton shirt did not provide the best protection against the cold, it was much better than the dress I had initially came in and the soles of the shoes made me feel as if I was walking on clouds rather than hard, cemented terrain.

I had to move, I had to move, I had to move.

I had to find Ansgar.

I had to…light. In the distance. Behind me.

I heard voices and more torches as they inched closer, trapping me in the darkness.

I heard Rhylan's voice moments before strong arms gripped my shoulders, then circled around my neck.

"Where do you think you are going, sprout?"

I kicked the bars until my knees started hurting, until the tension of the iron cracked through my bones and made my joints shiver in pain. I couldn't escape. I was trapped in there, locked away just like last time, in the same bedroom I had shared with Ansgar.

Rhylan's energy must have knocked me unconscious for a long while. I had no recollection of the journey back, my return to the room or the installation of the iron bars, which must have taken a long while.

There was a tiny space which I could reach through and grab things, like a doggy door that allowed me to get food or return the plates they brought for me. Not that I touched the food. A silly form of protest really, because I was only hurting myself and my stomach, but I still had to do it.

I needed to let those guards know that I would not eat or drink until Rhylan came to talk to me. I couldn't even spot the clock, which I stupidly left in the living room, so I had no idea how long it had passed since I woke up. They tried to feed me twice and I wasn't sleepy, so I assumed I had skipped breakfast and lunch. My eyes didn't focus on what was on the plates in front of me before I threw them through the bars and made a tantrum.

I shouted everything that came to mind, lots of fuck you's and curses that would make my mom hide under a rock, trying to order them to open the door as the princess of their kingdom that I was, but clearly had no authority over whatever orders they received, and

I tried threatening them with the arrival of my mate who would kick their asses, then once again I tried crying, pleading and then shouting Rhylan's name until my throat became sore.

One of the soldiers went into the kitchen and filled a glass of water for me, but I kicked it and refused to drink. I then sneakily tried to go to the bathroom — luckily that door remained on my side of the cell — and turned on the tap, but only a dry noise came from the sink. Or the shower. Or the bathtub. Only the toilet worked. Of course the freaking bastard thought about everything.

I started to shout for Cressi, hoping that she might hear me and came to my rescue, but something told me that she too, might be trapped in a similar situation.

Then I tried to shout Ansgar's name, as if I could open a portal for my voice to reach him, but then my vocal cords gave up completely. So, I remained silent and kicked.

I planned to kick until my legs broke, or until one of the soldiers realised I was prone to hurting myself in the process and bring Rhylan in. I really hoped the second option happened sooner rather than later.

"Are you done acting like a spoiled little brat?"

I jerked upright to find Rhylan by the iron bars, looking at me through the gate that kept me prisoner. I took momentum and slammed my body against the bars, as if the motion would miraculously set me free. It didn't.

"Let me out, you son of a bitch!" I shouted, shoving my hands through the metal bars and trying to get to him. To hurt him, to kick him…anything really.

"No," he simply replied, then looked at me with curiosity for a couple of seconds, studying my rage, before turning to leave.

"No, please!! I shouted. "Please, don't go!" I heard myself beg. I couldn't be alone, I needed someone to talk to. "Please…" I said again, leaning back and removing myself from the bars, to show that I would be complacent. That I only needed company.

"Well, well, well, the sprout has finally learnt her place," Rhylan grinned in satisfaction, though his features looked tired. Worried.

"Why are you keeping me locked in? Why are you punishing me like this?" I demanded, settling myself on the edge of the bed to look at him through the open door. And the bars that separated us.

"I cannot let you do whatever you want, sprout. Not to my kingdom. And especially not to my queen."

"But Cressi is fine, she can stay here with you, where she is safe, and I can just go. Please," I heard myself trying to reason with him. "Just for a few days, just to find Ansgar and make sure he is safe. Then we'll come right back, the both of us."

A lie. I wouldn't bring Ansgar back here if my life depended on it. I would not put him through torture and pain, just because I had been an idiot. Again.

"Cressida is far from fine," he raised his voice, making the soldiers behind him shake, their armour suddenly clanking. "She is stressed, highly sensitive and worried. Also, she is in danger."

"She's not fragile, you know?" I stopped him. How dare he say those things about my friend? He had no idea how strong Cressi really was, how many things she had gone through, coming out more powerful and more confident. He only knew her for months.

"You keep looking at her like this fragile human, and I don't know why, probably because she loves you so much and doesn't want you to worry, that she is taking this place. Playing that part. Your pretty, useless queen that needs to be defended against everyone, that is incapable to fend for herself. You have no idea who Cressida Thompson is. You have no idea what she's been through!" Fine, emotional blackmail it is. I hoped that at least this would do something to get him back to his senses.

A few seconds passed before Rhylan started leaking blackness, dark smoke surrounding him and the room, seeping through the iron bars and coming so, so close to me. I knew it would hurt me. I knew I had to stay away.

"I do not know Cressida? *I* DO NOT KNOW CRESSIDA?" he shouted, his voice rising to the extent that the room started shaking. Along with the iron bars, the walls and even my bed. Everything trembled under the echo of Rhylan's wrath.

"How many times did you use her? How many times did you abandon her without caring about her feelings? How many times did she have to care for your ungrateful ass?" he continued to spread rumbles around me, that cloud of smoke stopping inches away. "When I met her, Anwen, she was a broken woman. Struggling to stay above the surface, fighting every single day for those smiles she so mindlessly shares with everyone. So don't you dare tell me how MY WIFE might be feeling, because you have no idea!"

"I…" I stopped. Was he right? Was Cressi lonely? Was she struggling?

Every time I saw her, she looked cheerful and happy, always ready for fun, always joking. Even in the hardest situations, even facing the unknown, she had been there for me. Supporting me on every single step. No...Rhylan had to be mistaken.

"I am sorry," I said softly. "Where is she? I would like to talk to her and apologise."

"Talk to her..." he huffed. "You've done enough, Anwen dearest. You have done enough," he said again, voice turning to lament. Darkness engulfed him in the next beat.

Next time they brought me a plate of food, I accepted it. I dragged the tray into bed and ate every spoonful of the cauliflower soup, finished all the mash and the two sausages that tasted of sage and not meat. Two apples remained on the tray, and I finished them off as well before I fell asleep.

Something hard hit my back, spinning pain close to my spine. I shifted and massaged the injured area, half-asleep, then shifted on my pillow and closed my eyes once more. But something hit me again, this time in my right calf.

"Anwen!" a barely audible voice came to my ears.

Cressi.

I was instantly awake.

"Fucking finally," she groaned again, barely audible, waving her hands through the iron bars to grab my attention.

"What are you doing here?" I jumped from the mattress and rushed to her, whispering as softly as she did.

As soon as I reached what was supposed to be the door, I realised why our voices needed to maintain the hushed tones. The guards remained in the living room, one of them asleep on the sofa and the other on a chair by the kitchen.

"How did you manage to sneak in here? Where is Rhylan?" I quickly asked, suddenly concerned for my friend.

"He was called in the middle of the night. Armies are coming. They are looking to attack," she whispered, trying to give me as much information as she could in a single breath.

"Are you okay? Are you safe?" I grabbed her hands in mine through the iron bars.

"Yeah, yeah, I'm fine. But Rhy..." she shook her head, eyes filling with tears. "I'm really worried, Anwen, I've never seen him like this. He is possessed with rage, he barely eats, he jumps at the smallest sound... I'm really worried," she repeated.

"Yeah...he is..." I stopped, Rhylan's words coming to mind. "He's worried about you; he wants to make sure you are safe." I paused again. "He loves you very much, Cressi."

My friend released a slow, heavy breath which sounded more like a sigh. "I know... He has gone through so much, Anwen, he suffered so much...you have no idea," she pressed her lips together, allowing me to read pity in her eyes.

Pity.

For Rhylan.

"He said the same thing about you, "I couldn't help my observation. "You guys need a long honeymoon after this is over. "

"Yeah..." she halted, nodding a few times.

"Can you get me out of here?" I squeezed her hands, trying to bring her back to the present.

"I tried to, but I can't seem to find a lock. I think this is sealed with magic or something, there's no way for me to open. I tried checking these two as well, but they don't have a key," she murmured.

"Cressi, I need to get out of here," I widened my eyes, pleading with my friend.

"I'll go get help!" she said before releasing my hands and running out the door.

Ansgar

Chapter Twenty-Seven

Thousands of shields shone in the midday sun, carried by some of the best warriors I had ever met. The Wind army was small, smaller than they had been centuries ago, but their fighters passed such rigorous training that all of them could have easily taken down a dozen opponents.

I barely helped a proud smile watching Amara and Marreth approached us, both cladded in armour, both holding their heads high and gazes sharp. Which meant that Queen Jyanna had welcomed them with open arms and with kind ears.

"The new prince of Wind," I mounted to welcome them in our camp, my horse slowly trotting in their path.

"Shut up, you jerk," Marreth greeted me with a smile while Amara displayed a slight blush underneath that helmet.

"So, I assume the return home went well?" I pointed the obvious.

"Yes..."Amara smiled, "And no," she added quickly.

"We'll tell you all about it once we get your girl back," Marreth added as soon as they reached me. "What news?"

By the time we dismounted and walked to our station to show them our points of attack and strategy, I offered some updates. Not much had happened in the meanwhile, no news of Anwen yet, which troubled me greatly, the information Eidothea gave us about the presence of the mermaids and their involvement in this and how we planned to initiate the strike.

"Is she not joining us?" Marreth turned to Vikram, greeting my brother.

"She wanted to, but I forbade it." I pressed my lips and widened my eyes to Amara, signalling to her the dramatic events I had to suffer through during our departure and by the small smile she shot to me, she fully understood.

Eidothea, a siren queen, the second in command nonetheless was not a being to be ordered. And my brother, the commander of an entire region of our army, was not a male to be told no. The two turned the kingdom upside down in the most dramatic couple's fight I had witnessed in my life, making Damaris and I take mental notes and learn from our brother's mistake.

The screams I heard from my brother's chambers bested the most terrifying torture screams, but by the end of the session, Vikram came our victorious, shutting the door behind him. Victorious if we did not count the various scratch marks on his face and neck.

"So..." Marreth, as always, did not show the same royal tact as the rest of us, "you tried to order around a siren queen, huh?" the commander crossed his arms and tilted his head to better observe the swollen fingernail marks on my brother's cheek.

"I did not say I came out of it unscathed," Vikram groaned in annoyance, making us all chuckle.

"In all fairness, she struggled to walk, "I defended my brother who had been tending to his mate for the past three days, caring for her every need. If there was any doubt of his love, one only needed to see the attention and care he dedicated to Eidothea. I guessed that, deep down, she also knew she would be a distraction rather than help on the battlefield, which is why she must have allowed Vikram to come out alive of that room.

"Every surface needs getting used to, and she hates shoes," I added.

"It can't be easy for her, "Amara said.

"She did contact her harem and some of her army, they are on standby should we need reinforcements. Which, hopefully we will not," Vikram advised.

"How is that working for you?" Again, Marreth and that big mouth. "To know that your mate has a harem?" The commander kept his head tilted, scanning Vikram's face for any reaction.

Amara and I stopped as well, suddenly curious to know the answer and notice the pleased smirk on Vikram's face.

"It makes things very interesting," my brother threw the commander a feline smirk that said it all. If there were going to be orgies on our floor, Anwen and I needed to move to a different side of the palace.

"Can we return to thinking with our brains and discuss strategy?" Amara snapped her fingers, bringing us back to the subject in question.

"Please, follow me," I invited the princess, leading her and Marreth to a massive table where various maps rested. Along with a carafe of wine because Vikram had needed to calm down before their arrival. I had spent the past two days with the kingdom's cartographers and Damaris, pouring over everything my brain remembered. Every tunnel, every passageway, the training locations, the exit tunnels, the direction to the nearest forest and tried to create some sort of underground map of the Fire Kingdom. My brother calculated the attack strategies and number of warriors required in various scenarios, both of us determining the best course of action each time.

Vikram had remained with Eidothea, who struggled with her adjustment, but the siren queen insisted on visiting and offering some advice and the contact information should we require assistance from the waterlings. They would be stationed near the island, ready to infiltrate and help should we summon them.

"The least I can do…" Eidothea had shared a broken smile before limping away, too proud to ask my brother to carry her again. Too proud to let us see her struggle.

"You kept busy…" Amara noted when I pointed out our plan, showing her the various figurines used to mark troops, entrances and defence lines.

"I did not have a choice," I swallowed tightly, the anticipation too great. I had always been weary before battle, just like any other soldier, but this time I was leading the most important fight of all.

To recover my mate. To bring back my goddess. To finally be free.

"Alright then, I shall go speak to our commanders and alert the troops," Marreth nodded before placing his helmet back, allowing me to only see his eyes and part of the scar on his neck, his hair carefully tucked away.

"We will be ready to proceed within the hour," Vikram advised.

Thousands of soldiers surrounded the Fire Kingdom. Every entrance, every blade of grass, every rock or tunnel remained fully guarded and under strict supervision. Layers of shields clinked against the roughness of the new wind, the sea scorched the battle terrain with the eagerness of the mermaids who wanted to get a better view of the action.

A horn blew.

A horn to announce our attack, banners flying around and signalling the armies to advance, to progress and not to stop until a new order was given. Until they reclaimed the benefit of rest.

I did not stay behind, not wanting to shield or linger beyond the attacking troops. Instead, I pushed them forward, urging them on, abandoning the horses and advancing through the main tunnels and through the darkness of the cold kingdom that laid before our eyes.

The windling army progressed from the side, trying to intercept any attempt to flee, their battle steeds chasing away all dreams of liberation, striking blow after blow until no fireling remained alive.

We would not give them a chance to band together, nor to form a battalion or even a troop, we would destroy them as and when they resurfaced, mercilessly striking to earn more space through the tunnels, to advance and to gain terrain.

I walked along with my own platoon, with the males I had shared battles and wounds, males I grew up with, told jokes to and attended classes together. They trusted my sword as I trusted theirs, having remained at one another's merciless strength to protect the company on various occasions.

They didn't even need commands, they knew what to do, reading the orders in my stance, the way I stepped or moved my arms, the way my sword struck.

We did not need torches, did not offer the enemy any chance of reprise, only a swift passing. I remembered the core soldiers, the battalion I had been put in charge of during my forced stay in their kingdom, the males without hopes and dreams, ones that had become machines, listening and following orders. I tried not to think how many of them had perished by my own sword, males that had once covered my back, males I had trained.

My eyes protected themselves and averted from their faces, scanning only the lit torchlights they arrived through the tunnels with, a prior attempt at self-defence which only signalled their death quicker.

Time passed into oblivion, it could have been minutes, hours or centuries, I did not know.

I did not care as we pushed forward, moved our steps within the core of the kingdom, striking our way through the tunnels until blood painted our faces, our swords and our fate.

Still, we did not stop. We progressed through flesh and bone, we cut armour and responded to fire with fire, unrelenting and unyielding.

We hadn't planned for a battle of this magnitude, we merely needed to make way through the kingdom and reach the entrance, but the firelings did not stop. They kept coming through the night, through the darkness and down the corridor, forcing their lives into our weapons rather than surrendering, rather than giving way.

We did not stop, my warriors following the same orders as they had always been: never give up. Never surrender.

"Stop, please! STOP!" a female voice broke with desperation. "Can't you see they're killing you? Please, just stop!"

I knew the voice. I recognised that voice.

"Shield wall behind! Nobody moves, nobody passes," I ordered and did not look back to see if they followed the command. I already knew they would. Then I shouted as loudly as I could. "Cressida?"

A few seconds passed, three more attacks came my way. I managed on my own, telling the soldiers not to break rank.

"Ansgar?" I heard the echo, the calling for my name.

And I started running.

"Cressida? Cressida, where are you?"

"I'm here," she replied, her voice broken, sounding so far away. "I'm trying to stop them, please help me!" she begged, making me understand her meaning.

She was trying to stop the soldiers from progressing, from running into our blades.

"HALT!" I shouted, forcing my voice to pierce through the darkness and death. "By the order of Prince Ansgar of the Earth Kingdom, this passageway is closed. There is an entire army on your footsteps, do not progress to your death!"

Then I turned to my own battalion to utter the same information. "I am calling a halt. I will go in myself and speak to their leader. The tunnel is to remain blocked, let the Wind army know. We are on standby unless further attack."

Their armour jittered to tell me they were rushing to follow the command. To tell Amara and Marreth that I had made it, that I was in. There was no use spilling more blood, on either side. If the firelings remained complacent, we would not progress the attack, it was the conclusion we had all reached before starting the blow. None of us enjoyed killing. Not unless we had to.

"Cressida!" I called for her again, rushing through the darkness and through the barely lit torches, trying to find those golden locks, to find her ivory skin. "Cressida!" I called again, starting to doubt my senses. Had it all been in my head? Had I truly heard her?

"Ansgar!" a shadow reached me from the side, and I barely contained my sword to stop the blow, recognising those rays of sunshine.

"Cressi," I opened my arms to allow her to reach the safety she obviously needed. My friend's hands wrapped around my shoulders with desperation, holding onto me for dear life. I looked down at her, trying to wrap my arms around her back and offer her my warmth, the illusion of protection.

And I noticed blood. Blood dripping down her back, rivers of crimson staining those beautiful sandy locks.

"Cressi, are you hurt? What happened?"

She shook her head, crying softly into my chest, her body shaking along with whatever memory I had forced to resurface.

"Hey, you are safe now. The fight is stopped," I caressed her back gently, allowing my fingers to slowly trace her skin. To soothe and to find the source of the wounds. A blade that touched her shoulder, I realised. Not too deep, but definitely painful.

"Please, let me help clean your wound, it might get infected if we are not careful," I slid my fingers down her arm for emphasis, trying to tell her with my movement that I would not let her go, that I only wanted to care for her.

Yet, Cressida shifted away from me.

"No," she said quickly, her big blue eyes wider than usual, filled with the ghost of battle. They had witnessed death and would never keep the same shine again. "No, Anwen needs us. Anwen needs us," she repeated, then grabbed my hand and squeezed it in her shaking palms.

"Please," she said, "You have to come. You have to help her!"

Anwen
Chapter Twenty-Eight

The guards vanished hours ago, leaving me on my own, to think the worst. I heard muffled sounds starting to slither through the walls a few minutes after the two soldiers abandoned their posts, backs straight and faces grim. They left me without a word or a single glance, their legs shaking on the way out. Which could only mean trouble.

My voice was mostly recovered from the day before, but no amount of shouting brought them back. Or anyone for that matter. Cressi hadn't returned with an update, and I feared that something might have happened. That Rhylan got wind of what she tried to do and put her in a similar situation to me. It made sense to dispatch the guards to protect his queen rather than the useless daughter he never wanted.

I did not know if it was still night or morning, or how much time had passed for that matter. My stomach grumbled and no one came to bring me food, so I assumed it wasn't time for breakfast yet. But when my lips dried and I struggled to swallow from dehydration, the worry returned with a vengeance.

Something important was taking place outside these walls, and I remained here, locked away and forgotten. I heard screaming, I heard doors banging up and down, I heard soldiers shouting in the corridors, everyone too far away to hear my begging for help. They probably had much more important business to tend to.

Having to fight the dread and loss of hope, I tried to make myself useful, to keep my mind occupied with something, to find a solution to get myself out of this place if no one else would. I looked around the room, probably paying attention to my surroundings for the first time since I woke up in this newly formed cell. I checked the bed frame, the nightstands and the wardrobe to see if there was some kind of lever that I could use to push those bars and make room for myself, but everything was made out of wood.

I kicked the bed frame a few times to see if there was some sort of metal support, but I couldn't find anything. But the bathroom had pipes, the realisation hit me.

I rushed through the only door I had access to and tried to unscrew the tap from the bathtub, giving up fairly soon because there was no way in hell I could even move it. Then I turned my attention to the sink, looking around and opening the cupboard beneath it, in the hope to find something. Anything that would help.

"Anwen! Anwen, where are you?"

Cressi! Cressida returned for me. God bless you, you beautiful person, I internally shouted, because my throat was so dry that I wasn't sure if I could speak again until I had five glasses of water. I rushed back into the bedroom, hurrying to the iron bars.

To see my friend, face covered in blood, hair dishevelled and trapped on her shoulder, wearing some sort of dress that had been torn to pieces, leaving her legs bare and unprotected. And behind her…

"No…" I released a muffled sound, my entire weight dropping to the floor, knees unable to contain my weight. I felt my lips tremble, my hands shake, and I blinked so many times to banish the tears that filled my eyes, wanting to make sure it was truly him. That he had come for me.

"Fahrenor," Ansgar rushed to my side, his hands instinctively touching the bars to get to me. And immediately shifting away, my mate releasing a sudden grumble through his teeth.

"It's iron, don't touch them, you will hurt yourself," I begged him when I saw his hands moving again, forearms too big to fit through the bars and touch me, so they stopped and pressed against the iron, creating open flesh as Ansgar's hands tried to reach my face.

I shifted closer to him and put my cheek in his palm, desperate for contact, my hands wrapping around his wrist and pressing a wet kiss on his other palm.

"You came for me," I remarked the obvious, which I wasn't sure he understood between all the crying, the snot and my shrivelled up vocal cords.

"Told you I'd bring help," Cressi attempted a smile from behind him and I barely shifted my gaze to find my friend. To see how tired she looked. How scared.

"Rhy is in the throne room with the generals, I'll go find him and tell him the attack is halted," she announced and took a step back, before stopping and waving a finger from Ansgar to me. "Is this ok? Will you get her out?"

"Of course," my prince replied. "Do you want me to accompany you to find Rhylan? Do you need assistance?"

"No, no, I'll be fine," she shook her head with conviction. "It's better if I go alone and tell him the good news. He's a bit pissed off as you can imagine, seeing you might not be the best idea," she added. To which, surprisingly, Ansgar dipped his chin in agreement. "Seeing how I escaped my guards will piss him off as well, but hey, what can you do?" she shrugged.

What was happening out there?

"Just get our girl out, give her some food and make your way down there in a bit. Good luck."

"And to you," Ansgar responded and before I got a chance to say something, to ask what was happening, my friend rushed out the door.

When Ansgar's shadow-ridden eyes turned to me, my heart stopped beating. He did not know. He did not know what kind of monster I had become, that I was the one to combust all this mess around us, that I was the sole responsible for everything bad that happened in the past week. That, if he was punished in any way, it had been my fault.

"Ansgar," I tried to speak but my throat chose that exact moment to stop working, the words stopping midway to my tongue, stuck on their way to the path of confession.

As if suddenly coming to a realisation, my mate's eyes widened slightly, then he kissed my fingers and removed his forearms from the bars, rushing into the kitchen. I heard noise, I heard the sound of running water and a few moments later, I saw him leave the room with two glasses. Filled to the brim. Oh, thank god.

He handed one slowly to me, careful of his fingers not to touch the bars and drop the glass and I instantly grabbed it and gulped it down. My throat stretched like never before, becoming a whirl that chucked away all the liquid without even considering the concern of suffocating. Water dripping down my throat felt so good, so nourishing, taking all that pain away, all the swollen marks I had left behind when my raspy voice had forced through my oesophagus.

"Here's another one," Ansgar said and offered the second glass, placing it in my hand quickly enough for me to not have to stop drinking. As soon as the final gulp seeped into my mouth, he'd changed it with the new one.

"Thank you," I finally spoke, my heart palpitating with the sudden draw of oxygen, lungs expanding to new frontiers within my chest. "I really needed that," I said between pants, the urge to breathe taking over.

"Of course, fahrenor," my mate shared a sad smile, his gaze struggling to avoid scanning me with pity.

Fahrenor...No, he could not call me that anymore. I had lost the privilege.

"I did it," I heard myself speak, grabbing those bars for dear life, hoping they would keep me grounded, needing them to, because I knew. I knew the next words were probably going to sign our undoing. They will let my mate, the only man I had truly loved, the one I had dreamed a future with, know who I was. They would tell him he deserved so much better.

"I killed Branwyl." I uttered the words slowly, making the pronunciation smooth and perfectly placed, lest there be any mistakes. Hoping he would not ask me to repeat it.

To confirm that I too, was a murderer, just like the mermaid I had hated for so long.

"I know," Ansgar said, a slow nod, eyes still locked with my own, no sign of disgust on his face. No trace of betrayal. He only blinked at me, softly, with understanding, as if he knew I needed to say it out loud, I needed to accept what I had done.

"How?" I asked instead.

"I guessed… When Eidothea returned and told us what happened, that she left you on your own with Branwyl in the throne room…when I saw the damage, I assumed it was your power. I recognised it," he almost wanted to smile, his lips curling just slightly before coming back to a straight shape.

I felt it then. A whimper. An exasperated whimper, one that I had to keep locked away for days made its way out, causing my chest to shudder, my lungs to contort and my breath to jitter.

"I killed her," I said again, this time louder, forcing my ears to listen to my confession, to learn of what I had done. Deep sobs forced me on my knees again, letting my body fall, muscles lost into oblivion while I cried, colossal tears springing down my face.

"Fahrenor…" Ansgar's voice hit like a soft caress, one I knew I did not deserve. I instantly shook my head. "No, don't call me that. I can't be that anymore…"

As if understanding my need to divulge my actions, my prince reached for me through the bars, sliding his fingers down my shoulder and caressing with soft strokes. "How did it happen?"

I let my mind float away then, take me back to the moment, to her laughter, to the way she mocked my brother's life.

"I don't know what happened. Initially I wanted to hear her say it, to admit that she killed Erik. Cressi started to push her into the topic, then I took over and she started...she started making fun of him. She said she had enjoyed it, and I just...I don't know, I was so angry. I summoned the night, I started screaming...everything, his name, insults, everything I could think of and then...there was blood everywhere, and Cressi was shaking." I stopped, drowning in sighs and weeps, struggling to find my breath while those fingers continued their calming motion. "By the time the night vanished, so did she. She was gone....only blood remained...I..."

"I know, fahrenor, I saw it."

I had to continue, I had to tell him that I was responsible for everything. Had to make him understand that I was deserving of hate, not this unconditional love he did not stop giving me. "Rhylan came rushing in. He felt me using his power and...Cressi wasn't okay. He said we needed to leave, that they would come for us, that I had put Cressi in danger. He was right."

Only then, Ansgar's lips started pressing together under the pressure of a tight jaw and I almost heard his teeth grinding. His fingers stopped caressing me for a mere second, before he regained his composure and continued. "Did he hurt you?" His eyes had become storm clouds, ready to bring down hell on whomever would drown in them.

"What? No! No, of course not, I went with him willingly."

That seemed to surprise him. "Why?" my mate added a small frown to his expression.

"We needed to go, if the sirens found out what I had done, they would want to punish us. And Cressi cannot defend herself, so Rhylan said it was the best option, to leave there peacefully."

Ansgar's brows shot up.

"Rhylan wanted to leave peacefully?"

"Yeah…we ran through the glass tunnels, Cressi wasn't really moving, I think she was still in shock, with all that blood on her face…She was crying, then she was shaking, but as soon as Rhylan came in, she just turned into a ball in his arms and said nothing. We had to get her out," I said again.

"But the tear? The attack?"

"We were close to the exit when Eidothea appeared, out of nowhere and she carried the tear. That's where things got crazy, her and Rhylan fought, he wanted to get the tear and have leverage, to keep Cressi safe and make sure no one would come after us. But she pushed it into my chest, it dissolved somehow, I don't really remember. I was passed out for a long time."

"How are you feeling now?" his forearms pushed through the bars again, scorching his skin at the contact, but he did not even flinch.

"Why are you still being so nice to me?" I sighed again, shifting away from his touch to wipe more tears. "When will you start hating me?" It was a stupid thing to say, to make him admit, because I did not want to know when his love would turn into hate. I did not want that to happen. Ever. Yet here I was, asking for it. Idiot, idiot Anwen.

"Hate you?" my prince blinked, looking at me in surprise. "Why would I hate you, fahrenor?"

"Because I am a murderer?" I felt my voice shake with the admission.

Ansgar huffed.

Then looked up at me and smiled.

"Fahrenor, you could burn down the world and I would not hate you."

Then, with sudden determination, he stood and grunted under his breath. "I am sick of this." Then my mate drew his sword and, after telling me to move away towards safety, he started hacking at the iron bars. And when he managed to split some of them up, he started pulling at them, using his bare hands, his shoulders, his back and legs until he created an opening big enough for me to squeeze through.

He stepped back then, burnt and bleeding, opening his arms to me.

"Come to me, my love."

Ansgar

Chapter Twenty-Nine

"My love." I finally had her back to her rightful place. Back in my arms. I allowed myself to feel her breathing, to capture the warmth of her body. It repelled off my armor, the protective breastplates not letting me fully enjoy this moment.

"One second," I spoke softly, slightly shifting away from her, enough to reach behind my neck and pull the straps that kept the armor in place. I did the same to my biceps and forearms, remaining in the shirt underneath, still carrying the leather overlays sewn into it. Anwen did not say a word, only looked at me as I unhooked the royal armor, watching me with curious eyes.

"That's better," I said and grabbed her tighter, letting my heart beat in the same rhythm as hers, our chests finally able to join and share warmth. Goddess, I finally had her back.

"I love you," she sniffled against my shirt, not daring to gaze up at me. Without letting go of my hold, I shifted my hand enough to allow my fingers to reach her chin and slowly lifted it, forcing her eyes to gaze up at me.

"I will always love you, fahrenor. Always," I said again, trying to drill the message into her mind, forcing the truth to her heart and spirit. To never be forgotten again. I could not help it, not when she was this close, not when she was mine again. I leaned down to find those beautiful lips I missed too much, to taste her mouth again, allowing my tongue to greet hers.

She did not protest, did not shy away from my touch and kissed me eagerly, both of us allowing the moment to reconnect our energies, to make one another whole again. The world stopped spinning, time froze in place and neither of us even dared breathe from fear to break this moment. To allow our spirits to rejoice in their closeness.

She was back in my arms.

"I'm so sorry I put you through this," I heard her say, the words muffled by the tight embrace. And then, she slowly released the admission that broke my heart, her deepest fear, that she had kept hidden, locked away in that trembling heart. "I didn't think you were coming. I didn't think…" Anwen stopped then, forcing the words back.

"I will always come for you, fahrenor. Always," I reassured her, draping my arms around her trembling body, allowing her to keep my warmth, my support, my love.

Then her head shook, slightly. Another thought. "Rhylan was only trying to protect Cressi. He does not want this war, he said so himself. He wants to live in peace. We need to stop this." Then her enormous hazel eyes shone into me. "Please."

I dipped my chin. If this could find its end without further bloodshed, I was in full support of the idea.

"Of course, my love. We shall go to him right away." I hoped that by then, Cressi had reached him and offered him the news, so Fear Gorta knew that the tunnel and entrance to his kingdom were blocked by a full army. Hopefully, the information would make him more complacent.

"Wait," Anwen grabbed my arm when I showed my intention of wanting to shift away from her, to move into action. "I need to give you the tear," she blinked, her eyes wide and hopeful.

"Is it still with you?" I could not believe it, I had fully expected Rhylan to rip it out of her chest, especially when I found her locked away. I could not help but notice that the bastard had shoved her in the old room we had shared, nourishing her fear of abandonment. For how would she find calm, in a bed we had slept in, made love in? How would she hide from her thoughts, her fears, when everything reminded her of us?

"Rhylan said he wanted to take it away, but then I tried to run, and he locked me in here," Anwen spoke softly, the memories oozing with pain. She had tried to run. Part of me felt pride at her statement, her attempt to, no doubt, come back to me. The other part thought with terror what would have happened if Rhylan hadn't been so merciful.

"I...I don't know what to do."

Truth be told, I didn't either, for none of the training I had received ever prepared me for this. We would join the three energies of the kingdoms and if legend spoke true, we would summon the goddesses. That is, if they willed their return. And that is, if Anwen and I managed to extract the third piece of energy.

"It's in my chest," Anwen said, stretching her back and opening her chest wider for me, as if expecting my hand to poke through and grab whatever I needed. I sensed her heart beat faster, with anticipation or fear, I did not know.

"Did it hurt? The first time?"

"I don't remember, I think I passed out. Rhylan did say I needed to eat a lot and get my energy back because he couldn't take it otherwise. And then he locked me away and seemed to kind of forget about it," she shrugged, as if to say she did not know why he didn't do it earlier.

I scanned my mind for all the information I had. It used to be a pearl, which Eidothea pushed into my mate's chest. The energy dissolved, so it did not necessarily have to remain in the same place. It had to be willingly given.

"Do you want me to have it?" If Anwen held even a shred of a doubt, there would be no point in trying. I did not want to cause harm to my mate by trying to extract something which would not be given freely.

"Of course I do! I need it out of me," she shook her shoulders, as if trying to shake the energy away from within her. I could not help a small smile, then nodded.

"Let's see what we can do about that."

I asked my mate to take a seat, not knowing how long this would take and what effects it would have on her, so I wanted her to rest comfortably. Without protest, she circled the sofa and planted herself right in the center of the fluffed-up pillows, enjoying the new sensation of comfort.

I told her to breathe, deeply, slowly, to allow her mind to relax and lose herself in pleasant memories. While she did so, I started telling her about Eidothea's first visit, Takara's reactions and the fight Vikram and the former siren queen had just before she left. She asked about my brother and my family, about our nephew and I told her everything that happened since we departed, careful to offer calming details, to bring her memories that would slow down her pulse and allow her to relax, allow her to dream and remember better days.

"Does this hurt?" I asked as soon as I placed my hand on her chest, caressing the area above her heart in an attempt to feel any strand of new energy. If Takara were here, this would have been so much easier. Instead, I had to rely on her teachings and trust my senses. Which, in a kingdom that kept me prisoner, with guards all around and with the possibility of a war starting, I could not really find my best focus. But my mate was in danger, so I had to try my best.

"No, it doesn't," she shook her head, keeping her eyes squeezed closed as if she had expected pain as soon as my touch arrived. We exhaled in relief, almost simultaneously.

I grew more confident, allowing my fingers to slowly touch her chest, right above her breasts and let my fingers wander along the bones, trying to feel for any changes, for anything that might prove useful. After a few more minutes, Anwen fully relaxed into my touch.

Her head dropped on the pillows as if she was preparing to sleep and her breathing became even, a soft smile on her face, no doubt from the small caresses I was creating on her chest and around her bra, because my mate insisted to remove her shirt. And I was sure she wanted to add to my torture, knowing what touching her breasts would do to me.

I felt something by the side of her left breast, and I pushed my fingers deeper into her bra, hoping to find victory. There was some sort of…tightness, right above her heart, trapped within her sternum. As soon as I touched the area, I felt it.

The raw power, the palpitating force, begging to be released.

"Anwen, please give me the tear," I murmured, asking my mate for permission before I tried to take it away from her, wanting to ensure, one more time, it was freely given. But my mate did not say anything, did not respond and I don't even think she realised I had found it. She laid relaxed on the pillows, enjoying my touch and slightly biting her lip, just the way she knew drove me to absolute madness.

My fahrenor, goddess how I love her.

There was a small pearl in my hand, no bigger than a ring.

There was a pearl in my hand, I barely breathed.

"Anwen…"

My mate did not reply.

"Anwen!" I shouted and spread my fingers on her chest, shaking her abruptly.

"What?" she opened her eyes with a slight frown, and I realised…she was falling asleep. She did not feel a thing and my caresses had probably relaxed her to the point of wanting to take a stroll in the world of dreams.

"I have it," I barely murmured, inundated with relief. She was fine. Anwen was completely fine. And I had the tear.

"What?" she blinked at me and inched closer, her eyes wide and curious, gazing at the pearl in my hand with slight disbelief.

"Is that it?" she frowned, confusion draped across her eyebrows.

"Yes. Yes." I said it again, wanting to convince both her and myself. Because I did not feel anything. Catalina's energy did not buzz inside of me like I expected it to, it did not recognize its sisters. "Yes, this is it," I said again.

"So? Call the goddesses, bring them back!" she urged me, inching closer to me on the sofa, looking at me as if she was expecting a magic trick or some sort of entertainment.

"I…I don't think it works, Anwen," I frowned again at the small bead in my palm, trying to shift it, to activate it somehow, but it remained limp in my hand. The same thing happened when we collected Zaleen's tear, only that time I did not expect a jolt of energy since its sister was missing.

But now…now I had all three tears. And nothing happened.

"Maybe you need to put it in your mouth?" my mate suggested, and I looked at her with a half-grin.

"What?" I frowned.

"I don't know, it was inside of me, maybe you need to like…I don't know? Put it inside you. Swallow it like a marble?"

I smiled at her innocence with endearment. Then I shook my head.

"It does not work like that, baby. I do not think it works at all. It was all a lie..." I barely let the words slip, not wanting to drown in a sea of disappointment. I had let myself hope, let myself believe the legends, believe Rhylan and the siren queen when *I* should have known better.

The goddess never called upon my summons, never once answered even one of my callings. And I was part of her!

They would not hear our prayers this time either.

This was not the moment to break into pain. It had all been a dream, but I had to live in reality.

"At least we have the pearl, which we can return to the sirens, they will withdraw, and everyone will be safe. Eidothea will not spend eternity cursed and you and I..." I swallowed a huge lump. If the goddess was not here, I could not ask for a favour. I could not ask to be unbound from Amara. Which meant that after all this was over, I needed to return to Wind.

"What is it?" she blinked, her eyes fearful of my reaction. Broken and pitiful at the same time.

I forced a smile, this was not the time nor the place. We had to stop a war.

"Nothing, fahrenor. Let us go to the throne room and stop this nonsense once and for all."

I helped her up, both of us struggling to shake the disappointment that weighed heavily on every step. We had dared to hope, we had dared to make plans and think of a better world, when we should have known from the beginning that we could not expect a deity to come and sort our problems. We had to fight for redemption ourselves.

Anwen took a while to find her footing, leaning onto me as we passed through the corridors, exhausted and ready to regain peace. I used the tip of my sword as a walking stick and levered part of my weight into it, while letting my mate find her own rhythm and follow through the torches and discarded shields.

I would not leave the weapon out of my hand, I would not trust our safety on the whims of someone who was going to get very angry, very soon, so I allowed my body the respite it needed, all the while feeling possessed by the sheer weight of failure.

"Earthlings!" a male voice called for us, struggling to find its path through the darkness of the main entrance. I turned to spot Marreth in the distance, his Wind Kingdom armor weighing on his shoulders, adorned with new blood. Behind him, a shorter comrade in the same armor sent us a smile that illuminated the hallways.

Anwen and I stopped, both shifting towards them and waiting for their advancement to reach us.

"You guys look impressive as hell," my mate exclaimed, and I knew, even without looking at her, that she was smiling, happy to see our friends. Happy for this to be over.

"We did what we could," Amara shared the same smile, her golden locks braided and tucked inside her armor. She leaned in to offer Anwen an embrace, pushing me to the side to get to my mate.

"Is this the welcome you give your husband?" I joked. Amara had made so many plans, plans that I would have to break. My heart sored for her.

"Urgh, I've seen your face recently. It's not that pretty that I have to gaze upon it all the time, you know," she elbowed me with affection while keeping my mate trapped in her arms.

"This is perfect, Anwen has the tear, the army is halted, we can all go home," Vikram appeared out of nowhere, his adamant skin reeling through the darkness.

My mate and I looked at each other then, sharing the sudden realization that we would have to be the bearers of bad news. Wanting to spare me suffering, she took the lead.

"The tears don't work," Anwen pressed her lips after making the announcement and looked at each of our friends in turn. Our partners through danger, through training, through so many events that would seem unspeakable to anyone else. We had shared so much together, been through so much that the bond of friendship hung stronger than ever.

"What do you mean?" Marreth asked, stepping closer to my mate as if he hadn't heard her correctly.

I appreciated what she was trying to do, that she wanted to spare me the same questions she had asked. Maybe I didn't do it correctly, maybe there was another way, maybe we needed to wait. Only I knew, only I could feel it, so it was only right that I should be the one to offer the information that would break their dreams.

"It was all a lie. I put the three tears together, tried to summon the goddesses and nothing happened." I sighed, then felt the need to repeat. "It was all a lie."

"But...there's...that means..." Amara struggled to find the words, her expression suddenly grim.

"We will find a way," I reached out and squeezed her shoulder, trying to reassure her. "I promise you that we will find a way."

She nodded, though her gaze dropped to the ground.

"But have you tried summoning them? Have you —"

"Ansgar was our best chance," Vikram intervened, aware of the full truth. One that I could never share with the rest of them, not even with my mate. "If he can't do it, no one else can."

"But we can return the pearl to Thelssha, make Rhylan surrender," Anwen interjected, the hope in her voice heart breaking to us all. "We can at least stop the war, right?"

"Right," I dipped my chin in agreement. If we could not improve our world, we could at least return it to the way it was.

"Rhylan is going to be pissed," Marreth noted.

"Cressi went ahead to talk to him, we should follow and give him the rest of the news," my mate exclaimed, taking a step forward, through the tunnel that would lead us closer to the throne room.

"We should follow," I agreed and signaled the rest to follow in our footsteps as we walked silently through the darkness.

As we advanced through the corridors, holding hands and pressing our steps with a newly discovered determination, I thought about all the plans I had involuntarily made. In the few days since Amara had asked to disband our union, I allowed myself to daydream about everything I would do with my mate returned to my arms.

I imagined us celebrating human holidays with her parents, going to those restaurants she loved to take me to, walking through the enormous park I had completely fallen in love with and working on her family business, growing plants and discovering their properties. I imagined myself taking business advice from Jason and attending every one of Elsa's afternoon tea parties, where she gathered with several ladies and discussed common interests.

I saw Anwen sharing dinner with my family, playing with baby Ansgar and our new nephew, taunting Vikram, sharing laughter with Takara and getting lost in shopping sprees through the regnum, just like she had loved to do since her arrival.

But the goddess did not arrive, which meant that none of these could happen. That Amara and I had to remain married and connected, with the risk of breaking both our hearts. That I would have to give up Anwen yet again, unless there was to be some sort of arrangement to see each other from time to time.

Selfishly, I would do anything to keep my mate with me. I would get on my knees in front of Jyanna if she would grant permission for Anwen to live in the kingdom, even though I knew it would not be fair on her. I could not ask Anwen to renounce her life and her own dreams, just for the illusion of being together.

"Here they are," Cressida's voice welcomed us into the throne room, to find Rhylan, along with a few other firelings, which I assumed were his new set of commanders.

As soon as she saw her friend, Anwen let go of her hold on me and rushed to the Fire Queen, both of them running into each other's arms. I smiled softly, the expression of true friendship developing right in front of us was the perfect way to start this conversation.

"We have you surrounded, there is no need to fight unless you want to claim more loss of life," I announced, instinctively stepping closer to my mate.

"I know…" Rhylan's voice rumbled through the room, waves of

darkness seeping from his mouth as he released the words.

"Rhylan, stop this madness. There is no point. It was not real." I watched his eyes turn from dark crimson, his capillary veins filled with night, return to the Rhylan I had come to know, to the male who had shown kindness from time to time, even if he was forced into it by his new queen.

"What is that supposed to mean?"

I felt more than saw Vikram, Marreth and Amara stepping behind me, as if to flank me should Rhylan start a fight, telling me that they would be right behind me should reinforcements be needed.

"Commander, how quickly you forget your place," Fear Gorta threw Marreth a disgusted look. "Drown in cunt for a little while and you forget all about your plans."

Marreth tensed behind me, but, to his merit, he maintained his calm. "Stop this, king. There's no use. You are surrounded."

"That means nothing, I still have all my power and can use it to rip the lives out of you in a second, if I will it so."

Cressida and Anwen stopped their embrace right in that moment, both gazing at Rhylan. His daughter and his wife, so beautiful, they could make any heart drop. Looking at him with pleading eyes.

"Rhy…" Cressida spoke.

Anwen continued. "We put the tears together, Rhylan. Nothing happened."

I watched how his wrath turned to terror. How his terror turned to pain, how his knees gave out, making him fall to the ground.

Defeated.

Completely and utterly defeated.

"Rhy, my darling, I am so sorry," Cressi was instantly by his side, kneeling alongside him, cupping his jaw and offering slow caresses, trying to bring him back to her, to get him out of that frozen, defeated state.

His gaze shifted to me, questioning, as if hoping that I would be able to change the information, to tell him otherwise. Instead, I nodded. "I have all three tears. They are not here."

I recognized the heartbreak on his features, I read the sorrow in his eyes, in his entire shape, the shoulder that stood straight for centuries now becoming nothing but sanded pillars.

"We need to end this, Rhylan. Please, there's no need to fight, no point to do so. It was all for nothing," Anwen spoke softly, stepping closer to him, as if she too wanted to caress the wounded soldier.

Who had fought alone for so long, his strength seeping from a single purpose.

Now, nothing but dust.

"It wasn't all for nothing," Cressida repeated, straightening her back and gently picking Rhylan's dagger from the ground, where he had let it fall while his life purpose crumbled alongside his defeated body. Her voice sounded strange, as if coming from deep within, as if she had been hollowed of feeling.

"It is time to claim revenge," Cressida spoke, a cruel smirk on her face while the dagger she held dug into Rhylan's ribs.

Anwen

Chapter Thirty

"Cresi, what are you—"

My breath stopped, eyes not believing what they had just witnessed. Cressida. Cressida, who had been in love with Rhylan since the moment she laid eyes on him. Cressida, who looked at Rhylan as if he held the secrets of the universe. Cressida, who could not shut up about all the qualities her king possessed.

Cressida, shoving a dagger into his rib cage.

I heard how the air escaped Rhylan's throat, how his lungs pushed the pain out of his chest and how he turned, his face filled with pain and surprise, to his wife.

"Sunshine," his lips barely parted, the expression of pure unadulterated pain lining his dark eyes, fanning over his long lashes and finding its escape with a tear that ran down his cheek. "What are you doing?" his mouth barely worded, head dipping down to find the source of that pain and betrayal.

Cressida only blinked with her gorgeous neutral features, as if no feeling passed through her heart. She only stepped back and looked at him, analysing what she had done, looking at the wound that had started gushing dark rivers of blood. My friend tilted her head and watched as Rhylan lost his balance, his body falling to the floor, no doubt succumbing to the pain and the sharpness of the wound. She then shook her head slightly.

"Not enough," my sister allowed a grimace to form, then kneeled in front of Rhylan.

"Cressida," I stepped closer to them, part of me wanting to protect Rhylan. From the pain, from the betrayal. I did not know what hurt him more, if the wound that by this point coloured the rest of him in crimson or the fact that its cause came to be from the love of his life.

The love of this life, at least.

My friend did not even acknowledge me as she kneeled in front of her husband and bent to find his eyes, to see him panting, so broken and damaged. She touched his face, gently, with a delicate motion, as if wanting to caress the ache away, cupping his jaw and allowing her fingers to fall to his neck, down the unbuttoned top of his shirt and even lower, towards his chest and finally, to the dagger that remained clutched in between his ribs.

"It's not enough, is it? Not when you deserve so much more."

With that, her hand moved like a flash, and I barely had time to react when she removed the dagger from his flesh, taking along with it a stream of gore and hurt, only to change the location of the weapon's resting place into his chest. I saw her hand sliding backward, finding the momentum she needed to pierce through bone and as soon as I spotted the blade pierce right through his chest, I screamed.

"Cressida, stop! Please, just stop!"

I ran to Rhylan and wrapped my hands around his shoulders, just in time to feel how he lost control of his weight and had to lean into me, forcing me to fall to the ground alongside him. I would not let him go; I would not let her kill him.

"What the hell is wrong with you?" Before the question was even out of my mouth, my friend was surrounded by the fireling soldiers, who had remained in the room, as stunned as the rest of us. By the fact that Cressida kept trying to kill her husband, by the fact that he had not done a single thing to stop it.

"No..." he barely worded the command, "let her go. Evacuate the throne room at once."

"What? Why?" I squeezed his shoulders to make him change his mind, to make him take back that order, but the soldiers stepped back and turned simultaneously, with every intent to leave the room.

"No! No, stop! Come back!" I shouted, but my words were nothing but crumbled pieces of sound, deaf to their ears. "No, please help!" I shouted again, this time causing Cressida to smile.

"Are you going to die with him, princess?" my friend spoke, only it was not her voice at all. Those were not her eyes, that was not her soul, those were not her hands. Cressida wouldn't hurt anyone. Ever.

"There's not going to be any dying here, queen," it was Vikram who said it, his arms suddenly wrapping around Cressida's hand. I watched Ansgar do the same with the other one, both earthling princes keeping my friend trapped in their hold.

"Release me at once," she spoke. "Do not place your dirty fingers on me," she shouted again, trying to escape her new leash, but the two princes did not listen, only dragged her back, forcing her body to twist and contort in a way that was unnatural. Unhuman.

"Don't hurt her...please," Rhylan mumbled from within my arms, his body shaking and dripping blood everywhere, barely able to move. But somehow, his hand reached out to her.

The two brothers stopped, only for a moment to look at him, their eyes suddenly kinder, then they dipped their chin in agreement. No one said anything for a few seconds, Rhylan struggling to breathe, me barely able to hold him in a more upright position to keep that blood from fleeing his body and the two brothers holding my friend with sharpness and slight care, while she tried to jerk away in such abrupt movements, that I wondered how her bones were not broken yet.

"She's it, isn't she, Fear Gorta?" Cressida started screaming from the other side of the room, her voice raspy and uneven. "She is your weakness, she is the only one you will not touch."

"What the hell is wrong with her?" I didn't realise I had said the words out loud, until Rhylan wheezed a reply.

"Thelssha has her body."

Oh my god. Of course!

Cressi wouldn't hurt Rhylan like that, of course she would not behave like a psychotic lunatic. Of course, there had to be an explanation. That's why no one interfered, I realised. Because they did not want to hurt my friend, whose body had been trapped by that beast of a woman.

"I will kill her, I will kill her with my own hands," I said and squeezed him reassuringly, letting him know that this would not be the end. That the sirens couldn't just come barging in here, use whomever they wanted to and expect things to be normal again.

"We can't," Rhylan shook his head and tried to tilt it to reach my gaze. "We cannot risk hurting Cress."

My heart broke for him. Having him in my arms, so broken, trembling with pain and betrayal and still, trying to protect the one he loved. I felt a rush inside me, I felt my chest palpitating and demanding the words to come out. The feeling I was experiencing and needed to share.

"I fucking love you, you know?" I sniffled, sudden tears sprouting down my lashes. "I don't know why, because you are an absolute bastard, but I love you."

He chuckled, then started coughing, no doubt caused by that blade still stuck in his chest.

"You drive me mad every single day, sprout, but I wouldn't change you for the world. I love you too."

"What a beautiful family reunion…"

This time, another voice came from behind us, carrying the same rage and disgust. I looked at Cressida to see that Marreth had joined the band and the three of them tried to place a chain around Cressida's waist, while she struggled to break free.

"Amara, stop. Please, don't do this," I instantly shifted and spotted the windling princess, a foot away from us, gripping another dagger. Did everyone have a dagger all of a sudden?

"Amara, stop!" I shouted. Hopefully, enough to make the boys hear us, to make at least one of them aware of the new threat and hope they would be here in time. "Amara, please, this is not you, it's that fucking queen, please, just stop. Don't do it."

I don't know what possessed me, but I released Rhylan's body and tried to push him away. He could not move much so he fell to the ground like a sack of potatoes. But instead of running, instead of fighting her, I opened my arms, I tried to make myself a guard and cover her view of Rhylan with my own body. Hoping she would not reach him. Hoping she would not sacrifice someone else to get to her goals.

I was wrong.

Amara smiled. "His heir makes for a nice payment against the life you took."

And with that, Amara shoved the blade into me.

My stomach twisted, trying to get away from the incoming blade or to soften the blow. All those techniques that Rhylan had tried to drill into me during training came to mind. How I could shift my energy into creating a shield, how to tighten my muscles to make any injury hurt less, how to stop an incoming shot. I did not know how my mind reacted, how my body followed, but I found myself on the floor, with the blade making a deep cut into my right side.

In front of me, a curtain of darkness pulled Amara to the ground, her body falling with the same thump as Rhylan's hand did behind me, leaving an adamant spear pierced through her heart.

"Amara?" my voice shook, trembling with what was right in front of me. With what I witnessed. "Amara?" I asked again, the words barely a whimper compared to the hurricane of howls that came from the other side of the room. From Marreth's throat.

I started crying, pushing myself back, trying to get away from the blood that kept gushing out of her chest, out of that wound pierced by the crystal spear. It could not touch me, I would not have it near me.

I pushed back, pushed back into Rhylan, whose injuries kept bleeding, I was trapped between new and old blood, trapped between dead and dying. Because that's what Amara was. Dead.

I couldn't see it; I couldn't see her like this.

I kept pushing back.

No, no it could not be.

I didn't realise that my own body kept shivering until Ansgar was by my side, catching me in his arms, moving me away from Rhylan whose hand still shook. Who still bared marks of that crystal spear he had sent into our friend.

To save me.

To keep me from sharing the same fate.

No, no it couldn't be.

Marreth kept yelling, ordering Amara to wake up, shouting at her and shaking her shoulders, begging her body to revive, to retake the functions it used to hold only seconds ago.

"Anwen…" I felt Ansgar squeeze me tighter, suddenly aware of the injury piercing right above my hip, of the dagger that still remained tucked into bone.

"Anwen…" another voice, a guiltier one said my name, forcing those waves of darkness, the same ones he had used to resurface through me.

I grabbed at the dagger stuck in between muscle and pulled it out in a single movement, while pushing Ansgar back.

Away. Away from him.

The blade pointed to Rhylan, my wrist trembling, my fingers barely able to hold onto the hilt.

"You stay away! Stay away from us!" I shouted at Rhylan, tears making me choke.

I couldn't look. Couldn't look at Amara, couldn't see that limp body of the princess, of the person who had become my friend, whom I had shared so much with.

She wasn't breathing. She couldn't breathe anymore.

Never again.

I needed to protect Ansgar, I needed to take him away.

His hands wrapped around me, suddenly focused on my hip, on the wound that kept making everything wet. My pants were wet, my left thigh was wet.

Ansgar kept pressing onto me, preventing me to move, shouting at me not to, but all I wanted was to get away from Rhylan.

He couldn't hurt Ansgar too.

I would not let him.

Ansgar

Chapter Thirty-One

Anwen shook in my arms, the shock quivering her entire body. She kept pointing the dagger she pulled out of her own flesh at Rhylan, who could barely breathe, barely defend himself against the gushing wound in his chest and the terror of his own actions.

He did not want to do it.

That, at least, was obvious in his gaze. So lost and unaware, still not able to process what had truly happened. What he had to do to protect his daughter.

And for the first time ever, I realized how much Anwen meant to him. How much he cared about her, not just as his kin, his heir, but her as a person, as a friend even. Because the way he looked at my mate, with so much guilt and desperation, was the look of a male who knew would never find forgiveness.

I tried to shout her name, to call her to me but she was obsessed. She kept threatening Fear Gorta with that small dagger, one that was not enough to permanently wound him, but one that would break him and rip his energy apart. And I prayed.

Prayed to anyone who would listen, to any goddess that still remained trapped in this chaos to help us, to prevent the siren queen from taking my mate too.

To spare Anwen from all of this.

Because, just like Rhylan had, I would do anything to protect her.

There was so much screaming that my ears buzzed with what sounded like centuries of howls, all trapped within the same room. All floating in the air and crawling under my skin.

Cressida continued shouting insults and threats to her husband and king, uttering phrases that would break even the heart of a statue, while Anwen shouted at Rhylan from deep within my arms, asking him to stay away. Demanding to put distance in between us. She kept pushing me back, not realizing that we were already trapped by the side of the wall with no other place to go but forward. Anwen kept pushing into me, kept trying to get away from a shaking Rhylan, covered in blood.

Marreth wailed in pain, holding his lover in his arms and screaming, pleading for her return. The commander cupped her face and kept kissing her while his dripping tears started to clean the blood specks on her face, without wanting to look further down, to see that line of adamant block that pierced through her heart, to see all the dark blood that had been released underneath her armor and down her legs.

He did not want to do it. I knew this. We all did. We all saw how he tried to take Anwen away, how he tried to shift her from the line of the weapon and how Amara had pushed herself into his power, into that cloud of darkness that ended up spiking through her heart.

He only wanted to defend his daughter.

"AMARA!" Marreth's screams did not stop for minutes, desperately calling for her return, shivering hands trying to touch her face, her shoulders, trying to make her react and come back to him.

Vikram had managed to keep Cressida trapped and covered her mouth with his palm, allowing her to release only muffled sounds but he too looked utterly destroyed. My brother hadn't known Amara long, they only met on the frugal occasions we had to discuss strategy and future plans, yet his tears responded to her pain.

Same as mine.

I lost a friend. I lost a dear friend.

"YOU!" the commander's voice shifted, flourishing with sudden determination, the need for revenge taking hold of him. Amara's body remained limp on the ground while Marreth caught strength in his legs, raising his fury towards Rhylan. "You will pay for this!"

"Marreth..." the broken fire king's voice came out broken, barely audible, the sorrow in his tone a calling for forgiveness.

"Don't even dare speak! Do not even dare find an excuse for what you did. YOU KILLED HER!" the commander yelled, his steps coming dangerously close to Rhylan, who, having nothing to defend himself with, not wanting to summon his power again, ripped the dagger from his own flesh and pointed it to his friend, just like Anwen had done minutes ago.

"Don't come near us," I heard her scream, still shaking and

trapped in my hold, that shivering hand still gripping the blade. I knew there would be no use, if either of them decided to come our way, she would be unable to defend us with that small dagger.

It calmed her to have a weapon in her hand. To think that she was defending me. Us. So, I let her, all the while making sure she was safe.

We focused on Marreth, who continued his march towards Rhylan, watching how the new king did not move, did not make a gesture to defend himself but remained limp, bleeding into the ground, heavy breaths wheezing out of his lungs. The commander did not stop, unyielding and relentless, nourished with hatred and loss. Ready to strike.

I found my body shifting involuntarily, letting Anwen go from my arms, listening to her scream for me to come back as my steps led me towards them, forcing me to stand in between Marreth's need for revenge and Rhylan's urgency for forgiveness.

My fingers dropped the sword I carried, signaling to the commander that I had no intention to fight, the sound of metal dropping on the marble floor making his gaze sharpen, his body to stiffen and look at me.

"Don't…" I tilted my head slowly, making him understand my request. "Marreth, don't…" I said again, stretching my back to cover Fear Gorta out of his sight, just like Anwen had done from Amara.

"Move away, Ansgar. Move away or I'll have to go through you," the commander threatened, no sign of my friend remaining in his dark eyes.

"You won't. You will not stain Amara's sacrifice with more

bloodshed," I begged him, forcing my voice to come out as even as my throat allowed it.

He stopped, the words capturing my intended meaning. A deep sigh overpowered him, a gust of pain crawling a new path into his spirit.

Marreth fell on his knees, sobbing like a youngling would. Shouting around a crumbling world.

"I lost her…I lost her again," the defeated warrior cried, his once sturdy hands shaking like leaves in the October winds.

I let myself reach my friend, kneeled alongside him and grabbed his shoulders to prevent him from crumbling down. My hands felt his lungs expand with the newly acquired pain, a sentiment they would now have to carry for the rest of his life. His chest pumped with desperation, blood having to carry a life without love in his heart.

"I lost her," Marreth cried again, his fingernails scraping through the marble floor. Abruptly, his breath stopped. Eyes lifted, finding a new target.

"It is all her fault," he pointed a threatening gaze towards Cressida, who remained trapped in Vikram's arms, chained to one of the pillars.

Anwen

Chapter Thirty-Two

No, no, no, this was not happening to me again. Not again. I had to get him away, I had to get him away from danger. I would not lose Ansgar again, not again.

I had to protect him, I had to...

Sprout. The voice pierced through my skull, shoving itself into my mind, an unwelcome intrusion.

Get the fuck away from me, I instantly thought, sending my message against adamant sculpted columns, forcing the words to gush away, the contact to stop. I did not want him in my mind, I did not want him anywhere near me.

Sprout, he came back. *Sprout, please listen. Calm your breath and listen. You are in shock.*

"I said get the fuck away!" I shouted, out loud this time, hearing how the echo of my voice travelled in waves of darkness that I did not mean to release. They were going towards Ansgar, towards Marreth and Rhylan.

No, no, no, no. I stopped. I took a breath. I urged them to vanish. They did.

That was very good, princess. Try to keep your calm, we do not want any kind of accidents again. Too much blood has already been spilled.

Fuck you, you fucking murderer. You criminal. Get the fuck away from my mind!

Anwen...

You killed Amara, you son of a bitch. I was glad this was just a thought, just a mind-to-mind word exchange because I could not have said it out loud. I could not have heard myself admitting it, the sound of my voice somehow making it true. Taking all the hope away.

Anwen... Rhylan came back to my mind and for some reason, my eyes darted to him. To where he sat on the ground, fallen and injured, to where Ansgar was still standing in front of him, shielding him with his own body against Marreth, just like I had done with Amara minutes before.

Had it only been minutes?

Only minutes since we lost our friend? Our ally?

That was not Amara, it was one of the sirens. In Amara's body. And she was aiming for your heart, sprout.

My heart, I huffed. The bastard had the nerve to lie to me, even now. To make me think that this reasoning would somehow be justified? Because he wanted to defend me, he had to kill her?

My mind went blank. I tried to remember, tried to take memories back to that moment. I forced the image in front of my eyes, Amara's dagger, the way I shifted to protect Rhylan, the way I stood and how she pierced the blade...

I saw Amara's hand, coming from above, coming straight to my chest, but somehow, she only reached my hip, somehow, I turned, I shifted to protect myself.

I shifted to protect myself. Only I hadn't. In the hundreds of hours of training, I hadn't managed to do it once. Not one time. So, I couldn't have instantly done it via muscle memory, there was no such thing.

I remembered the murmur of darkness whispering into me, shifting my body, I remembered spikes of adamant and blood. I remembered Rhylan's reaction as soon as the clouds vanished. His dread. His horror.

You did not mean to do it. You didn't do it on purpose.

"It's all her fault," I heard a shout, the accusation finding a stance into the newly crimson coloured marble floor.

Marreth.

Marreth was going after Cressida.

Cressida, who was still trying to break free, a desperate Vikram struggling to hold her in place. Cressida, who was not my friend right now, just like Amara wasn't. She was a vessel, used for purposes beyond our control. Used for revenge.

And Marreth's fury was aiming towards her.

"No, Marreth, no, please," I heard myself say, my legs stumbling and trying to find their hold, trying and failing to give me enough strength to rise and protect my sister.

Cressida could not be an accident.

"Marreth, no!" I said again, shouted, screamed, tried to get to him through the sound of my voice, my hands reaching out for him.

A line of darkness escaped my fingers.

And another one.

They tied around Marreth's feet, cords that I could use and control, preventing him from moving forwards, from reaching my friend. His dark eyes turned to me, oblivious of my existence.

Then, with a single flowing motion, he cut through them. Ansgar's sword somehow got in his hand. Or was it his own sword? I did not know, did not care as I tried again, this time strengthening the lines into thick rope, using night, magic and fear to interweave and wrap around his legs, around his waist, raising to his chest and tying up both of his arms.

"Anwen!" he shouted, fury screeching out of him as he tried to squeeze and scratch his way out. I felt the pain, just like I had when he cut those first lines, it was coming back to me, through the hold I had on that power. It became sentient, a part of me that he was struggling to hurt, to cut through, to break.

Ansgar was suddenly there, disarming the commander, taking away his sword and placing his arms around his friend, cupping his jaw and speaking things I could not possibly hear. That I forced my ears not to listen to.

I allowed my attention to move to Vikram, just enough to see that he was already in a fighting stance, waiting for the blow Marreth was supposed to bring, his legs stretched wide, knees slightly bent and sword out, that beautiful armor he always wore ready to take the blow.

"Marreth," Rhylan stood somehow, covering that open wound with the palm of his hand and commanding the blood to stop escaping his veins. He walked slowly, barely placing his steps, away from the place where he had been laying,

Where Amara's body still remained.

Limp and damaged.

Her armor looked twisted, scarred by the rain of crystal spikes it had received, tiny cracks lining the entirety of her chest, her arms and the pieces of metal that covered her legs. Her hair, once braided and arranged for battle, now fell limp, so different to the golden locks she had always loved to display, dry and lifeless.

Her hand rested on the marble floor, distant and far away from her body, her fingers remaining in an awkward stance, some of them twisted in a way that looked unnatural, unhuman.

An avalanche of blood had possessed her body, digging away from her torso, from where a massive crystal bolt remained embedded into her chest, making her back arch past its ability to accommodate the blow.

She had once been a rival. I spent her entire wedding day hating her, jealousy taking everything I owned. She had then become an ally, helping Ansgar and I on every occasion. And she had become a friend. In the month that we all spent together in Canada, she cooked, she shared stories, she laughed and she danced, she loved passionately and she dared to dream.

My brain could not piece together the pathway we had followed to get to this moment, where one of us gave their life. Where one of us would not return to the life we had involuntarily planned, dreaming of our freedom.

"Marreth," Rhylan said again, his limping motions finally reaching the commander. "Please…"

Words I never expected to hear from Rhylan's mouth, a word

that he seemed to utter to mark the passage of each minute. Every time his voice becoming more estranged, more broken and damaged.

Ansgar stopped speaking, letting Marreth's ears gain a break until Rhylan prepared what he had to say. My prince continued to support the commander's body, his friend's body. They had been inseparable in the past few months, during training, through the kingdoms we had visited, and I knew their friendship had started long ago.

Only the roles were reversed then, Ansgar being the one lost and afraid, my prince now turning into an unshakable pillar.

"Marreth, I did not mean to... you have to understand. It was...she's my daughter..."

A shiver crawled down my spine. His daughter. Rhylan had done it for me, to defend me. To take me away from that killing blow Amara prepared to bring.

To save me.

Because I was his *daughter.*

I never expected to hear those words from his mouth, never thought that he would be the one to acknowledge our connection, especially when we spent our life bickering and cursing at one another with every chance we got. But he was my family.

I felt it, I knew it, the words I had said not so long before rang true in my heart.

"Very well then. It was an accident," Marreth's voice echoed on the brink of summoning thunder. "Then you will not mind if another accident happens. Right, king?" The last word flew like an arrow into Rhylan's chest, with every intention to hurt, to damage.

"Marreth, you don't have to do this. It will not bring her back, trust me brother." It was Ansgar this time, still holding Marreth's shoulders, elbows pushing into his chest with a grip firm enough to help sustain the commander's body weight.

"He killed mine, so I will kill his!"

"That is youth's talk, that is nonsense. Marreth!" Ansgar pushed again. "What are you turning into, commander? Do you want to become a fireling? Do you want to become a female killer? Is that who you are now? Is it?"

Every word drilled into Marreth, everything that Ansgar said finding its mark. Into his chest. Into his arms. Into his body.

His knees suddenly crumbled, forcing the tall male to fall down in defeat, making his fingers unwrap from the weapon he had squeezed with so much hatred, with the need for revenge.

Understanding dawned on him.

There was nothing he could do, there was nothing anyone could do to bring Amara back and hurting Cressi would only cause more damage.

Ansgar was instantly by Marreth's side, kneeling in front of his friend, nursing the pain that threatened to take away his will to live.

Meanwhile, Cressida struggled in Vikram's hold. Struggled so much that from time to time clinks of shattered bone resounded into the room. Her body contorted in ways I had never seen before, trying to pull her own bones out of their sockets, trying to hurt and damage the insides of her own body. If she could not go free, she would do as much damage as possible from the location she had been forced into.

"Please, stop hurting her!" Rhylan shouted, just when Cressida's shoulder popped out, piercing through her damaged dress and created a lump near her neck, her veins swollen and flesh ripping apart.

"Please, stop!" Rhylan took a few more steps and fell on his knees in front of Cressida. In front of the siren queen. Her body instantly calmed, my friend gaining a new attitude. She blinked at Rhylan with interest, the purpose of hurting her own body long forgotten.

"Please, let her speak. We need to end this," Rhylan tried, this time addressing Vikram, who still held my friend trapped. Trapped in chains, trapped in his arms, trapped within the marble of the column holding her prisoner.

"Are you sure?" the earthling prince asked and as soon as Rhylan nodded, he released Cressida's mouth who shook away from his hold, gazing at the prince with disgust.

"I never understood what my sister sees in you."

"And I will never understand what she saw in you, to stand by your side and waste her life away," Vikram retorted, then turned to scan the room, taking in his surroundings. He first checked Marreth and Ansgar, both of them sat on the ground, Ansgar still grabbing hold of his friend, then he found the pool of blood and Amara's body, his eyes filling with sorrow.

Then he finally gazed at me and started taking determined steps in my direction.

"It will all be over soon," Vikram said while he threw his body next to mine and grabbed me in an embrace. I didn't know if he needed the warmth or if I was still shaking but having someone hold me felt better than expected.

"What will happen to Cressi?" I asked below my breath, eyes too focused on Rhylan and the insults he was powering through.

"The queen needs to release her, there is no other way," Vikram spoke, tilting his head back to look at the woman he had guarded for this long.

"Thelssha, please. Whatever you want, it is yours. Just stop hurting her," Rhylan pleaded, his hands trying to reach his wife, who still shifted away from his embrace, not willing to accept his touch.

Cressida stopped then, blinked a couple of times as if trying to read the truth in her husband's words. My friend took a deep breath before she slammed herself against the wall, forcing her shoulder back into place. No sound escaped her mouth, not even a grimace to acknowledge the pain.

"A gesture of good will," she tilted her head slowly, then fluttered her eyelashes at Rhylan.

"Thank you," his voice came out ruffled, grim, expecting the worst.

"Now, you do the same and release me. Remove these dreadful chains from your lover's skin, can't you see they are hurting her?"

Rhylan nodded, then moved to release Cressi, ripping the chains around her with his bare hands. He did not use his power, which would have done the job without him having to move a finger. He did not dare use his power again, I came to realize. Not when the last time he had tried to protect someone, it ended up taking an innocent life.

Cressi stretched her back and rolled her neck, allowing us all to witness the song of her cracking bones.

"Much better," she nodded to Rhylan, who remained in front of her, observing Cressida. Observing what the queen planned to do to his wife's body.

"Now, kneel," she demanded, recuperating that sweet, melodious tone.

I couldn't believe my eyes.

Without even a protest, without a snarky remark or one of the insults that had become so familiar to him, to all of those around him, Rhylan did as commanded and pressed his knees to the floor, head bowing before the siren queen.

Cressi smiled, visibly pleased with herself.

"Finally, you learn your place."

"What is it that you want, Thelssha? Ask it and be done with this."

"Oh, no, Fear Gorta. This is about what you want, what you've always wanted." Cressi started pacing around him, pressing her steps in such a way that her voice echoed perfectly around the room, as if she wanted us all to hear her command. To hear the request we all seem to need to follow in order to get Cressi back.

"You want the world to go back to the way it was. You want a life before the kingdoms gained their powers. You want retribution."

Rhylan nodded, chin touching his chest, head bowed so low that I finally had a chance to spot the line of tattoos flowing down his neck. Symbols I never understood, symbols I never cared enough to ask about.

"I'll do anything, queen. All I want is my wife back," he murmured, so low that his words turned to smoke before they reached the room.

"Very well, Fear Gorta. I shall release your wife. I shall release her as soon as you open Belgarath's tomb."

"It is done," he instantly nodded, then turned towards Ansgar and Marreth, who remained a few steps behind.

"Get away from the throne," Rhylan demanded, his tone gaining more command with every sound he uttered.

Ansgar did as told and stood, forcing Marreth to come along. The commander wobbled on shaky feet but listened to my mate and they slowly walked towards the wall, away from the throne. Only Marreth stopped, turning suddenly.

"No…" he spoke, the sound broken and void. "No, I will not leave her," he said again, then shifted towards Amara's body. "I will not leave her," he repeated and started walking back, feet heavy and dragging until he reached her limp body.

"I will not leave her," he said again as he kneeled and grabbed her in his arms, struggling to reach her with the crystal still embedded in her chest. Ansgar was instantly there, helping Marreth drag Amara's body away and towards the side of the room, close to where Vikram and I remained.

Only when we had all reached safety, Ansgar's hand wrapping in my own and Marreth shedding silent tears over his lover's hair that Rhylan turned back to the queen to nod.

"It shall be done," he announced and, with a deep expansion of his chest, which poured more blood from the wound that did not seem to close, the fire king summoned the night.

This time it was focused, line after line of energy pouring into the throne, the enormous marble seat situated at the very centre of the room, carved by centuries of history and bloodshed.

Night, darkness and onyx strands poured into it, Rhylan pushing more and more of his power until we all heard an explosion, along with a shout that reverberated across the room.

Darkness did not go away.

Smoke created a curtain where the throne used to lie, now shattered pieces of marble and...a massive hole seeped into the floor, scorching the entire room, the temperature suddenly emanating so much heat, it started to burn our skin.

"It is done, you have it. The centre of the earth," he turned back to Cressi. "Now give me back what is mine," he begged again, defeated, tired and powerless.

"You will destroy the tomb, Fear Gorta. There will be no more gods, there will be no more tears. Each kingdom shall start anew. That is my condition."

Cressida smiled then, pleased with herself, with the demand she had uttered, because Rhylan looked absolutely destroyed. She had won.

The siren queen won.

"It is not only up to me..." Rhylan finally said, his head suddenly turning to us, to where we sat with hands raised, trying to protect our faces from the unbearable heat.

"Will it stop the war? Do you swear to remain in your own

kingdom?" It was Ansgar who spoke, surprising us all.

Cressida dipped her chin. "I do, prince."

Then Ansgar nodded. Nodded towards Rhylan. But instead of taking the agreement with joy, Rhylan's gaze propelled pity. His eyes filled with sorrow, with the impossibility of his task. And he looked at Ansgar, at all of us, as if we too would be sharing the same feelings very soon.

"The rest are to remain unharmed and free," he demanded.

"Better yet, Fear Gorta," Cressida threw him a mischievous smile. "I will even give you time to say your goodbyes."

"We are in agreement then."

"Farewell, Fear Gorta," Cressi smiled again and waved a hand nonchalantly to Rhylan. She then took a step back, keeping her pleased smile for a while longer, before her entire expression turned to stone. No feeling lined her body, no movement in her muscles, no sign of life.

"Sunshine," Rhylan spoke softly, struggling to stand, to get closer to her.

Cressida blinked. Once. Twice, looking around the room. Taking in her surroundings.

"Rhy?"

Cressi blinked again, suddenly filled with worry at the sight of him. This was my friend, I recognized the sound of her voice, the kindness in her features, that unconditional love her eyes always displayed for Rhylan.

"Sunshine," he reached for her with shaky hands, with crumbling powers, with the last shred of hope. "Sunshine," he said again, wrapping Cressi in an embrace, shaking with the arduous need for connection.

I finally allowed myself to breathe and squeezed Ansgar's hand tighter, letting myself to shift my eyes towards him and display a small smile. It felt so inappropriate, so out of place, but somehow, I had to do it.

Hope took seed inside my heart, and I needed to share it with my mate.

Only his features were tense, raw, filled with something I could not understand. Worry and pain and…something else, something I did not know how to read. Ever since Rhylan had agreed to destroy the tears, Vikram and Ansgar had remained tense, as if struck by the command of the queen and Vikram kept trying to reach his brother, kept trying to speak, but Ansgar did not allow him to, fully focused on Cressida's release.

Now, however, the middle prince did not shy away from uttering his feelings.

"You are not seriously considering this?"

No answer.

"Ansgar! You are not doing this!"

I turned to Vikram to find him looking at me, through me, desperately trying to reach his brother's suddenly deaf ears.

"Anwen, tell him!" He tried again, this time shoving me into his brother's arms, as if forcing him to grab hold of me might change something about this decision, the promise Rhylan had made. As if feeling our connection would change Ansgar's mind.

I started to get worried.

"Ansgar, what is happening?"

Only then he turned, my words gaining the reaction Vikram's had failed to achieve.

"Nothing we need to worry about right now, fahrenor," he pressed his lips in the weakest attempt of a smile I had ever seen, then planted a kiss on my temple. "I love you," he spoke softly, as if the words hurt coming out of his mouth.

"Ansgar!" Vikram shouted again, trying to get to his brother and taking me along if he needed to, using me as a shield to clear up whatever this confusion was.

"Vikram... please!" I heard Ansgar's tense tone. "Do not make this harder than it is."

His eyes looked stormy, lost, scanning for something...they were filled with loss, but I could not understand why. We were here, we were safe, we could go home.

We had Cressi back.

Leaving Vikram's tension behind, I focused my attention back to Cressida and Rhylan, to their embrace, to the multiple kisses and caresses they shared, to their happy faces. Happy to be together again. Happy to find each other in this falling kingdom.

Happy...

The feeling remained so distant, yet, within reach. We could be happy. We could get away from this and return home. With immense loss, with our hearts heavy.

But we could go home.

By the time we reached Cressi and Rhylan, my friend started shedding tears, no doubt learning about Amara and what had happened. Rhylan tried to calm her down, tried to place soothing caresses on her but the shock was too great, and Cressida's tears did not stop.

"Sunshine, we need to talk. Please..." Rhylan said, desperately trying to calm her down. I wrapped my arms around her and squeezed her in an embrace, telling her that it was okay, that we would all be okay, that she was finally free, and we could all leave this behind.

We could return home.

This was over.

It was over.

Rhylan and Ansgar tensed, with a very unhappy Vikram trailing behind them. I didn't understand what the hell was happening, and we really needed to get out of here because the heat Rhylan had opened up from that throne scorched our skins to the point of becoming painful.

"If the tears don't bring back the gods, can they return life?" Cressi's voice caressed our ears with the idea.

"We can definitely try," Rhylan said, gazing at Ansgar for approval.

This dynamic had shifted so abruptly that I did not have a chance to process it. Rhylan, asking Ansgar for permission. Twice now.

"We can try," my mate nodded. "We can try," he said again, looking at Marreth, whose eyes lit up, cascading with hope.

Ansgar

Chapter Thirty-Three

Calm down, calm down, calm down.

I could not start thinking about it right now, not when there was still so much left to live. Not when Anwen was smiling at me, newly found hope in her eyes.

Not when my mate told me she loved me.

I still had time.

We still had time.

And I had to make the most of it. If I could try and bring our friend back, then that was the immediate focus of my full attention.

We could try to use the tears that had brought us so much sorrow, so much pain and had broken every dream we had hoped to follow. If at least this part proved to be true, it was not all for nothing.

"I need a knife," I turned to Rhylan, then to Marreth and my brother, hoping that one of them still held their weapons. We were all gathered around Rhylan and Cressida, the two unable to stop sharing that embrace.

I knew why, I understood Rhylan's reasons for not caring about anything else.

I would soon have to do the same.

But not yet.

I forced my mind to be strong, to reinforce the self-imposed pillars that still kept me up, still kept my back straight and prevented my legs from shaking. I had to do this.

Marreth passed me a dagger with shaky hands, then he asked Vikram's help to bring Amara's body back to us.

I watched how the two struggled to carry our friend, her body limp and damaged through the scorching heat, to the curtain of smoke that had started to dance across the room, filling it with shadow and doom. One that we would soon have to embrace.

My eyes darted to Anwen, her gaze serene, finally relaxed, looking at me in awe as if I was the main source of her happiness.

I swallowed a dry lump.

Not yet, Ansgar, not yet. Do not break down just yet. Do not take her with you.

Not until we brought Amara back. I had to focus, I had to keep that shy smile on Anwen's face for as long as I could, for as long as time allowed.

Rhylan kept squeezing Cressida in his arms, kept pressing kisses on her cheek, on her skin, her neck, shoulders. He could not stop. He could not let her go. Bastard.

"Ready," Marreth and Vikram said in unison as soon as Amara's body returned to our proximity. Marreth had removed his shirt and covered her wound, the crystal spear now out of her chest. I appreciated the gesture, the care he showed to his lover, even now.

"Rhylan, your help is needed," I demanded, pure jealousy striking through me. I needed to be doing the same, I needed to spend every second with my mate.

No. No. Not yet.

"I'm ready, prince," he spoke, finding strength within himself to release Cressida from his hold and step closer to us, to where Amara laid.

As soon as he nodded, showing his readiness to offer help, maybe for the first time in his life, I prepared myself for the pain that was to come. I shoved the dagger into my biceps, cutting and rummaging through muscle until the blade crushed against the crystal, showing its location.

"Oh my god, baby..." Anwen covered her face with her hands, muffling her whimper at the sight of what I was doing. My fahrenor, always taking care of me. Always feeling my pain as if it was hers.

Only it did not hurt, not this time. Not when I knew what was coming. I even embraced the pain, the tingling sensations of my muscles parting, the screech of my bone against the knife. As soon as the blade touched the crystal, I shoved it deeper, cutting through skin and tilting the dagger, trying to push the tear out.

After a couple attempts, a small lump came out from my muscle, a speck of light filled with blood that took our breaths away.

"Is that it?" Anwen whispered in awe, her voice a song of amazement.

"Let us hope it fulfils its purpose," I replied, reaching out with the tear still in my hand and offering it to Marreth.

The commander blinked, his hands shaking, not knowing what

to do. Neither of us did.

"Maybe it works better if it's coming from a place of love?" Cressi asked from behind Rhylan, her hands wrapped around his waist, peaking through the side of his shoulders, not wanting to let herself see the entirety of the gore Amara had been through.

Marreth nodded and kneeled again, placing himself next to his lover, the tear still shining in his hand. With shaky fingers, he removed the cover, letting Amara's wound become visible, the hole in her chest piercing through and creating ripples of pain within us all.

"I love you, please come back to me," he said to her, voice trembling and eyes filled with tears before he dropped the crystal into her chest, letting the light fill the cracks that used to be Amara's heart.

"Please come back to me," he said again, grabbing her body tighter in his hold, hands wrapping around her shoulder and waist, trapping her in an embrace.

Rhylan raised a hand as a rain of darkness peeled through, so focused and ready, like small beads of energy that floated through us, around us, all of them swimming to the princess, towards the tear shining in her chest.

A second later, the light exploded, Amara becoming an ember of energy, her body jolting with the strength of Rhylan's power. Only for a second.

The tear was destroyed. Zaleen's energy floated down Amara's chest, making all of us hope. Plead. Beg.

"Please. Please my love, please come back to me."

Marreth kept uttering the words, the prayer repeated with religiousness. He did not stop, he did not stop for minutes, he did not stop until his throat became sore and until his tears dried out.

I watched the moment when each of us realized this too, had been a legend.

And like all legends, no truth came out of it. Rhylan was the first, stepping behind Cressida and wrapping her protectively in his arms. My brother was the second one, his eyes averting to me, realization dawning his features. Then Cressida gave up, turning from the weeping commander and into the protection of her king's arms.

Finally, Anwen lifted her teary eyes to me.

"It was all a lie," she said, voice shaking with remorse and just like Cressida, she found a haven in my arms. I allowed myself to feel it then. The dread, the loss, the sorrow.

Fear.

I was afraid.

One look at Rhylan's tight jaw and I knew. I knew it was time.

I sighed, our gazes locking, both of us holding the love of our lives to our chest.

"When did you know?"

"After you got Zaleen's tear," Rhylan smiled. Actually smiled at the ridicule of it all. "We had the tear right under our noses for the entire year…" he shook his head, those dark times now becoming obsolete. Fading in the light of the present.

Anwen's eyes lifted to me then.

"What are you talking about?"

But it was Rhylan who responded, his arms wrapping tighter

around his wife.

"It's the moment for goodbyes, prince."

I nodded, Fear Gorta following the same motion of agreement and releasing a disorientated Cressida from his hold. To step towards me, towards Anwen, who still remained in my arms.

I appreciated this final kindness, the sacrifice he made to release his love and not asking me to do the same yet.

"Sprout," he spoke softly, with kindness, as one does to a babe. He was close enough to grab Anwen's hand, making her shift in my arms, turning to face him.

"Rhylan, what the hell is happening?" my mate asked, the hand she kept locked on my back squeezing me tighter. Her desperation growing.

"Sprout," Rhylan repeated, without letting go of her hand. "You were brilliant. I could not have asked for a better heir. And I thank you for bringing me into your life, for offering me a chance at happiness. I hope your heart will mend and you will enjoy a long, happy life. You truly deserve it, princess," he smiled at her.

"Rhylan, what in the —"

Before she had a chance to speak, Rhylan uttered the words that would seal his fate. "I accept your blood as mine, your life as mine, your energy as my own. For we are one and the same."

Anwen's body stretched, ripping through our hold and releasing ages of night, of darkness, of power and wrath, all summoned back into Rhylan. The two remained enveloped in a whirlwind of obsidian, power and energy floating through them.

Until Anwen stepped back, panting heavily, her chest expanding with dread.

"What did you do?" she barely exhaled. "What did you do to me?"

But Rhylan did not reply. He would not say the word, he would not deliver the news.

I had to do that.

Taking advantage of the space, of the sudden freedom of my arms and not wanting to keep it for long, I turned to Vikram, who remained only a step away, watching the exchange of power with horror.

"Brother…" I tried to offer him a smile but only managed to give him my tears.

"Ansgar…no…" Vikram shook, his hands shaking, his eyes creating beautiful rivers of pain.

"I love you. I love you all so much. You have brought me so much happiness and joy. Please tell everyone, tell them…" my throat stopped, unable to share the words.

Unable to release them.

"I will," Vikram sniffled, grabbing me into a tight hold. "I will, my brother. I love you."

"Be happy, Vikram. You deserve it, more than anyone. Enjoy that stunning mate of yours and please…please take care of mine."

I felt him nod against my shoulder, tears preventing both of us from speaking.

"Go," he briskly released me. "Go to her, go."

I nodded, struggling to find a smile on my trembling face and stepped away from my brother.

I found Anwen gazing at me, abandoned in the centre of the room, her body wrapped in the smoke emanating from the open tomb.

"Fahrenor…"

"Ansgar! Ansgar, what is happening?" Her voice shook, her mind already realizing what her heart did not allow her to accept. From the other side of the room Cressida's screaming wails started to make a dent in our breaking hearts.

"Ansgar, what is happening?" Anwen cried again; her hands desperate to grab hold of me. As soon as I stepped to her, she cupped my face, caressed my jaw and wrapped her hands around my shoulders. Checking me, checking me for damage, checking me for wounds, not understanding what was developing right in front of her eyes.

"Fahrenor."

I took a deep breath, forcing my lungs to take their fill, to allow me to hold this conversation.

"The earthling royal family has a long-standing tradition, we call it the blessed rule of three. Births of a third heir are the most celebrated, though no one knows why."

My mate frowned, her hands shaking hard, filled with the panic caused by Cressida, whose sorrow resounded across the room, her hands wrapped around Rhylan's neck and desperately crying on his shoulder. I forced myself to continue.

"Only a member of the royal family, born or gained by alliance can be made aware of the information. If they tell anyone else, the goddess will claim their life for the betrayal. I tried, fahrenor, I tried to tell you so many times but…" I shook my head.

It didn't matter now. I felt the pull on my energy, the threat of what would happen should I release the words.

It did not matter.

"Catalina's tear is not a pearl or a crystal. It is a heart."

"What? Ansgar, what are you saying?" She blinked tears away, trying with desperation to cling onto my words. To understand what I was trying to say.

"We are the beginning and the end…" Anwen said then, her eyes wide. "That's what you said to me once. When I told you I had Rhylan's power…" She stopped. "Belgarath's power…."

"The beginning," I nodded. I was so proud of her. She had become a strong female, a fighter. And now, now she understood.

"Catalina was the last goddess," Anwen barely murmured. "The beginning and the end…Ansgar…Ansgar, no!" her fingernails shoved into my shoulders, piercing through my shirt and into my skin, begging for a firmer grip. Begging her to not let go.

"I am Catalina's tear, my love. And it needs to be destroyed," I swallowed again, fighting back tears.

"No, no, no, no, what are you saying? What are you saying? Ansgar, what are you saying?" She shook, her legs gave out, making both of us fall, our knees too weak to sustain this much sorrow.

"No, no, no, no please, no…" she started clawing at me, she started ripping through my shirt, grabbing at me as tightly as she could as if that would stop me from going.

"This is it fahrenor, this is all the time we get," I wrapped my arms around her, allowing my hands to feel her warmth for the last time. I leaned in to smell her hair, those undulated locks that always tickled my nose. I pressed a kiss on her head. And a few more. Unable to stop. Unable to let her go.

"Please, please, please," she kept saying, kept begging. "Ansgar please, I love you so much, please!"

I pulled her head back then, forced her to look at me, to let me see those beautiful hazel eyes once more.

"Fahrenor…"

"Ansgar, please!" she kept shouting, her pain overpowering Cressida's. Both of them broken. Both of them filled by the same loss.

"Anwen, my love. I would not have stopped loving you in a thousand lives and if I can love you after death, know that I always will. Always, fahrenor. Hie vaedrum teim."

"I love you.." she barely spoke, the words muttered and barely audible. "I love you," she said again, this time her voice becoming stronger, more determined. "I love you. I love you so much and I will not let you go. You won't do this. I won't let you," she kept saying, a promise she must have made to herself, her legs now wrapped around my body, her fingers still digging into me, trying to keep me with her, trying to keep me in her arms.

"I won't let you, I won't let you," she kept repeating, over and over and over.

"I love you, baby," I gave her another kiss, this time on her cheek, closer to her lips, through the tears that kept oozing out with such deep pain.

I looked at Vikram, pleading once again for his help.

I could not let her go, I could not force her away from me. I did not have the strength to do it.

My heart would not allow it.

Vikram was there in an instant, his hands tucked underneath Anwen's shoulders, slowly peeling her body away from mine.

"No! What are you doing, no!" she started shouting, screaming to be returned to me, her hands reaching out and grabbing onto me as hard as they could, with desperation and need.

"I love you, fahrenor," I said again, allowing myself a final caress. A final kiss.

A final dance of our lips, companions in sharing so much joy. One last kiss. That was all we had.

And I made the most of it.

But as soon as her arms relaxed on my shoulders, I allowed myself to get lost through their hold.

I took a step back, away from my mate. Away from the female that had brought me so much joy. That taught me how to love.

"Ansgar please!" Anwen started begging, her body fighting my brother's hold, both of them shedding tears.

I took another step from the life I had envisioned, from the children we wanted to have, from the dreams we had planned.

I took one step back from my future, from everything I could have accomplished, from the long happy life I had hoped to have.

I took a step away from her. From the love of my life.

From my mate.

I forced my ears to become deaf to her shouts, to her desperate screams begging me to return, to the cries and pain I knew I had caused. That I knew would follow her for a long time.

I met Rhylan at the edge of the earth, both of us looking down at the fire waiting to devour our bodies. To fulfil our promise and destroy all godly energies.

To bring the world back to its beginnings.

"Together, prince?" I heard Rhylan ask, his trembling shoulder telling me he too, was scared.

Scared to die.

Scared to stop existing.

Scared to give up the love that brought him happiness.

"Together, Rhylan," I replied.

We took that step, the step that would lead us to destruction. The step that would cover us in death.

Anwen.

My love.

My last thought.

The final beating of my heart.

Anwen.

Whether you want to continue crying or need a reason to smile, this is the place you need to be.

The last chapter is your choice, because these characters are as much yours as they are mine. Give them the ending of your choosing.

Read chapter 34A if you want to continue feeling the loss. Happiness awaits at chapter 34B.

Summer

Anwen

Chapter Thirty-Four – A

"Are you sure you don't want me to come with you?" Vikram asked for what felt like the millionth time, to which Cressi and I replied in unison.

"No."

"I can always go for a plane ride," Marreth said from behind him, trying to cheer us up.

Not that it worked.

Not that Cressi or me even remembered how to smile.

We had cried until there were no more tears. Sometimes together, sometimes separately, the truth was still the same.

We were alone.

There was no joy left in the world.

So we cried, we passed out from crying, then we woke up and cried again. It sort of became our living cycle.

And I would be sure to follow it.

No matter what I did, no matter where I was, I kept returning to that room. Seeing Ansgar smile his final goodbye before stepping into that pit of fire.

I had fought with flesh and blood to get myself free from

Vikram's hold, but without Rhylan's powers, I had turned back into a useless human. One that could not do anything but watch her mate die.

And cry about it.

All of us were destroyed really, all of us had suffered massive losses. A brother, a lover, a friend.

I don't remember the rest of the day. I don't even remember the rest of the week.

Vikram was there for a long time, then Takara came in, trying to convince me to return to the kingdom.

I refused.

Marreth, to his credit, directed all of his pain into healing, into regrowing what was lost. The commander became leader of the Fire Kingdom, with the full support of the soldiers, the court and mine and Cressida's.

Neither of us even thought about the responsibilities we suddenly had, neither of us were capable of doing anything but suffer and split from the gushing pain.

So Marreth took over.

He rebuilt the throne room, sealing Belgarath's tomb shut. It took days of hard work, days of drilling and pouring rock and powder into that life-claiming hole, but he managed to cover it. He even managed to rebuild the throne room to its exact replica.

He asked us to come and see it.

We refused.

We wanted nothing to do with the place where love goes to die.

We soon came to realize that without Ansgar and Rhylan, we

wanted nothing to do with the faerie world.

The mermaids kept their promise, Water Kingdom sent a new treaty to ensure all borders were kept and no alliances were made in the future in an attempt to overthrow one of the kingdoms, wanting to establish new trading routes and better cooperation between the regnums.

I did not care. It was the least they could do after taking my mate away.

Every day I woke up full of hatred, full of loss and sorrow and wondering what was the point of living.

What was the point of trying to have a life without Ansgar in it.

When I told Cressida this, she made the decision to go back home, saying that it was finally time to cut our ties with the fae.

I had no feelings towards the matter, so I agreed.

We asked Marreth to arrange our departure, to prepare everything he needed for us to renounce our official titles in the kingdom and he reluctantly, after much arguing and trying to make us reconsider, did so.

Vikram came to help us jump out and to say his goodbyes, making me, of course, cry again.

He brought me news from home, as he called it. Eidothea was feeling better, slowly getting used to her new life, Takara's babe started to kick. I did not ask about the rest. I did not want to think about them, how they might be feeling after losing a son or a brother.

"We wish you both happiness. I am thankful for your assistance and help through this time, I couldn't have done it on my own. If you ever need anything, I will be happy to return the favour." Cressi said her goodbyes, then shared a quick hug with the each of them and went up the stairs of the jet, saying she would wait for me inside.

I forced a smile to Marreth. "Like she said, I hope you find happiness, king." I did not mention love. I was never going to mention love again.

"Thank you, Anwen. If you ever need a second home…" he tilted his head with half a smile. The truth was, Marreth had flourished since becoming king. He drowned all his pain into something new, into a new way of life. The soldiers loved him, the court loved him. And he loved them all in return.

Marreth had once tried to tell me about all the plans he had, about how he wanted to propose commerce to the Earth and Wind kingdoms and start new trade, with a new fresh perspective and on peaceful terms.

"Hm…and all it was needed was for my mate to die."

The new king instantly stopped talking and never mentioned the subject again.

"If I'm ever in New York…" Vikram tried to make another joke.

"Don't," I replied, my features grim, absolutely no shade of a smile. "I can't do it."

"Anwen…you are family. You can always come see us, live with us even," the prince insisted again, just like every single time he saw me.

"I need to go home, Vikram, there is nothing left for me here."

He nodded. He knew. He understood.

"Goodbye boo boo," the prince whispered as we shared a quick embrace. It was uncomfortable. I hated his arms. I hated how they kept me away from Ansgar.

"Goodbye."

As soon as the seat belt sign disappeared, Cressi passed me a brand-new phone.

"We have Wi-Fi," she announced, then focused her attention on her own screen.

I grabbed it and opened the box, connected to the plane Wi-Fi and set up my account, watching how all my passwords, all my socials, playlists, photos, videos and digital wallets were installed.

My fingers hated me, because they went straight to the photo section, making me watch how thousands of photos of Ansgar unrolled in front of my eyes.

Ansgar sleeping.

Ansgar eating a banana.

Ansgar sat at the table, chatting to Marreth.

Ansgar in bed, half naked.

Ansgar smiling.

Ansgar making a face.

Ansgar grimacing and trying to cover his ass that day I caught him in the shower.

I didn't realize my chest was wet from tears until Cressi passed me a tissue.

I thanked her and kept scrolling.

"We also have a TV if you want to see what happened in the world while we were away," she announced.

I did not reply but after a few seconds I heard a TV anchor making some comments in the background.

I continued to scroll, this time through the videos. I pressed one at random.

Ansgar appeared on the screen, eyes droopy with sleep, blinking lazily at the camera.

"Fahrenor here is so tired after a very sexy night she shared with this handsome fae," he snickered, making the camera record his pecs and his abs for emphasis. It then shifted to me, wrapped in blankets, my hair all over the place, sleeping.

"My lady is very tired indeed," he threw a proud smirk to the camera.

I paused the video, hating myself for sleeping, for wasting so many moments we could have had together.

I rested my head back, settling into the seat and started listening to the TV.

"Plant species have started to disappear at a faster pace. In the past two decades, over six hundred species have gone extinct. The most recent one coming as a shock to biologists, according to the Botanical Society of America. The gardenia jasminoides, commonly known as the gardenia, a plant that many of us have owned or admired in a bouquet is now extinct. Two months ago, the species of gardenia jasminnoides started wilting at an alarming rate…"

5 summers later

Anwen

Chapter Thirty-Four – B

I hate Alexa. I just hate her. I despise that device with sheer conviction. The nerve on her to wake me up at half six on the dot, every single morning and not stop playing her cheery songs until I physically got out of bed to turn her off.

I had set it up like that, it would have been too easy to just shout at her from the comfort of my own pillow and order her to stop playing. So she ended up torturing me, every weekday to her cyber-heart's content.

The bed felt so cosy, so welcoming and that new mattress that we bought heated up my side of the bed in the perfect way, begging me to remain there, cuddled up in blankets and wrapped in his arms.

I loved the feeling; I loved my life. And above all, I loved him.

I turned slowly, tilting my head to the rhythm of the song and turning to his cold side of the mattress to place a small kiss on his cheek. It gained no reaction, so I added another and another, my lips forming a slow trail until I got to his lips and lingered a while. Just enough to make him react and brush a smile against my kiss before he responded with a lazy caress of his tongue.

"In what world am I the one waking you up?" I chuckled,

shifting away the loose strands of hair that prevented me from seeing those gorgeous eyes of his.

"Someone kept me up most of the night…" he threw me a proud smirk, a reminder of the long hours we had spent devouring each other. A tradition we liked to maintain as often as we could.

"So, am I to tell my dad that his Global Product Manager is late on his first day?"

I pronounced his new job title slowly, letting myself bask in the sound. My heart swell with pride, he had worked so hard to launch a new fully organic line and it had proved so successful that the promotion was the cherry on top. Needless to say, we had taken the night to celebrate at length.

"Actually, oh little impatient one," he smirked and wrapped me tighter in his arms, "Jason guessed we would need a lazy morning, so my first meeting is at eleven." He returned my kiss with more intensity, eyes suddenly alight with new desire.

"Well, I have to be in the office early, I have to…" his kisses started trailing down my neck, on my shoulder, making me forget my words.

"You have to stay in this bed, with your husband. I think that is your main task of the morning," he giggled against my breast. "I believe we have a more important task at hand," he lowered his lips and passed my breasts, his tongue caressing and teasing my lower belly. Only to go lower to the line of my lace panties.

Well, if he wanted to start his morning like this, I would not argue.

Smiling, I relaxed into my pillow and allowed him to lift my hips, removing my pyjama bottoms in a swift motion, already much too experienced in removing my clothing to stumble on anything that entailed undressing me.

My panties were next. This morning he woke up ravenous and I would soon turn into the main course.

His tongue started rolling on my skin, hot and ravenous, trailing in all the right spots, all the places he had made a mission to learn for years, obsessed with bringing me to the point of madness every single time.

I released a slow breath, sensation already trapped in my lower belly and by the time his teeth started nipping at my clit, I was ready to be undone.

A finger pierced into me abruptly, making me jolt.

"Ansgar!" I shouted his name, hands automatically reaching out for his shoulders, curling into his hair, trying to prepare me for what was to come. For reaching the end of the world.

"Mmhm…so eager my fahrenor this morning," he chuckled, the echo of the sound falling from his lips raising goosebumps all over my skin. Then his eyes averted to me and oh my god the sight of him. The sight of him panting between my legs, the desire in his eyes almost made me cum right then and there.

"Are you eager, my love?" As soon as he said it, his finger started piercing deeper into my core, finding that soft spot that raised waves of pleasure into my lower belly.

"Yes…" I moaned. "Yes, please…"

I didn't finish speaking before his mouth returned to the sweet torture, caressing me expertly with his tongue, suckling while his finger danced inside of me in a way that—

My phone started buzzing.

No, no, no.

Ansgar didn't stop, didn't even acknowledge the interruption, but I knew better. My phone never rang this early. Never.

"I have to take it," I told him, begging him to stop eating me so desperately but his arm rested on my hips, keeping me prisoner.

"Don't you dare…" he bit my clit with intent, punishing me for even thinking to stop.

God, this man knew my own body better than I did.

"Please…it could be important." I curled my tummy just enough for my eyes to reach his. "I'll make it up to you, I promise."

"Oh, you *will* make it up to me," he instantly said, but removed his hand to let me tilt upwards to reach my phone. But before I answered, two fingers pierced back into me and started moving with desperation, making my entire body shiver, my muscles trembling with the newly found pleasure, the mix of delight and slight pain driving me mad.

"Ansgar, don't…"

"You insisted on answering, baby. Now talk."

Fuck, fuck, fuck. I tried to control my breath, tried to find some sort of reason beyond the accumulating pleasure and grabbed my phone.

My heart instantly dropped.

"It's Cressi!"

Ansgar stopped, his eyes pinned on me, his full attention on the incoming call.

"Morning, sexy...How are...things?" I barely spoke between deep pants. I was so close, so close that my body still shivered, begging for the contact, begging to find that release.

"Are you fucking?" Rhylan's tone came out sharp, admonishing,

"N..no," I immediately said, looking at Ansgar and watching how his attention dropped back at the pulsating desire in between my legs,

"Sprout, I think we know each other for long enough now to spot when you are lying to me. Don't get me wrong, fucking is good, it increases serotonin and that can help with the production of collagen, so, great for you. Keep the princeling young."

Rhylan had become obsessed with youth. With maintaining it. He made it a mission to learn everything there was to know about keeping his new human body healthy and preserving his youth for as long as possible.

This new passion started a year after their return, when, according to Cressi, he spotted a grey hair in the mirror and swore to himself that he would do anything to stop new ones from appearing. Needless to say, Rhylan still struggled to accept life as a human with all its consequences.

Neither of them remembered what happened, how they came back. One day, a few months after Cressi's and my departure, when Marreth prepared for a visit from Wind, he ordered for the throne room to be prepared. When the soldiers went to make the arrangements, as per their new king's request, they found two bodies, wrapped in some sort of clay.

Marreth was instantly summoned, and he started crying with joy at the discovery of the two. It took them a few weeks to wake up and come back to their senses, but Cressi and I never left their bedside.

Vikram was the one to pick us up. Initially, we did not want to go, did not want to return to the place where we had lost everything, but Marreth, the newly appointed King of Fire, kept insisting to the point that we reluctantly accepted.

We reached the Fire Kingdom to find everything transformed and to find...windows. Everywhere. The Wind Kingdom had helped with some sort of magic transformation that allowed the underground to mirror the surface. It gave the entire place a new life.

Marreth was shining, so happy and proud, leading us through the newly decorated hallways and barely containing his joy.

It was beautiful, but we did not understand why we needed to see it all, why we had to return.

Until he asked us to follow him to a massive room that looked like some sort of studio, equipped with a fully stocked kitchen, a bathroom, lots of medical equipment and two large beds, one for Ansgar and one for Rhylan, who were asleep and unmoving.

None of us knew what was happening, if what we were living was even real or some sort of illusion. The entire royal family of the earthlings came too, checking on their son and bringing in healer after healer to try to wake the two of them up.

Three weeks later, when we had started to lose hope, Rhylan opened his eyes.

Ansgar did too, four days after that.

Both of them woke up human. No power left, no burdens to

carry. With a full life ahead.

"Rhylan, what is it?" I snapped, the need to return myself to Ansgar's mouth making me a bit grouchy.

"We're at the hospital now, I need to go in soon, the doctor says it won't be long."

"We'll be right there."

Rhylan gave me the details once again, not that I needed them, not when I'd gone with Cressida to so many doctor's appointments.

"We need to go to hospital," I told Ansgar, who pouted for a few seconds before jumping into action, fully prepared to react under pressure.

Twenty minutes later, we were showered and dressed, hurrying down the stairs to find mom and dad.

"Why are you two up so early?" Mom looked at us in surprise, instantly extending her cheek for Ansgar to give her a kiss. In the last few years, they had become so close, that I knew mom loved him like her own son.

"Rhylan just called. Cressida is in labor," he explained while stealing a piece of toast from her plate and grabbing a donut from the tray for me. "Jason, could Ian cover today's meeting?"

Dad nodded, a wide smile on his face. "Sure son, don't worry about it, I'll cover it myself if I have to."

Another few minutes later, we were out the door and into the car, Ansgar reciting the GPS directions to me while checking his phone as well, using every satellite at his disposal to make sure the roads were clear.

It took him a few months to learn technology, but once he

discovered the iPhone, there was no turning back. I even had to buy him blue light filter glasses to make sure his eyes were protected from all that screen time. He did not waste his minutes on socials or TikTok, like the rest of us. Instead, my husband kept reading and listening to news, wanting to learn everything there was to know about the world, read every botanical journal and article he could find and kept in touch with his family.

We spent every summer with them, dedicating three months a year to the Earth Kingdom. We had made an arrangement with my dad, asking that Ansgar's job would be covered by the team for the summer, after inventing some excuses about Ansgar's family and how they could not come visit as often as their son Vikram did. Of course, dad instantly accepted, too happy to have us home for nine months a year to protest.

Damaris and Takara were working on their third son, both of them enormously happy to not have to worry about any bursts of godly energy coming their way while Eidothea and Vikram travelled the world and enjoyed one another, sometimes very publicly. They came to visit every couple of months, stopping by for a week or two before they were off to some new country that needed to be discovered. Always by the sea.

Queen Bathysia had started dropping hints about wanting more grandchildren, with the full support of the king, and we promised to do our best to bring them some good news the next time we visited.

I had stopped getting the contraceptive injections two months ago, after having a long discussion about our future and agreeing that we were ready to become parents.

We were now enjoying the fun part, the trying to make a baby part, which gave Ansgar an excuse to visit my office very often, with any kind of pretense just to get me alone at lunch time.

We also talked about getting our own home once the family grew, but we ended up deciding against it. We loved family dinners too much and we wanted our kids to experience the same love and affection we had grown up with. To get to know their family, their grandparents, aunts and uncles.

We rushed through the hospital halls and took the elevator to the main VIP birthing suite because of course, Rhylan would not get anything but the best for Cressi. I carried a bunch of balloons while Ansgar struggled to drag a massive basket of flowers, stopping by the door and waiting for the good news.

We paced and paced, watching how doctors walked past us, nodding their heads in slight acknowledgement. Ansgar got us breakfast and we ate on the uncomfortable chairs, our hearts beating faster with every sound squeezing through the door.

At three fourteen in the afternoon, the door finally opened to display a fully-grown man crying his heart out.

"They're here," Rhylan barely spoke between sobs, the widest smile I had ever seen plastered on his face, his lips shaking.

"Congratulations, dad," Ansgar was suddenly there to offer a tight embrace, both of them squeaking with joy.

Two enemies, two rivals, two unlikely friends. Now brothers.

After congratulating Rhylan, I hurried into the birthing suite to find Cressida in bed, looking as fabulous as always, holding two small bundles in her arms.

"Congratulations, mama," I smiled at her, tears of joy dripping down my face.

"Come see them," she tilted her head in an invitation, the nurse rapidly jumping into action to help her move the girls so I could see them better.

Rhylan and Ansgar walked to us, my mate's arms wrapped around my waist, covering my lower belly, both of us shivering in anticipation of the day we too, would live this moment.

"This is Amara," Cressida said, showing us a small blue-eyed bundle that barely made a noise while breathing.

"And this is Catherine," Rhylan said softly, as if fearing to wake up the babies. He then looked at Ansgar to give the explanation. "Catalina was more difficult to pronounce."

"They are perfect," I felt Ansgar's smile on my neck, recognizing it by the way he exhaled. "May they both be blessed with health and joy," he continued, "and may the rays of sunshine illuminate their path."

Rhylan nodded, containing a sudden lump in his throat, no doubt at the words which I could only assume, symbolized a faerie tradition.

Ansgar chuckled. "So, how does it feel to have three daughters, Rhylan?"

We all started laughing, enjoying this moment.

Enjoying happiness.

And hoping that the rays of sunshine will illuminate our paths too.

For a new author, reviews are everything, so if you enjoyed this book, feel free to give it some stars!

More from the author

Discover the Tales of Earth and Leaves series
Tales of Earth and Leaves
Tales of Fire and Embers
Tales of Forever and Now
Tales of Wind and Storm
Tales of Water and Blood

Discover *Love, Will, an LGBT historical fiction*

Thank you for choosing to have a read.

Printed in Great Britain
by Amazon